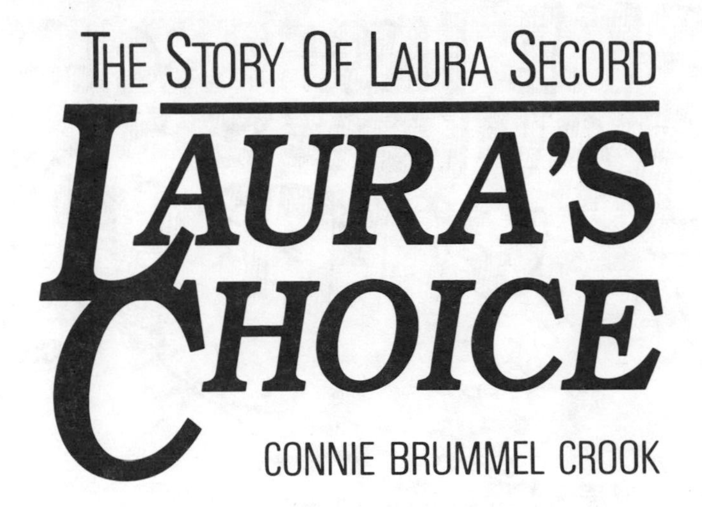
THE STORY OF LAURA SECORD
LAURA'S
CHOICE
CONNIE BRUMMEL CROOK

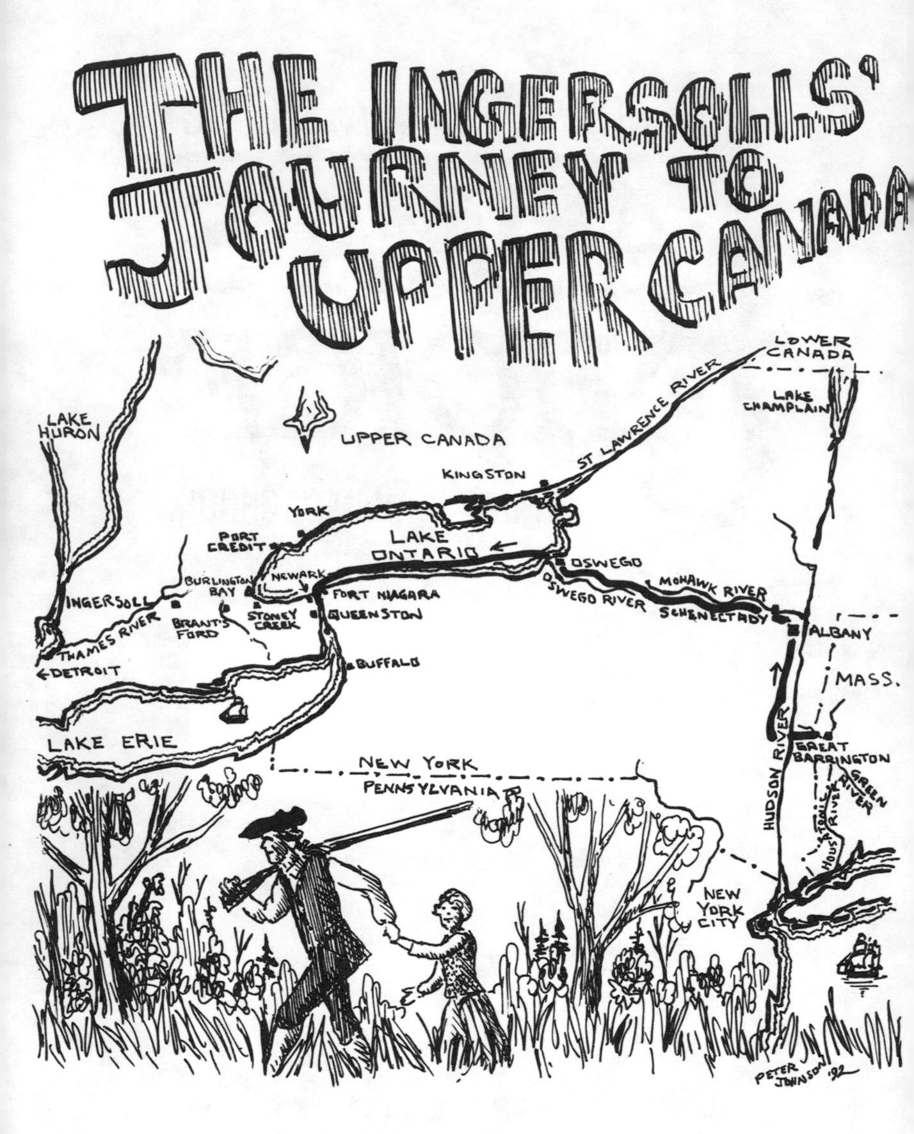
THE INGERSOLLS' JOURNEY TO UPPER CANADA
LOWER CANADA
LAKE CHAMPLAIN
LAKE HURON
UPPER CANADA
ST LAWRENCE RIVER
KINGSTON
YORK
PORT CREDIT
LAKE ONTARIO
OSWEGO
OSWEGO RIVER
MOHAWK RIVER
SCHENECTADY
ALBANY
BURLINGTON BAY
NEWARK
FORT NIAGARA
QUEENSTON
INGERSOLL
THAMES RIVER
BRANT'S FORD
STONEY CREEK
DETROIT
BUFFALO
MASS.
LAKE ERIE
HUDSON RIVER
GREAT BARRINGTON
GREEN RIVER
HOUSATONIC RIVER
NEW YORK
PENNSYLVANIA
NEW YORK CITY
PETER JOHNSON '92

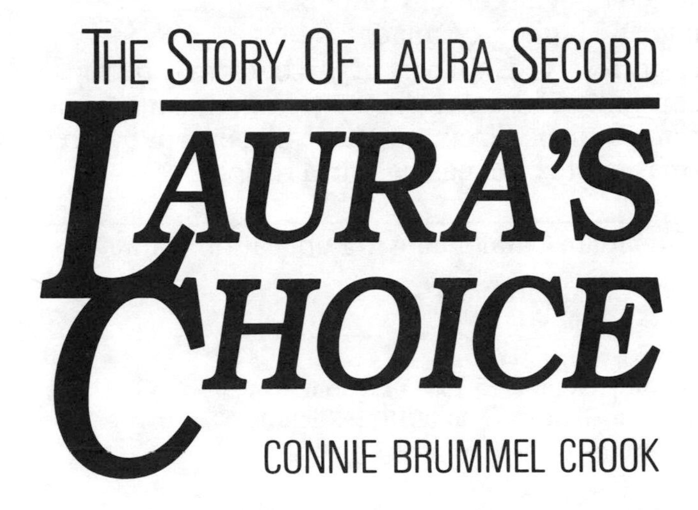

WINDFLOWER COMMUNICATIONS
WINNIPEG, MANITOBA

LAURA'S CHOICE

Published by Windflower Communications,
Winnipeg, Manitoba, Canada

Canadian Cataloguing in Publication Data

Crook, Connie Brummel
Laura's choice
ISBN 1-895308-12-7
1. Secord, Laura, 1775-1868 - Fiction.
2. Canada - History - War of 1812 - Fiction. *
I> Title.

PS8555.R6113L3 1993 C813'.54 C93-098062-X
PR9199.3.C7611L3 1993

Cover art by David Craig, Toronto, Ontario
Maps by Peter Johnson, Scarborough, Ontario
Design by Publishing Services, Winnipeg, MB
Printed in Canada by Derksen Printers, Steinbach, MB

International Standard Book Number: 1-895308-12-7

Acknowledgements

I would like to thank the Niagara Falls Public Library for allowing me to read their files on Laura Secord; the reference department of Peterborough Public Library for obtaining books and photocopied materials for me through the inter-library loan programme; and the reference department of Trent University Bata Library for helping me find historical background material.

A special thanks to my cousin, Lorena Montgomery of Niagara Falls, Ontario, who accompanied me to the Laura Secord sites and helped me to trace the route of her famous walk.

Thanks also to Gavin K. Watt of King City, Ontario, President of the Museum of Applied Military History, who was the military consultant for the film Divided Loyalities, for his help in answering my many questions about the military, firearms, equipment and grooming; Nancy Watt, a teacher, and director of Period Fashion Seminars, whom I consulted about clothing; Cynthia Rankin, a teacher and former resource consultant with the Peterborough County Board of Education, for preparing a study guide; Debbie Floyd and Beth Beranger, teachers in Oshawa and Maple Grove, Ontario and Eleanor Bruce, a teacher in Madoc Township for their helpful suggestions; Debbie Floyd along with Nancy and Gavin Watt for the title; Kathryn Dean for her advice and editing; and Gilbert Brandt, President of Windflower Communications for his support and encouragement.

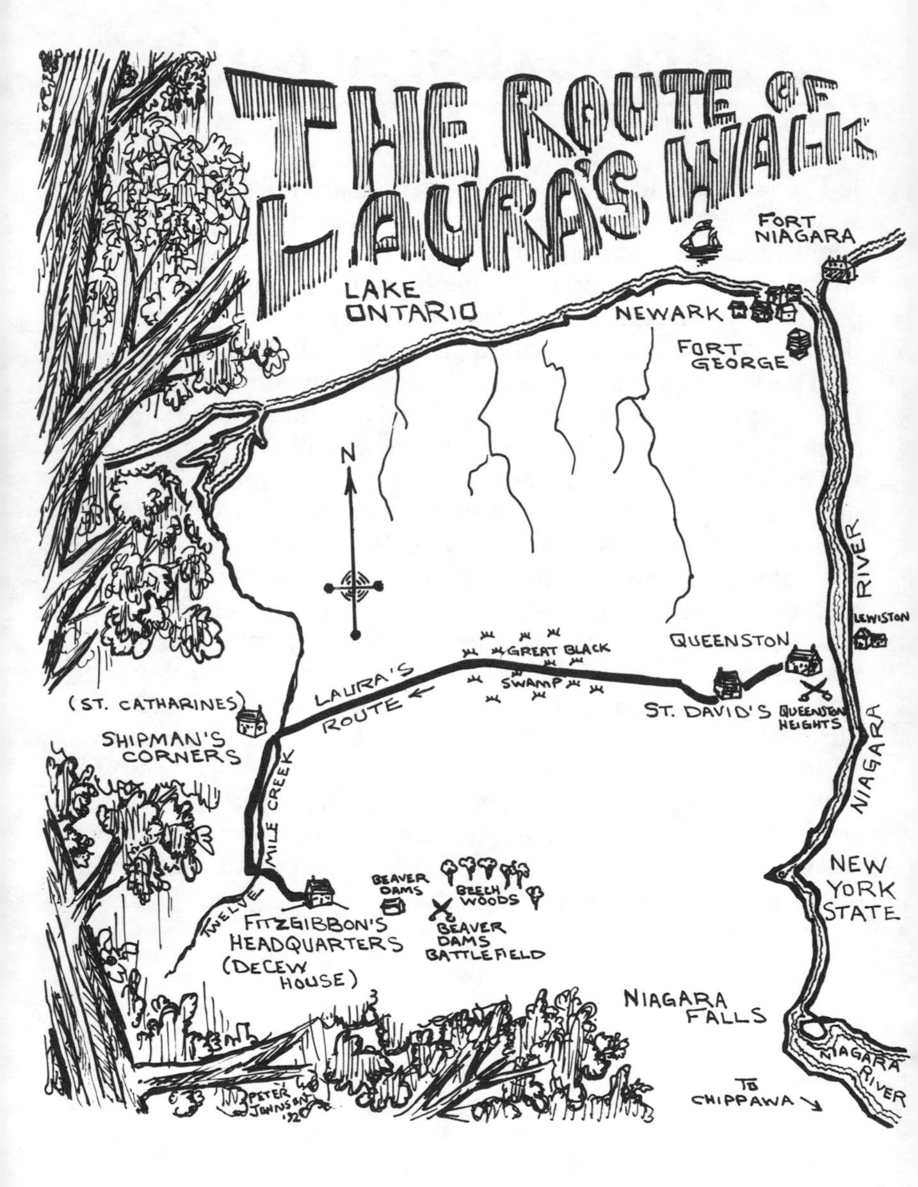
THE ROUTE OF LAURA'S WALK
LAKE ONTARIO
FORT NIAGARA
NEWARK
FORT GEORGE
N
NIAGARA RIVER
LEWISTON
QUEENSTON
GREAT BLACK SWAMP
LAURA'S ROUTE
(ST. CATHARINES)
SHIPMAN'S CORNERS
ST. DAVID'S
QUEENSTON HEIGHTS
TWELVE MILE CREEK
BEAVER DAMS
BEECH WOODS
FITZGIBBON'S HEADQUARTERS (DECEW HOUSE)
BEAVER DAMS BATTLEFIELD
NEW YORK STATE
NIAGARA FALLS
NIAGARA RIVER
TO CHIPPAWA
PETER JOHNSON '92

To my father, Elick T. Brummel, 1907 - 1992,
who loved to read and retell tales
of our own Canadian past,
including this one.

Contents

PART ONE

RED

ONE

Laura Ingersoll slid down behind her wooden desk as far as she could go. She braced her feet against the legs of the bench in front of her and pressed her chin firmly against her chest. That way she didn't have to look at Elizabeth reading in front of the class.

Elizabeth Bachus had moved to Great Barrington from New York City just after the Christmas holidays a little over a month ago, and everyone thought she was great—especially the boys. Laura couldn't figure out what everyone saw in her, except maybe her clothes. She always wore grand petticoats that made her look older than she was, like the long, full yellow linen one with a blue silk waist-sash that she had on today. Laura was sure that Elizabeth was not thirteen yet; she was probably almost twelve like Laura herself, or maybe even younger, but the Mayo brothers were stretched across their desks staring up at her as if she were much older. Her blonde hair was beautiful, the way it was curled up high on top and then fell in soft curls down her back. It was just the shade of light blonde hair Laura had always wanted to have.

"An excellent reading, Elizabeth," said Mr. Salisbury, the teaching master, as he peered at her over the top of his gold-rimmed glasses. Then he closed his book. Mr. Salisbury couldn't have been listening too hard, Laura decided. "That will be our last reading for today. Clean your slates, students, and prepare to leave."

There was a great clatter as the students put their books away and shut their desk lids. Laura chucked her slate into her desk and looked over to the Mayo brothers, who lived on the next farm. They were still gaping at Elizabeth as she walked back to her seat. When she passed the boys she looked down shyly, but that did not fool Laura.

Just as the noise of the class was dying down, Laura heard the sound of heavy footsteps coming from the front porch of the small frame schoolhouse. The door burst open and a gust of raw wind blew across the room as the town watchman, his face red from the cold, strode over to Mr. Salisbury. A hushed silence fell on the students, for his serious expression told them he had brought bad news. They watched as he spoke in a low mumble to the schoolmaster.

Mr. Salisbury straightened his glasses and cleared his throat. "All after-school lessons and practices are cancelled," he announced. "Go straight home. Do not linger along the roadside and do not take any shortcuts across fields."

"Why?" asked Thomas Mayo. He didn't look worried. In fact, he had a smug look on his face. Laura wondered if the rumours were true that Thomas secretly belonged to the rebels. She knew many farmers supported them.

"Because the agitators are on the prowl again," the schoolmaster explained. "They have never hurt children, but it would be best to avoid them. Keep to the main roads. Now hurry and go."

As she raced down the front steps of the school, Laura shivered inside her red wool cloak and pulled the hood tightly over her head. She bet the Mayo brothers would be walking the new girl home today, so there was no point in waiting around. Anyway she was used to seeing soldiers and bands of men passing along this way to Great Barrington. The town was close to the main boundary between Massachusetts and New York, and it had been a centre of traffic during the Revolutionary War that had ended four years before in 1783.

The sun was shining so brightly in the southwestern sky that Laura had to squint her eyes. It was going to be a bitter February evening, she thought, as she hurried along the road with the hard snow crunching under her feet. Her family lived just south of the town, almost a mile away. She passed sleighs with waiting parents—but not hers. She knew no one would be waiting for her. Of course, it couldn't be helped, for her mother had died three years before, her new stepmother, Mercy, was always sick, and her father was never home.

Turning off the front street of Great Barrington and onto the main highway leading south out of town, Laura could not help wondering if Thomas and Levi really were walking Elizabeth home. They would come along this same road, for Elizabeth lived with her mother on her grandparents' estate, just a mile beyond Laura's house. Finally Laura turned around to look. To her surprise, she saw Elizabeth a few yards behind her, walking alone. Her head was bent down against the cold and her fur tippet, wrapped snugly around her neck, swirled out behind her in a sudden gust of wind.

In a few minutes, Laura heard the crunch of footsteps just behind but didn't turn her head. She didn't know why but she didn't like Elizabeth. "Wait up, Laura," shouted Elizabeth.

Laura turned then and looked right at Elizabeth. She was wearing a cloak trimmed with fox, and her mittened hands were almost hidden inside her fur muff. In spite of her warm clothing, she was shivering and her face was beet red from the raw wind. Laura almost felt sorry for her.

"This is a dreadful place to live," said Elizabeth with a frown. "Are all the winters this cold?"

"Oh, worse," said Laura. She didn't think the weather was all that bad but didn't mind upsetting Elizabeth. "This is nothing compared to some winters."

"Well, I wish Mother would take us right back to New York City, but she won't, no matter how much I beg her."

"Why not?"

"It's too hard to manage. My father was killed in the war, you know."

"But it ended four years ago. Why are you moving here now ?" Laura asked even though she had heard the rumour that Judge Whiting was tired of paying his daughter's expenses in New York City.

"My grandparents were lonesome in that big house. They persuaded Mother to come home, and she runs the household staff now since Grandma took sick."

"My stepmother is sick a lot, too."

"You mean you don't have a real mother?" said Elizabeth with surprise.

"Of course I have a real mother . . . but she's dead."

"Can you remember her?"

"Of course I can remember her. She died just three years ago."

"And you have a new stepmother already. . . . Well, I can't remember my father. He was killed when I was a baby, so I don't miss him."

"My father is still living, but he's always away."

"Why is that? My grandpa was never away much when *he* was Judge of Great Barrington . . . before he retired."

"My father's more than just Judge of Great Barrington. He's also Captain of the local militia."

"So I suppose he's out chasing rebels today. That's too bad."

Laura did wish her father would stay at home more, but she would never admit that to Elizabeth. "His job is very secret. It's too important for me to discuss," she said with pride. Actually, she wasn't even sure that she was proud of her father helping put down the uprising. After all, many of the farmers were rebelling because they couldn't pay their taxes. Many had their farms taken away and some had even been sent to prison for debts. But Elizabeth didn't need to know that.

"Do you think there'll be a real battle? My mother says . . ." Elizabeth's words were cut short by the sound of tramping feet and loud laughter just up ahead.

"It's them. It must be," gasped Elizabeth.

Three men were walking towards them on the opposite side of the road. The first two were middle-aged farmers with unshaven faces and straggly hair. Laura wouldn't have wanted to meet them alone! Just as she was thinking how glad she was to have Elizabeth there, Elizabeth grabbed Laura's arm. Gripping hands tightly, the girls plodded along the outer edge of their own side of the road towards the strangers in their tattered homespun breeches and woolen coats. There was no escape across the snow-filled fields, and if they turned and ran towards town, the men would soon catch them. Elizabeth stopped suddenly, but Laura pulled her ahead, for she knew it was better to keep going. Even now they were in sight of Laura's home across the fields.

"Well, if it isn't Little Red Riding Hood," yelled one of the men. He was pointing at Laura's red cloak and laughing through his nose.

"Going to Grandma's house?" the man jeered, stepping into the middle of the road, closer to the trembling girls.

Laura noticed a boy behind them. His red hair blew wildly in the wind and his tattered doeskin coat hung loosely from his shoulders. He looked no older than the boys in her class. Laura could hardly believe it. Her father hadn't told her there would be boys that young in this rebellion. But she did remember him saying that the militia would stop the rebels before they reached Great Barrington. So what were they doing here?

"What're you afraid of?" the nearest man sneered at Elizabeth, whose hands were shaking hard now. "The big bad wolf?" Yanking Elizabeth by the hand, Laura started to run from the men.

Her heart was thumping heavily, and with the strain of pulling Elizabeth she was soon winded. On impulse she looked over her shoulder and saw only the men's backs. They were heading on toward town. She thought she heard a ripple of laughter coming from their direction.

"They've gone on," she said bravely, now that the crisis was passed.

"Are you sure?" Elizabeth too was gasping for breath. "Come on, in case they change their minds." Letting go of Laura's hand, she stumbled on ahead.

Laura turned back for one more look. The men were just two dark figures by now, but the boy was still easy to see. He was walking some distance behind the others. She couldn't help admiring the defiant way he marched down the road. Then, unexpectedly, he spun around and seemed to stare at Laura before he turned back and sauntered on behind the men.

"What are you staring at those rogues for?" Elizabeth shouted. Laura turned and started walking towards home again. "I just can't understand why you'd stop to look at that grubby bunch. It's a good job you had me along to drag you away."

"*I'm* the one who dragged *you* away! I only stopped after we were past them."

"Really. So why did you take the time to stare at that stupid boy?"

"I was just looking at . . . ." Laura couldn't think of any reason but she knew she was getting very annoyed with Elizabeth. Tomorrow she would walk to school without her. She clenched her mittened hands tightly together underneath her cloak and, taking long strides, pushed ahead of her. Elizabeth followed a few steps behind, unable to keep up to Laura's pace.

They had not walked much farther when sleigh bells rang out just ahead of them. "It's Grandpa!" Elizabeth ran toward the sleigh.

Judge Whiting made a sharp turn in his covered cutter and drew up beside the girls. "Hop in," he smiled. "You, too, Laura Ingersoll. I'm sorry to be late. It looks as if you didn't have games after school today."

"I don't need a ride, thank you," Laura said, "I'm almost home. I'll walk."

"Young lady, you get in the sleigh this minute. I'm taking you right to your door." Laura could see there was no point in arguing. She stepped up onto the iron footstep on the side of the cutter and sat beside Elizabeth, who had wrapped herself up in the bearskin lap rug. She unfolded a side of the rug and threw it across Laura's lap.

"Now girls," said the Judge, "next time school gets out before you expect me, wait at the school until I get there. You can't be too careful these days. And Laura, I know your father is away on business, but you should have waited until one of his servants came for you."

"Bett and Sam are too busy. My stepmother had another bad spell and Bett's afraid it's pneumonia. Mira's still at home, you know. She's only six and Bett has to take care of her too."

"I see." The Judge took out his handkerchief and blew his nose. "Well, we'll stop for you tomorrow morning. Be ready at eight. I always like Elizabeth to be on time."

Laura did not reply but she certainly was not going to be ready at eight. And she did not intend to ride to school with Elizabeth and Judge Whiting. She wasn't sure at the moment how she would avoid it, but she would think of something.

They rode on in silence, right to the long lane leading to Laura's home. Judge Whiting turned the cutter in towards the house, between the cedar and red pine that stood on either side of the lane. Through the trees, Laura could see part of the thirty acres of land that her father owned. It was enough to raise a few young cattle and grow a vegetable garden to supply most of the family's food.

As they came up to the house, Laura saw Sam, their black slave, heading across the dooryard towards the barn to do the chores.

"Whoa!" The Judge drew his horses to a halt in front of the white frame house.

Laura jumped down into the deep snow beside the cutter before it came to a full stop. "Thank you, sir," she shouted as she stepped onto the path leading to the front of the house. She ran up to the verandah and hurried along it to the side kitchen door. She was shivering from the cold and snow.

Inside the kitchen, her cheeks tingled in the warmth from the fire crackling in the hearth.

"Where's Bett?" Laura asked Mira, who had run up to her sister and put her arms around Laura's snowy cloak.

"Putting a mustard plaster on Mama. Ooo, you're all wet. She coughs all the time now."

"Has Father come home?"

"No. Want to see my new doll? Sam made it." Mira held up a small wooden doll with an acorn head.

"That's nice," said Laura without looking at the doll. She walked into the front hall and hung her red cloak on its hook. She could hear her stepmother's sharp coughing from the room at the top of the stairs.

Back in the kitchen, Laura sat down beside Mira on the horsehair couch in front of the fireplace. As Mira snuggled up to her, Laura gazed out the back kitchen window. Through the swirling snow, she could see three dark figures making their way along the west side of the barn. Laura's heart beat faster as she realized who they were: the same two men she and Elizabeth had met on the way home from school. And the red-headed boy was there too, straggling along behind.

Laura rushed to the door and flung it open, but they had vanished. All she could hear was the howling of the wind as it whipped across the bare verandah.

TWO

A shaft of light beaming through the iced-up windows wakened Laura. The rest of the family was already downstairs eating breakfast. She could hear spoons scraping against the wooden porridge bowls and Mira whining about something to Bett. Laura pulled the quilt over her head to muffle the sounds and keep out the cold. If she stayed in bed for just a little longer, she might be able to walk to school by herself; she was determined not to ride to school with Elizabeth, and besides, she was freezing. There was no point in getting out from under the quilts before she had to.

She had not lain there long before she heard the back kitchen door slam shut and Bett saying, "No, don't wait, Elizabeth. Laura isn't up yet. So she'll just have to walk. Thank your grandpa for callin' though." Then after the front door closed, "Now where's that Laura? It isn't like her to lie in bed after me callin' her twice."

Laura was out of bed in a bound. It might be cold out there, but it would be worse to get a scolding from Bett. She had a way of saying things that were true that you didn't want to hear. In minutes, Laura was almost dressed and downstairs. She still had to lace up the front of her gown and put her boots on.

"Why there you are! What ever came over you to lie in bed so long?" Bett opened her eyes wide at Laura and raised one eyebrow.

"Well, . . . " Laura began.

"Oh, never mind now. I see you're all ready and rarin' to go, so eat your porridge quick and get out that door." Laura did up her boots and gown as quickly as she could and gulped down her breakfast, then grabbed her wool cloak off the peg in the hallway, and raced out the back. Bett's words followed her. "Hurry on to school, now. Those agitators are still out on the roads and the longer you linger, the more's the chance you'll be in their way. Lord help us. This is no place for children to grow up in."

It was a snowy day. The wind was blowing, but between gusts, the sun shone down in blinding rays. She rounded the side of the house and went down the front lane. She had just turned to the left onto the highway that led to Great Barrington when she heard men's voices and laughter carried on the wind from the cedar woods to the east of the highway. As she kept walking along the road to Great Barrington, she looked in the direction of the sounds and thought she saw glinting steel between the cedar branches about one hundred feet away. She knew she should head back home, but curiosity got the better of her, and she stepped off the left side of the road, opposite the sound, and hid behind a clump of wild raspberry bushes and thick cedars.

Through the swirling snow, she saw a crowd of men, as many as a hundred, emerging from the woods and striding toward the highway. Most were well armed with rifles and muskets, and some carried other supplies. A few, who appeared to be no older than Thomas and Levi, straggled along farther back. Some were regular soldiers, but many wore tattered farmers' clothes that still gave off the sharp smell of pig manure.

The band of men turned down the highway towards town, passing right by her. Just as Laura was thinking she should risk making a run for it back home, she heard more heavy tramping and saw the next group coming towards her. They were prodding a prisoner along the way ahead of them. With a start, Laura realized it was Solomon Gleazen, the schoolmaster from the nearby town of Stockbridge. He looked straight ahead, the way he had when he'd led their spelling bee, but he walked with a noticeable limp and he was shivering in his light woolen waistcoat. The man just behind him was wearing a tailored coat much like the one the schoolmaster had worn the week before.

Laura shivered. She had to get moving or she would freeze. As the men disappeared from view in the distance, she slowly stepped back onto the road. There was no question of going to school now. She would head for home.

"Where ya goin' miss?" said a voice with a strong Irish accent. She turned and almost bumped into the boy she had seen the day before. He was sullen-looking now, and she noticed again the red hair and ragged doeskin coat. He must have been standing right behind her as she watched the men pass by.

"None of your business." Laura swerved around him and fell headlong to the ground. She had tripped over the boy's extended boot. Gritty snow bit into her face as she sprawled on the side of the road.

"Look, you can't go back to warn nobody 'bout us. The men up ahead has got business to take care of, an' they don't need the militia called out because of some gabbin', little girl."

The boy reached out his hand to help Laura up, and still short of breath from having her wind knocked out by the fall, she did not resist. Then unexpectedly, he pulled her over to a clump of young cedar trees farther back in the woods and yanked her down beside him. In a gentler voice, he said, "We'll just stay here till they've had time to do their job. Then you can go on back wherever it was you was goin'. I'm not gonna harm you none, Miss."

Red-faced and angry, Laura gasped, "Well, that's a fine way to show it, knocking me over like that and then dragging me over here."

"Sorry 'bout that, but I had to stop you fast."

Laura studied him intently as they huddled behind the cedars. The boy's fiery red hair blew around his freckled face. His worn twill breeches were made of farmer's homespun, and one sleeve of his doeskin coat was torn and hung loosely from the shoulder. He was shivering. When he noticed Laura staring at him, he pulled the pieces of his sleeve together.

"Where are you from, anyway?" Laura asked in a whisper.

He stared straight into the trees.

"What are all those men doing in our town?" she asked.

He pushed down a cedar bough and peered out towards the road.

Laura became braver and raised her voice. "How long do you think you can keep me here? I'm not far from home, you know."

He was a little bigger than she was, but she bet he wasn't any older, probably around twelve too.

Finally, he turned to her and mumbled, "Not long." He stared at her for a minute, "Where was you goin' anyway by yourself this mornin'?"

"To school. Where else?"

"Not very many girls go to school."

"Well, I do. My father's the judge in this town. He wants his daughter to go to school."

"Really! Is he down at the court house now?"

"No, he's . . . ." She stopped abruptly.

"It don't matter none if you don't tell me. We'll all be goin' soon. We don't mean no harm to nobody in Great Barrington, anyway."

"Then why'd you have the Stockbridge schoolmaster tied up?"

"I don't rightly know. I was here ahead as a scout, you might say. They just picked him up this morning along the way, I guess."

"I know he's the schoolmaster over at Stockbridge. His students visit our school for tournaments and spelling bees and such. We just beat them at a spelling bee last week."

"Spelling bees. Boy, am I glad I don't have to be bothered with that kind of stuff and nonsense."

"What a stupid thing to say! They're fun, especially when you win. You're just jealous 'cause all you do is follow soldiers around the countryside in the freezing snow all day."

"I don't put much store by book learnin'. You think learnin' ABC's is going to put food in the bellies of the starvin' farmers? It didn't help back home in Ireland and it won't help here. Everywhere I go the farmers have problems. My father shipped me off from Ireland because his farm was too small for my three brothers and three sisters. He could barely grow enough food for the lot of us. 'Go to America,' he says. 'Uncle Gerald's got no sons to help him to work that farm. Four times as big as ours, it is. And when he's gone it'll be yours.' So I came. Then once I got out here to my uncle's farm what happens? He can't pay the taxes because he can't sell the crop. There was no one with the money to buy it. That's the whole problem. People don't need more schoolin'. They need more money. They need to stop those taxes."

"Well, if the farmers were more educated, maybe they'd manage their farms better. And the government can't help the taxes. They're just as poor as anyone else; my father says a war is very expensive—and so is starting up a new country. And we're paying for both right now. It won't last forever."

"Forever! Even a year is goin' to be too late, Miss. Don't you know nothing? There's farmers starving and going to jail because they can't pay their debts. And there's people like. . . ." The boy looked down to the ground and wiped his face with his sleeve. "There's people like my uncle," he continued, "farm just taken away like that. It wasn't his fault he couldn't pay the debts. And Aunt Mary couldn't take it. She just had a fit. She never spoke another word after that and she dropped right dead away four days later. Me and Uncle Gerald's alone now, and he's taken to drink."

"Well, why aren't you back helping him look for a job or something, instead of hanging around with these ruffians? He must be wondering where you are."

"Well, you must be a fine lady with a rich dad to be so ignorant. And what would you say if I were to tell you that my uncle just happened to be one of those ruffians and we joined up 'cause it was all that was left for us?" The boy's grey-green eyes turned dark. "There's no work for no one out there. So there's nothing left to do but fight. Safety in numbers, you know. At least I get to eat every now and then instead of not at all."

"Every now and then? You have to eat more regularly than that!"

"Yes, and what am I going to eat? Why, are you going to feed me?"

"Well, yes, in fact, I will," Laura blurted out, suddenly feeling more compassion than fear. The boy's face was stark white behind the freckles and his hands hung bare and gaunt, poking out of the too-short arms of his doeskin coat.

"You? Feed me breakfast? And how are you going to do that?"

"Well," said Laura, "you're going to follow me down the road a piece to that house at the end of the long lane—see the one with the verandah at the side?" She pulled back some cedar branches so he could see her house. "It's quite safe. There's no one around."

The boy hesitated for a moment and his eyes softened a bit, but then he seemed to come back to himself. "I won't be awantin' anything from you, Miss. More than likely you'd be leading me straight into a trap. Besides I have to stay here. The others are depending on me. And they're gettin' victuals anyway."

The boy's speech was interrupted by a commotion from the road. "Move along there," yelled a man. Then they heard the heavy steps of many men coming back along the highway from town. Laura and the boy peered out between the boughs.

One man was prodding another in front of him. "Step up, boy."

Laughter drowned out the rest of the man's words. "What a catch! Two cellars full of food and wine!" More loud laughing followed, and then they heard the tramping of a great mob of men heading towards them.

"Stay still," the boy whispered roughly. "I'll not give you away." Then, almost childishly, he added, "Promise me you'll not tell on us when we're gone."

"I promise," Laura repeated shakily. She certainly didn't want to get in the way of that gang.

Some of the men were drinking wine straight from the jugs as they marched along. All of them were dressed in homespun shirts and breeches—which gave little protection against the intense cold of wind and snow. Only a few wore warm wool coats, and even those were full of holes.

Then Laura noticed a man she knew. It was Nathaniel Sheffield, a man who had been caught stealing at the General Store in the centre of town.

"They've freed the prisoners!" Laura whispered hoarsely.

"Not so loud. Are you daft? If they see you, they'll more than likely take you hostage—especially a judge's daughter."

"He's not a judge today," Laura said, wondering why the boy wasn't hauling her onto the road and giving her over himself. "My father's . . ." Laura stopped herself just before giving away the fact that her father was also a captain, who had left very early yesterday morning to lead troops against rebel farmers just like these.

The men finally passed. The boy had not moved toward them, and Laura was thankful.

"I have to go now," he said gruffly. "Remember your promise."

"I will." Laura watched him start to wade through the snow, heading down the highway in the same direction as the men. "Be careful," she called out softly, surprised to hear herself say the words.

The boy turned and gave her a brief, friendly smile. Then he said sharply, "Better to die by the sword than the halter."

Laura knew then. It was against these rebels that her father would lead his troops today. Those were not the boy's words; they were the slogan of Shay's men.

THREE

"Land sake's, child, what you lookin' out the window so much fer to see?" asked Bett, who was folding fresh laundry. Laura had arrived late at school, only to discover that classes had been cancelled the rest of the week. She was relieved that school had been closed. Now she wouldn't have to make up excuses to avoid riding with Elizabeth. Even better, in the afternoon Judge Whiting had come by and told Bett that Elizabeth and her mother were planning to go back to New York City for two weeks to get away from the dangerous happenings around the countryside.

"Are you quite deaf already, Laura?" Bett sounded impatient.

"No . . . I'm sorry. I was just thinking."

"I asked you, what are you lookin' at, out that window?"

"Oh, I'm looking for those men I saw this morning."

"They're long gone now. It's not likely they'll be returnin' this way. Too many furious folks 'round Great Barrington. Folks don't take kindly to havin' a bunch of clumsy fellows stompin' through their homes takin' their victuals and wine."

"They didn't come to our house."

"No, and I don't rightly know why. Our house was the first they come by. Must be the good Lord protectin' us."

"I guess they were anxious to reach the jail before they stopped anywhere," Sam interrupted his wife. "I heard they let out all the prisoners. Some of 'em just ran loose, but most of 'em joined the rebels and marched on."

"Did they break into many houses after that?" Laura asked.

"Yes, I heard tell they did, but no one was hurt. It's hard to blame a man fer stealin' food when his belly's empty."

"Sam! Watch your tongue! Laura, you can help your sister get ready fer bed now. After that, you'd best go yourself."

Laura took one last look out the west window, but she could hardly see a thing. Night had rolled in over the fields as she had been talking to Bett and Sam. She gathered Mira up in her arms and carried her up the front stairs. The little girl stared up at her sister with her huge brown eyes and put her arms around Laura's neck. "Tell me the story about . . ."

"Sh-sh, Mira, we're going past Mother Mercy's room," said Laura. She never liked going past that room these days. There was always a painful sound of coughing or such a dark silence. Laura walked past on tiptoe and turned into their bedroom two doors down the hall. A beam of moonlight stretched over the two four-poster beds by the far wall and landed just short of the cherry-and-maple-wood dresser near the door. Laura remembered a night long ago when the moon was shining in just like that and her mother—her real one—had put her to bed, the way she was putting Mira to bed now.

Mother Mercy started coughing and Laura tried to drown out the noise by singing to Mira. It was then that Laura heard the low vibrating sound of marching feet. She tucked Mira in, rushed over to the window, and pulled back the heavy linen curtains.

There was just enough moonlight to see soldiers coming along the highway, prodding a crowd of captives ahead of them—maybe fifty altogether. Some of the prisoners were men from the morning's mob. At least three lifeless bodies were draped over the horses. Laura gasped. A small boy no taller than Laura herself stumbled along between two soldiers. It had to be the starving boy she'd met that morning.

Laura went back to Mira and whispered, "I'll be back soon," but the little girl was already asleep. Relieved, Laura crept out into the hallway, tiptoed down the front stairs, and took her red cloak off the hook in the downstairs hall. Bett and Sam were arguing about the day's events, so Laura was able to slip out the front door without being noticed. In the cold, still air of the night, she felt suddenly frightened and alone, but she forced herself to walk down the lane to the highway, keeping well behind the soldiers marching toward town. When they stopped, she stepped in behind the undergrowth of young cedar bushes that grew thick along their lane.

"That boy's bound to be nearby. We'll catch him later," she could hear one soldier saying. "He can't go far. Besides, we better put these fellows safely away first."

"Yeah," another soldier said. "We got to attend to the dead. Poor Solomon. It wasn't his battle. I wonder why they forced him along."

"As a hostage, I suppose. The miserable pigs! You can never tell what a mob will do. But this'll be the end of Daniel Shay and his motley rebels, I warrant. There'll be many a hanging after this day."

"They say our judge will soon be a major, instead of a captain."

"What's that got to do with anything?"

"Didn't you see how he led the defense? He's bound to be promoted for that."

"He isn't much like Judge Whiting, is he?"

"Oh?"

"Judge Whiting takes the side of the farmers in the rebellion. He says he can't blame them none. Times are rough for these guys."

"Still, there must be a better way. . . . Guess that kid's gone. We can pick him up later."

Laura stood in shocked silence. Those men were talking about her father, she was sure they were. But beyond that she didn't know what to think. Her relief at knowing he was still alive was soon replaced with anger at his so-called success. Who did he think he was, leading soldiers against these poor people and pummelling them to death? Couldn't he just frighten them into running back to their farms?

Suddenly a firm hand clamped over Laura's mouth. A cold fear gripped her as she tried to twist herself away.

"It's me, Miss. Don't yell, an' I'll let go."

Laura nodded. The hand gradually moved away from her mouth. She tasted dirt on her lips. She turned around gingerly, wiping her mouth with the back of her hand.

She was not surprised to see that it was the boy she had met in the morning. He looked tired but meaner. Laura was beginning to wish she'd never come out, but she didn't want to let on she was scared.

"What are you going to do now?" she said roughly.

"Don't know. Guess I'll head back through Stockbridge and to the hills. Lots of places to hide in them hills." At these words, the boy looked so defeated that Laura lost all her fear. His eyes were sunken and his face was cold and red.

"There's a storm starting," she said.

"Maybe so, but I can't stay here. They'll soon be searchin' everywhere for the strays." He looked at the flakes that were beginning to fall.

"They won't search our house because my father's a judge."

He stared back at her in disbelief before saying in a squeaky voice, "What 'bout the Judge, hisself?"

"He's away," she tried to reassure the boy. Now he was the one who was scared.

"Still, I don't like it." His tone was firmer now.

"I could take you to our neighbours. They're out in the country a bit."

"How do I know it's not a trap?"

"You don't. So you can strike out in the storm if you wish, and they'll soon be combing the countryside for you. If you don't collapse in the storm or get lost, the soldiers will pick you up for sure."

He glanced down the road where the soldiers had gone. Then, as he turned to leave, he looked at Laura and hesitated. He stood still for a minute and then, reluctantly, slumped down onto a fallen limb. He sat there staring ahead as the snow began to fall thick on the ground.

"Well . . . maybe it's not such a bad idea," he mumbled.

Laura and the ragged boy tramped through the snow across a field in the direction of Thomas and Levi's house, where Laura knew she could find a spot for the boy to hide. Of course, they would have to keep the whole thing from their father, but Thomas and Levi were good at that. As they walked past Laura's home, the wind picked up from the north and cut them with cold right to the bone. After they walked past the barn, Laura turned to look back at the house. For a moment, she was able to make out the candle still flickering in the side kitchen. Then the wind blew even harder and the light disappeared from view.

"It's not far," she said, although the farm was almost a mile away. Her weak companion was plodding along even more slowly than before, and without any warning, he stumbled and fell face first into the deep snow. Laura held out her mittened hand to help him, but he brushed the snow from his face and struggled to his feet by himself.

A few minutes later, he stumbled again and this time accepted Laura's offer to help. He slung his right arm over her right shoulder and staggered along behind her for what seemed like hours. By the time the light from the Mayo's house became visible through the snow, the boy was almost a dead weight on her shoulders and she didn't know whether they would even make it or not. She stopped for a minute, took a deep breath, and plodded forward to where the light was shining. At the farmhouse, she led the boy behind a snow-covered elderberry bush beyond the south kitchen window, where he collapsed half conscious into the snow, sheltered from the freezing wind.

Laura peered inside the kitchen window at Thomas and Levi seated by the fireplace. Fortunately, the boys were alone. She walked around to the back stoop and tapped lightly on the door with her snowy mittens.

A chair scraped on the rough floorboards, footsteps came towards her, and the door creaked open an inch. Thomas poked his nose out the door. "Laura Ingersoll! Whatever are you doing here at this hour? Hey, Levi, it's little Laura! Maybe she's brought over another stray."

They would never stop teasing her about that sick kitten she'd brought them, and then found out it was a baby raccoon. But she ignored the remark and put a finger to her lips and beckoned Thomas out onto the stone stoop. "I've brought a farm lad who needs help." She knew Thomas and Levi were sympathetic toward the rebels. In fact, she'd even heard Sam say that they might have been involved in Shay's uprising.

Thomas stopped himself in the middle of a snicker. "I'll get Levi and we'll be right out." He left the door ajar as he stepped back inside.

Still struggling to get into their wool coats, the Mayo brothers hurried out onto the back stoop and followed Laura to where the boy was lying in a crumpled heap in the snow. They rolled him over onto his back and felt for his pulse. He made only a few groaning sounds.

"This boy's suffering from frostbite and exposure. We'll have to get him warm," Thomas said.

"We don't dare take him into the house or even the barn," Levi explained to her. "Lincoln's calling in more militia. It seems a number escaped today, and they'll be scouring the countryside for them. The word is they're going to make examples of all these fellows, and squash the rebellion once and for all."

"I have it!" said Thomas. "We'll take him to the potato hole. Levi, you go back and get a pot of live coals. That'll give us enough heat. I'll get a straw pallet to lie on and we'll be warm enough."

"You're not planning to stay with him, are you, Thomas?" Levi asked.

"Of course I am. He'll need someone. He's not in good shape. He might not make it through the night."

Laura sat shivering beside the boy. Was he asleep or unconscious? She pulled together the pieces of his torn doeskin sleeve and wished she had her needle and thread. She would bring them in the morning, she decided. The ragged boy would have to hide out for a few days until the hunt was over.

When the brothers finally returned with the pallet and coals, they rubbed snow on the boy's face to bring him back out of his faint. He opened his eyes and looked at them in a daze as they hauled him up onto his feet. Laura walked behind as Thomas and Levi each took onc arm and guided the boy across the snow-covered dooryard, into the first field behind the house, where a potato hole had been dug into a hill.

"I'm glad it's snowing like this," said Thomas. "It'll cover our tracks."

"Do your parents know . . . about the boy?"

"No, and it's best they don't find out. They've gone to be with old Mrs. Sloan, who took sick latc this afternoon. They may even stay the night. But Pa'll be back in the morning to see we get the chores done right. Maybe Ma too."

The entrance to the potato hole was small, about three feet by two. Thomas crawled in first and reached back for the boy, who had just enough strength left to worm his way inside behind him.

Levi loosely nailed the boards back to seal the entrance, and packed snow all around to hide them from sight.

"They'll be snug in there," he said to Laura. "I'll take food out to them first thing in the morning."

"Thank you, Levi," said Laura, turning to leave.

"Wait," Levi called after her.

"I must go. They'll miss me."

"I'll walk with you till we see your house lights. This is sure some storm and it's getting worse. I wouldn't want you lost."

They plodded ahead in silence through the deepening snow.

FOUR

Laura shivered into her long wool stockings, and fumbled over her knee garters with cold, stiff fingers. She drew her short gown over her shift, tied on her two pockets, which were held by a draw string around her waist, and covered them as fast as she could with her two petticoats. The outer thick one was quilted. She looked across the room at her sister, who was sleeping soundly in the morning light. Mira was warm and snug in her bed, not like Red, who even now might be freezing in the potato hole with Thomas. As soon as she was fully awake, Laura could only think of the rebel boy and how she would have to get over to the Mayos' to see how he was doing before the rest of the household was up. She sat down and put on her calf-high moccasins. On her way past the dresser, she took a needle and a spool of tough thread from the top right-hand drawer and tucked them into one of her pockets.

Bett was already in the kitchen, singing as she kneaded dough on the baking table. "Help yourself to some porridge, child," Bett said without turning around. "Your father come home last night, or I should say this mornin'. He was plenty done in. He'd been huntin' down them rebels all night. Seems they had quite a fight yesterday."

"Where?"

"Down somewhere near Egremont. Their leader was wounded pretty badly, they say. Five men was killed, including two government men. That teacher from over Stockbridge way was killed. Poor devil. He wasn't any part of it at all. He'd begun his day peaceful in his own classroom afore he was dragged off. But they've caught most of 'em now."

"What'll happen to them?"

"They'll hang 'em sure. What with their thievin' along the way, folks has no sympathy for 'em."

"When did Father come home?"

"I don't rightly know, but it wasn't long ago. He said the storm had blown out all tracks and he'd best wait till mornin' to carry on the hunt. He'll probably be up soon, though the poor man looked plum worn out. I hope he sleeps for a while."

Laura walked over to the washbasin that sat on a wooden stand near the back door. "He won't be here long," she said gloomily. "*He never ever is.*"

"One of these days, your father will be home more. He will." Bett patted Laura's shoulder. "It just takes time after a war to return things to normal. He's workin' on it. He's had his own troubles too. What with your mother passin' away so sudden, and now married again and his young wife ailin' so much, it's not been an easy life for the Captain."

Laura knew that, but still she wondered about her father's part in the battle that had gone on the day before. "Did he say much about yesterday, Bett?"

"Not much. Just said they still had to find some of those fellows."

"Maybe those men have a right to rebel." Laura sometimes thought out loud when she was talking to Bett, but this time she even surprised herself with her boldness. What if her father had heard her?

"Your poor father is terrible torn up, sympathizing with the farmers 'bout here and their situation and all. Still it's no excuse for lawlessness. An' your father's not 'bout to put up with it."

Laura finished her porridge silently. Then when Bett was busy cutting the bread dough into pieces for loaves, she slipped out to the front hallway and grabbed her cloak, then came back to the kitchen to get her fur tippet from the nail by the door. She could feel the extra mittens and stockings she had stuffed in the pockets of her cloak the evening before.

"Where are you goin', Laura?" It was surprising how Bett could always see behind herself.

"To feed my calf," Laura said and stepped out the back door to the woodshed before Bett had time to ask any more questions.

Grabbing her snowshoes from their hooks in the shed, Laura slung them over her shoulder and hurried out the back door. The snow from the night's storm had piled up in deep drifts against the barn and the fences. She made her way into the barn to make it look as if she were really doing chores, and tiptoed along the side of the small stable, past the switching tails of the cows. Sam was pitching hay down from the loft. The great forkfuls fell with dusty thumps to the landing in front of the cows' mangers. He hadn't even noticed the door opening.

Laura slipped out the back barn door to a stone landing protected by the roof overhang. She stopped there just long enough to put on the two extra pairs of heavy wool stockings and her boots, which she fastened to her snowshoes with leather thongs.

In twenty minutes, she was standing in the Mayos' barnyard, but there was no one about, and there were no tracks leading to the potato hole. She stopped for a moment, deciding what to do next. Should she peek into the barn or go up to the back kitchen where Mrs. Mayo, if she was home, would probably be preparing breakfast? She decided to wait.

It was the right decision. About ten minutes later, Levi came out the kitchen door. He was carrying a pot of steaming porridge and a small pail of milk.

"Morning, Laura," he smiled. "I'm taking the boys some breakfast. You don't need to worry. I'll take good care of them."

"Are your parents home?"

"They came back this morning, and I told Ma about last night. I haven't seen Pa. He went straight to the barn to do the milking. He'll just think Thomas and I slept in. We do sometimes."

"I hope the boys are all right."

"Don't you worry. Thomas'll be enjoying himself. He always loves a bit of adventure. But I'm glad I convinced him to stay home from the fighting yesterday."

Laura followed silently behind, carrying her snowshoes and stepping into the large footprints Levi was making in the snow.

As they passed the barn, Levi handed her his load. "Hold these a minute. I better fetch a shovel to dig them out." Laura leaned her snowshoes against the barn's stone foundation and took the milk and porridge.

Levi came back in a few minutes and took the food again. "Let's go," he whispered, handing Laura the shovel.

"Bett says she heard the fighting was bad yesterday," Laura told him. "She said some men were killed, including the schoolmaster from Stockbridge."

"Sorry to hear that."

"She says they'll hang the prisoners for treason. Would they hang the boy, do you think?"

"I doubt it, but let's hope they won't catch him. They probably won't hang all the prisoners either. Some say they had plenty reason to rebel."

When they got to the potato hole, Levi set his load down and started shoveling the snow away from the entrance. "It sure did snow some last night," he said. "I had no idea until I saw the drifts this morning. Not even any sign there's a hole here. It's a good cover, but they'll have to eat more than potatoes, and that's all they can get in there. If we didn't open it up now, they'd starve. Anyway, it won't be suspicious looking. We get potatoes here every day."

Laura reached into her pocket and took out the needle and thread she had brought.

"What'd you bring thread for?"

"His coat needs mending."

"I see." Levi smiled as he continued to shovel. "How much do you know about this boy?"

"Not much, but he was with those men." Laura looked away from Levi's searching glance.

"What's his name?" Levi asked.

Laura had no idea, so she blurted out, "Red."

"Well, it's not hard to figure out how he got that name. What's his last name?"

"He didn't say, but he did say that he lives with his uncle, and when his uncle joined these men he was forced to join up too. So Red didn't have any choice. He had to tag along."

"Too bad. He can't be much older than you, Laura, and already he's a wanted man." Levi stuck the shovel into the snowbank. He had reached the boards that covered the opening to the potato hole and with his hammer quickly pried them loose.

"Wake up!" he shouted but not too loudly, in case anyone came by.

There was no response.

Dropping to his knees, Levi stuck his head into the hole and crawled inside. Laura could see only the bottoms of his boots and heard no sounds from the hole. Soon Levi began to back out, pulling Thomas with him.

Laura looked over Levi's shoulder to see the still, silent face of his brother. Startled, she squatted down beside him to get a closer look.

Levi disappeared again and emerged more quickly with the boy. Then he dropped him and rushed over to his brother. He felt for a heart beat.

Ashen-faced, he looked up to Laura. "They've suffocated!"

FIVE

Laura stared in disbelief at the stone faces of Thomas and Red. Bending over his brother, Levi was choking with sobs. Laura reached out and slowly lifted one of the boy's hands out of the snow and onto his coat. It wasn't even cold yet. Then she stared at his face, certain that one eyelid had moved ever so slightly.

"Look! Look! Levi, he's alive!" She gasped. "Maybe Thomas is all right too!"

Levi grabbed his brother's wrist and felt again for a beat. They both waited. "I feel a faint pulse," he whispered. "Get Pa quick. He's in the barn."

As Laura turned and ran to get Mr. Mayo, she could hear one of the boys cough. "Come quick," she screamed as she got to the stable in the basement. "It's Thomas. He's suffocating."

Mr. Mayo was hard of hearing but he was startled by her hysterical shouting and instantly set down his milkpail. "Where? What happened?" he asked.

"The potato hole," Laura shouted. Mr. Mayo turned and ran out of the barn, reaching the potato hole before Laura, even though he was bent with rheumatism.

"Thomas! Wake up, Thomas!" he said hoarsely, lifting his son's head onto his arm while Levi placed his coat underneath.

Levi started rubbing fresh snow on Thomas' forehead and then felt for his pulse again. "It's getting stronger, Father. I think it is! I think he's coming around."

A few feet away, Laura knelt beside the rebel boy. His eyes were open now, and he was trying to get up on one elbow but sank back weakly to the ground with every attempt. She looked over at Thomas, who was now completely conscious. Mr. Mayo was still bending over his son, and Levi seemed to have forgotten all about the rebel boy, who had finally struggled into a sitting position. But no sooner was he up than he dropped his head forward on his bent knees.

"Is Thomas all right?" Laura hardly recognized her own squeaky voice.

"I think so, Laura," said Mr. Mayo, keeping his eyes on his son, "but hurry up to the house and get my wife to bring bed-quilts." Thomas' whole body was starting to shake.

Just then the boy glanced over at the men and then back at Laura, with a look of desperate fear in his grey-green eyes. Before she started for the house, she took off her cloak and covered him as he lay shivering.

It seemed to take forever to get through the snow, hopping in and out of Levi's large footprints. But finally Laura reached the pathway, where she broke into a run and made it to the stoop in seconds. She flung open the kitchen door and stood panting on the doorstep.

"Why, Laura, whatever are you doing here so early. Something wrong with Mercy or Mira?"

"It's Thomas," she said. "He needs blankets fast." Mrs. Mayo didn't ask any questions. She rushed into another room, came back in a minute with three quilts, and handed one of them to Laura. "Keep it out of the snow," she said quietly, "and lead the way."

It didn't take them long to reach Thomas, who was looking much livelier now, sitting on his brother's coat. When Mrs. Mayo pushed smelling salts under his nose he gasped, "What you trying to do, Ma? That's worse than the coal smoke."

Laura smiled with relief as they wrapped Thomas in the quilts and started to help him up. She turned then to help the boy, but there was only her cloak lying in the snow where he had been. "Where's Red?" she asked, forgetting that Mr. and Mrs. Mayo did not know him.

"We sent him into the barn where it's warmer. He seemed to pick up faster than Thomas," Levi said. Thomas' parents were helping him walk toward the house now. Laura was amazed that his father wasn't asking more questions. If it was her father, he would be asking all kinds of them. Then she remembered that Father was home, and he might be hunting for her even now. Still she must see the boy first, so she headed for the barn.

Red was sitting on a pile of hay that Mr. Mayo had already thrown down for feed between the two rows of cow mangers. "Hello, Red," she smiled. It was such a relief to see him looking alive again.

"That's not my name," the boy grumbled.

"What is it?"

The boy hesitated. "Red'll be just fine. Call me Red." He stood up then. "I have to be goin'. I suppose they're out searchin' the whole countryside for all us fellows."

"I'm afraid so, but you must be too weak to go far, and you'll need food."

"Well, I filled up on potatoes last night, that's for sure. I'm fine."

"Wait! I bet Levi left the porridge and milk right out by the potato hole. I'll get them. Will you wait?"

"Yes, but hurry. I should be footin' it away from here." Still shaky on his feet, he sat down again in the straw and wrapped his arms around his knees.

Laura had to hurry, for any minute now, Mr. Mayo might come back to the barn to turn the boy in to the authorities. As she hurried to the potato hole, she tried to think of a place he could hide until things calmed down. He couldn't stay at the Mayos. Mr. Mayo would be furious when he found out about Thomas' escapade. Even if Mr. Mayo did not report the boy—for Thomas would be questioned if he did—he could not let him hide on his property without endangering the whole family.

The milk and porridge were just where Levi had left them. The pail was only one-quarter full now, and Laura knew one of the Mayos' dogs must have found it first. But the porridge was covered, and there was still plenty of milk left for Red. She wouldn't tell him the dog had been in it. She picked the food up and turned back to the barn. There was a trail there now from all the walking in the snow. The trackers would have an easy time of it today.

She set down the food and pushed the heavy barn door closed behind her and dropped the bolt into place. If the militia came into the barn that way, she and Red wouldn't be surprised.

Red gulped down most of the milk in a single draught. Then he started to scoop up huge spoonfuls of porridge with the wooden ladle that Levi had left in the tin pot. The porridge was spilling out of the sides of his mouth and dropping back into the pot.

"I know the safest place for you to hide," said Laura.

"Where?" asked Red, slurping the last drop of the milk.

"At my place. I'll hide you in the barn with my pet calf. No one ever bothers with my calf but me. He's my sole responsibility."

"You have to be daft. You said your father was a judge. He'd turn me in." He was scraping the wooden spoon around the edge of the pan to get the last bit of porridge.

"My father is more than a judge. He's the Captain, who led the militia yesterday against this uprising. But that's the reason you'll be safest at our place. They'd never think to look for you at the home of Captain Ingersoll."

"Don't you think the Captain himself will search and find me there?"

"No. That's the one place he won't search. He's never home long enough. But our big problem is how to get you there. We could easily be spotted walking across the fields."

"I need something else to wear. Any old sacks around here?"

"That would only make them notice you. Here, wear my cloak. The hood'll cover you up better, and I'll wear your coat. I'll say you're my friend if they stop us."

"I don't want to wear no girl's cloak, I don't," sputtered Red.

Laura frowned. "If you don't want to save your hide that's one thing, but getting me into trouble for helping you is another. Now please put my cloak on. We're running out of time."

Red stared back at her in defiance. But Laura stood holding the cloak out to him. Finally with a shrug, he took off his torn jacket. She grabbed it and threw her cloak over to him. He put it on reluctantly.

Thump! Thump! They heard loud knocking on the stable door. Red burrowed into the pile of hay, and Laura fluffed more hay around the spot where he had sat.

"Open up, Laura. It's just me, Levi!"

Laura pulled back the bolt, and in walked Levi.

"How's Thomas?" Laura asked.

"He seems fine now, but Father has gone for the doctor. There may be questions. How's the boy?" Levi looked over at Red, who was crawling out of the pile of hay.

"Who's that? Little Red Riding Hood?"

"Go on! You don't look so great yourself. But you're a fine host, I'll grant you that! You go to no end of trouble to make a man feel at home. A bit too cozy, perhaps, but I felt quite at home with all those potatoes."

"Good! Because you'll have to leave now or you could be in danger and so could all of us."

"When will the doctor be here?" Laura asked.

"Soon. Now we plan to tell the doctor that Thomas just got trapped in the hole while he was digging out potatoes. He'll know we're hiding something, but he'll never guess the truth. Probably he'll think Thomas was in on the rebellion, but he won't turn him in."

"We're goin'," the boy said, grabbing Laura by the sleeve of the doeskin coat. He limped a little as he headed for the door.

"Go that way," said Levi as he pointed to the other door at the far end of the row of cattle. That's the cows' door into the barnyard and you can't see it from the house."

"Wait," Laura called. "I have to get my snowshoes."

"I have them here, Laura." Levi reached outside. He had picked them up from the side of the barn where she had left them. When she turned around, the boy was waiting.

Laura held out her snowshoes to Red. "Here, you need these more than I do." Red shook his head and walked to the cows' door. Laura put on her snowshoes and then followed. Levi closed the heavy cows' gate behind her as Laura strode out into the bright sunshine.

She soon caught up to Red and they walked on in silence. From a distance, they looked like two girls walking through the field. In his worn boots, through snow which at times was almost to his knees, Red was struggling to keep up, though he was trying not to show it. Twenty minutes later, Laura led the way into the barn and then to a far corner where her red and white calf was munching on crushed grain in the feed trough as if it were just any old ordinary day. She felt a bit jealous of its easy life compared to hers. The calf didn't even stop eating to look at the newcomer. Laura realized that Sam must have noticed she was gone because he had fed her calf.

"Now stay here," she said, pointing to a pile of straw on the other side of the calf's pen. "You are safest right here. I'll bring you food when I can. You know I have to come back here tonight to feed my calf." She turned to go.

"Hey, don't forget your cloak. It may be a daft colour but it sure was warm!"

"You're right. It is a bright red, isn't it?"

"Thanks, Laura, without you I might have either been in jail by now or worse. I lost Uncle Gerald early in the day, but most likely he's all right. He can take care of hisself, he can."

Laura could see that in spite of his words, he wasn't so sure. So she sat down on the hay beside him. She figured her father would leave again without even knowing she was gone, so what was the hurry to get back to the house? "I guess I'll just stay a while. Nobody'll miss me anyway," said Laura. "I bet it must be fun taking part in a real rebellion."

"Fun, no. That's not what I'd call it. But we had to do it, and since we was beat, I suppose it won't get any better for folks."

"I wouldn't say that. Lots of folks are in sympathy with the rebels. And I'm on your side now."

"Really? Even though your father's fightin' us?"

"I don't think he should be. I'll talk to him, if I ever get a chance." Red's large eyes looked bright green just now, and they were eagerly fixed on her. "It won't do any good though."

A big orange cat wedged its way through the calf's stall and strolled over between them. "This is Benje," said Laura. "He's mine. They sat there patting the purring cat, who rubbed against Laura with his tail high in the air.

After a few minutes of silence, Laura asked, "What will you do now after this all blows over?"

"Maybe go to sea. I think I'd like to be a sailor and see new countries. But maybe I'd just sail down to Florida where you live on oranges and swim and eat all the time."

"You wouldn't want to go there. Florida belongs to Spain again. And anyway, I'd rather be on a pirate ship."

"A *pirate* ship!" Red burst out laughing. Laura had never heard a laugh like that one. It was so merry that it made her want to laugh too.

"You've been reading too many nursery rhymes," Red said, leaning back on one elbow in the hay and chewing on a long piece of straw. He smiled a big lopsided smile. "No girl's goin' to get on a pirate ship."

"Bite your tongue, Red. Of course, I could get on the ship. I'd dress as a boy and cut off my hair." Her snapping brown eyes looked even bigger than ever, as she stared at him.

"So you're going to be on a pirate ship, are you? Well then I'm the cabin boy and you're the stowaway. So we need signals."

"Why?" What a strange boy, she thought.

"You'll have to come out sometimes. It can be mighty small and dark in a regular ship's cabin, let alone where a stowaway might hide. Have you ever been on a ship?"

"No, but . . . "

"So we need signals, one for 'all clear' and one for 'danger'."

"How about you whistle "Yankee Doodle" if it's all clear and ring the ship's bell if there's danger?"

"I can tell you know nothing about ships or stowaways. You have to do things quiet when you're hiding. Like maybe I should rub my nose if danger's near and keep my hands behind my back if all's clear."

"What do you mean in saying I know nothing about stowaways? I'm hiding you, aren't I? Maybe I don't know much about ships, but I know they have bells . . . and this is just a game anyway."

Just then a real bell started ringing.

"See, I told you," Laura collapsed laughing into the hay. "There it is ringing right now." Suddenly Laura stopped laughing.

"Oh, oh. That's our house bell. That means there's trouble. Bett never uses it unless there's an emergency, and I think I know what the emergency is. It's me. I'm missing."

Laura scrambled to her feet and ran towards the barn door, stopping just before she walked out, to wave at Red. He was lying on the hay with his right leg crossed over his left knee and his lopsided smile seemed to be saying "thank you" and "you're daft" at the same time.

"Laura Ingersoll, where have you been?" Bett boomed as Laura stepped into the kitchen. "Your father's callin' for you. Sam couldn't find you in the barn and we've been lookin' high and low for hours."

Laura flung her cloak onto the couch and started to untie her iced boot laces. "I went for a walk in the fresh snow. It is truly magnificent out there." She handed Bett her cloak.

"Well, my magnificent lady, this is a fine time to be appreciatin' the snow. Your father's waitin' in his study and wonderin' where in God's great winter you might be. Now here's your stockings." Bett handed Laura clean, dry stockings and moccasins, and hung her dripping ones by the fireplace.

Laura slipped them on and hurried down the hall and into the study. Her father, a tall wiry man, was sitting stiffly in a chair in front of the fireplace. He did not see her. With his head tilted sideways, he was gazing deeply into the flames, his deepset brow and bushy eyebrows shading his hazel eyes.

"Good morning, Father," Laura said as she spread her hands before the blazing hearth.

"A bit early for a walk, isn't it?" he said gruffly.

"I wasn't just out walking."

"That's what you just finished telling Bett." He was frowning even more than before as he looked up at her now.

"I was hunting for rabbits. I thought I might find some rabbits for pets for Mira. She's so sick of being inside."

"And just how would you catch a rabbit?" he said impatiently, starting to light his pipe.

Laura stared into the fire. Then it came to her. "I'd use my cloak. I'd just drop it over them, and they'd be so glad to be warm, they wouldn't move."

"How ridiculous! I don't really believe that you were out hunting rabbits. It's not safe today, Laura, whatever you were doing. There are still fugitives from the battle around here. I wish I could stay home and keep an eye on things, but I must leave now to continue the search."

Laura sighed. She didn't believe her father anymore. He was always saying he wanted to be home, but he was always finding some reason to leave. And it had been happening ever since she was born in 1775, the very year the American colonies had declared war against Britain. As a rebel soldier, he had been away for most of the next three years.

Then, as a captain, he had been stationed closer to home, and Laura could remember him visiting a few times. She could still see him in his dark blue uniform with the red lapels and cuffs, rushing in the front door and hugging Mother. Then he would grab Laura and throw her up in the air and catch her again. Mother was always so happy, and they would go for sleigh rides, just the three of them. But in the summer, he was always away fighting again and he was away the summer Mira was born. When the war finally ended, he moved home and Laura truly felt that this time he would stay, but before long, he was called away again.

He had been home when the last baby came, home to stay this time, he had told them. Laura remembered taking Mira outside to play all day so they couldn't hear the commotion in the house. They stayed nearby, however, and saw the midwife come.

At last, Father had called them inside to see their new baby sister, Abigail. Father must have been hoping for a boy, as he looked very sad, but Laura was glad to see the perfect little baby girl wrapped snugly in their old wooden cradle.

"She's beautiful," Laura whispered, bending over her. "May I see Mother?"

"Not now, Laura," her father replied. "Your mother's sleeping."

But Laura was determined to see her. So later that evening, when all was quiet, she tiptoed into the bedroom and walked up to the bed. As Laura was standing there, her mother opened her kind brown eyes and smiled. She had a smile that no one could match.

"Laura," she said tenderly.

"Mother! Mother! You're awake! Are you feeling fine now?"

"Yes, Laura, I'm fine. Have you seen the baby?"

"Oh, yes. She's beautiful."

"Watch out for her, Laura, and for Mira."

"Of course I will, Mother, but you'll be about soon."

"Not so soon this time, Laura. I'm very tired."

Laura gazed at her mother's pale, drawn face. "May I bring you anything?"

"No . . . just explain about the new baby to Mira."

Her mother's eyes closed and she lay very still, already asleep. Laura stood there for a few minutes, and suddenly she was afraid.

Reluctantly, she left her mother's room and started towards her own room but hesitated when she passed her father in the hall.

"Is Mother all right?" she asked directly.

"She's fine. Just tired, dear. Why do you ask?"

"She looks, well, different, and she was asking me to tell Mira about the baby. She sounded worried."

"She's always worrying about you girls," her father mumbled. His eyes were darkening. "She'll be fine in the morning after a good night's rest. Good night, Laura."

Laura hurried into her room and tucked the covers in around her sister before she climbed into her own bed.

Father had been wrong. Mother was not fine. She developed a fever, which gradually rose unchecked, and three weeks later she had died. Baby Abigail was sent to be brought up by Aunt Nash and Uncle Samuel, who lived in Sheffield.

Laura looked now at her father seated at the other side of the hearth. He was waiting for an answer. "Where did you go, Laura?" he repeated.

"Across the fields." Then she abruptly asked, "Did you know that Mother Mercy is very sick?"

"Bett told me she has a cold but that's nothing to worry about. Just because your mother died is no reason to believe Mercy will. There's no need for you to get upset about these things. Bett and Sam are capable. . . . I hear you're doing very well in school these days."

"Yes, thank you . . . and I must dress for school now."

"You shouldn't go out again today, Laura. School's been cancelled. We've got to flush out the rest of these fellows, poor devils. Then it will be safe for school to open again."

"Father, it's not fair!" Laura burst out.

"Laura, do not shout. Now what's not fair?"

"The way you're hunting all these men. You should be helping them!"

"That is quite enough, Laura. Now listen. These men have broken the law, robbing and killing, and it is my job to uphold the law."

"Who was killed?"

"Two government men and three of the rebels, along with the Stockbridge teacher." He was sorry to tell her this. She looked so much like her mother with her big brown eyes full of concern that he had to look away for a moment.

"Will this end it all?"

A tapping sound came at the window. Laura raised her eyes, and there in the window right behind her father was Red, making arm signals that she couldn't understand. She looked back quickly to her father and hoped he hadn't noticed her surprised expression.

"I don't know, Laura. I hope this will stop it. When I ride out to preside over the local courts, I never know if they'll come along and lock me out. It's very aggravating."

Laura dared not look out the window again, but she had to keep her father talking a little longer so Red would have time to return to the barn. "Sam heard that these men are only robbing because they're starving," she said while she started to rub her nose to warn Red.

"I wonder where he heard that rumour? It's not as bad as all that."

She must get out of the house to see what Red wanted. She hoped he was heading back to the barn. It was dangerous for him to stay there.

"Laura, what's the matter with your nose? It's as red as a cherry."

"Oh, I don't know. I guess I nipped it a bit when I was walking in the cold."

"Well, stop rubbing it! And I don't want you outside again today. I hate to leave home so soon again, but Shay's rebellion has got to be stopped."

Her father strode brusquely across the room and out the door.

Laura went to the window, which was stuck shut for the winter. There was no sign of the boy now, but as soon as Father had gone, she would rush out to find him. She couldn't help smiling as she went over to her father's chair and slumped into it. For once in her life, she was happy to see her father leave.

SIX

Laura watched her father ride his horse down the lane before she grabbed her red cloak from its hook in the front hall. She could hear Bett moving about in the kitchen, so she stepped lightly out the front door and hurried around the south side of the house to avoid being seen from the kitchen window. There was no sign of Red.

When Laura reached the barn, she slipped into the upper hay mow and scurried down the ladder into the stable and over to the small stall, where she had left Red. There was nothing there but the calf. It poked its little red and white head through an opening in the manger and nuzzled the rubbery grey-white end of its nose against her hand. She patted its head and wondered where Red could have gone.

"Surely he hasn't gone out again with the search still on?" she thought. Then she heard the heavy lower cowstable door creak open. In stumbled Red with Sam right behind him.

"What are you doin', boy? Up to no good, I'd say, just hangin' aroun'," grumbled Sam.

Sam sounded more worried than angry. So Laura stepped out from behind her calf's stall. "He's my friend, Sam," she said quietly but firmly. Would Sam defy her and turn the boy in?

"And how do you know him, Laura?"

Laura sputtered out, "We . . . we . . . met over at the Mayos'. I told him he could stay here for a few days."

"If you met him at the Mayos, how come he didn't stay there?"

"It's a long story, but he needs somewhere to stay. You won't tell on him, will you, Sam? Please Sam?" Laura had walked over beside Red now and was watching Sam anxiously. If Sam told her father, she would be in a lot of trouble, and she hated to think of what might happen to Red. He'd go to prison or worse if he were turned in to the authorities.

Sam stroked his right hand through his curly grey hair as he looked from one to the other. Laura knew he was having a hard time deciding. Sam had looked after their farm since Laura could remember, and he always carried out her father's orders, but he was a kind man, who seldom said "no" to Laura. She was counting on that now as she stood there staring at him with pleading eyes.

Red too stared straight at Sam as they both waited. Then Sam smiled kindly at Laura and said, "Can't see what there is to tell. I'm just doin' what the young miss of the house says. Your father'll not be home for a few more days until this hunt's over and if this child's gone by then, there'll be nothin' to explain."

"You won't tell him I hid a fugitive, will you?" asked Laura.

Sam smiled at Red. "What fugitive? All I see is a child. Where's your folks, boy?"

"Back home in Ireland. I come out here to live with my uncle, but he's too poor to keep hisself. So I set out on my own to find work. I haven't had any luck . . . yet."

"Well, you can only stay a few days, mind. Then you'd best be on your way. Laura, you better hurry on up to the house afore Bett misses you and starts askin' questions. I'll see the boy is looked after."

"Thank you, Sam. I'll be right along. I just want to feed my calf first," said Laura.

Sam started dishing out a little crushed grain into the mangers of the young cattle while Laura and Red walked over to her little calf. "Why were you waving at the window?" Laura mumbled.

"Sam found me. I thought he'd hand me over to your father, so I broke loose and ran away. But I stopped to wave goodbye to you. When he saw me waving, he believed my story about knowing you and said he'd talk to you first before he handed me over to the authorities."

"We'll all be in big trouble if Father finds out," said Laura.

"I'll leave in a couple of days. The hunt should be over then," Red said as he flopped down on a pile of hay. He looked tired and his smile was a bit weaker than it was before.

"I'd better go, Red. But don't worry. I'll think of something."

*****

Two days later in the early dawn, Laura was tiptoeing by her parents' bedroom. The pine boards creaked as she went past. She knew her Father had come home, for she had wakened a short time ago and heard him talking in a low voice to Bett about Mother Mercy. It seemed she now had pneumonia.

The fire in the kitchen hearth was low and she knew she must hurry because Sam would soon be there to build it up. Reaching into a lower bin, she took out a whole loaf of Bett's fresh bread. Then she grabbed a piece of cheese out of the top cupboard. She tucked them under one arm and grabbed her cloak and boots with the other hand and rushed out to the shed. She dropped the food in an old basket and threw on her cloak. Outside, a warmer dampness filled the air, and she could see a light fog lingering on the Green River that ran behind the barn across the southwest corner of their farm.

Laura stepped onto the stone stoop at the entrance to the lower barn and pushed open the heavy door. As she crept inside, she felt the moist warmth of the air around the sleeping animals. Her cat came up and brushed against her as she hurried past her calf to Red, who was now sitting up rubbing his eyes.

"Wake up," said Laura. "Father's home."

Startled, Red jumped to his feet, grabbing his doeskin coat. The sleeves were still inside out from when Laura had mended them. "I'm out of here. If he finds me, we're all in big trouble—you, Sam and me!"

"Don't worry. He just came in and I'm sure he's still asleep. He'll probably sleep till mid-morning. If he's up before then, it'll be to fetch the doctor for my stepmother. She's worse."

"I'm sorry, Laura." He sat down in the hay and started to pull the sleeves of his coat right-side out.

"It can't be helped, I guess. Bett takes good care of her." Laura handed him the bread and cheese. "Here's food for you to take with you. But it would be easier to carry in a sack. I'll get you one from the granary upstairs." She hurried over to the ladder and climbed up to the floor above.

Red was wearing his coat, and was ready to go when she returned. She handed him the sack. Red carefully put the food in the sack and slung it over his right shoulder. "Where'll you go now?" she asked.

He did not look at her. "To Canada, maybe. Me and Uncle Gerald planned to head up there if the rebellion failed."

"How's it any better up there, with the British in charge of things! It was the British taxes that started the Revolutionary War."

"Uncle Gerald said they're givin' the men tools, seed and land to set up their own farms."

"Your Uncle Gerald didn't fight for the British in the war, did he? So why would they give him anything?"

"Up in Canada, who knows which side he fought for?"

"Well, he's not here to go with you, and it's too far for you to go alone. Besides, they won't set up a boy in farming. So where will you go?"

"Don't you worry none about me. I'm used to takin' care of myself. I'll find work on a farm."

"I thought you said the farmers haven't got any money. How can they hire you?"

"Farmers can't afford to pay me, but they always have lots of work to be done. I can sleep in the barn and I don't eat much. Most farmers have some food around, haven't they?"

Laura thought he sounded a little uncertain, but she guessed there was no other choice—or was there? "Why don't I tell my father and ask him to help you?"

Red shook his head. "I'll take my chances with a farm family ahead of the Captain. Could you suggest a family?"

"I'm sorry, Red, I can't. But maybe Thomas or Levi could." They stepped outside, and Red pushed the heavy stable door shut behind them.

"Thanks for helping me. I'd most likely have frozen in a snowbank if you hadn't come along," he said in a husky voice.

In the grey cold dawn of the early March morning, Laura looked up at him and nodded again. A tear rolled down her cheek. She stood waiting for him to go. But he lingered there just looking at her and shifting from one foot to the other. Then suddenly he stepped right up to her, leaned over and kissed her on the cheek.

Laura was so surprised she almost fell backwards off the stone stoop. When she had got her balance again, he was across the barnyard and jumping over the rail fence. Then he was plodding through the snow-filled fields towards the northwest. She raised her hand to wave in case he turned around, but he didn't. She watched him grow smaller and smaller in the distance until he vanished over the knoll.

SEVEN

Elizabeth was back. That was bad enough, but worse still, Father had made Laura invite her on this picnic. Laura stared at her from behind as they made their way across the meadow next to the Mayos' woodlot. Who but Elizabeth would wear a light mauve satin gown with all the lace trimmings to a picnic? And she had mauve ribbons looped through her hair and a puffy bow at the back of her head. Laura was wearing a dark brown cambric outer petticoat and a woolen short-gown that draped down over her waist. She could move about freely in the full petticoat with no fear of dirt showing. Because of her practical clothing, however, Laura had been given the job of carrying the picnic basket, and it was heavier than it had looked when Bett gave it to her at the house. She strolled through the new grass that glistened under the April sun, with Mira hanging onto one hand and the basket in the other. The three girls had come along the cow path that ran from the Ingersolls' barn to the Green River at the back of their property.

"Ooo, oh, oh, I saw one! Oh, get it out of here!" Elizabeth was jumping sideways off the path, tugging her skirt in towards her as if something were biting at it.

"What are you shouting about, Elizabeth?" Laura was trying to sound polite, but was not succeeding.

"That! It's . . . it's a snake. I saw it. It was coming right for me."

"Where? Show me. Maybe we can take it home."

Elizabeth looked as if she was going to be sick. "Just get it away from me. Take it away."

"I don't see any snake. Did you notice what direction it was going?"

"Towards me! Can't you hear? It was sitting about over. . . ."

Zing-pfff! A loud crack came from the direction Elizabeth was pointing, followed by a puff of smoke. Mira screamed and grabbed Laura's leg. Laura dropped the picnic basket, but tried not to look scared. It was definitely a gunshot, but there was no sign of anyone around. All the same, the woods were nearby and anyone could be lingering there only fifteen feet away. She pushed Mira on ahead down the cowpath and told Elizabeth to get moving too. Elizabeth rushed along so close beside Mira that she nearly tripped over her.

"What's your hurry, girls?" shouted Thomas Mayo. He stepped out of the woods, his hands in his pockets, and flashed his usual teasing smile.

"Was that you shooting?" Laura turned and confronted Thomas.

"Yes, doggone it! I missed a rabbit."

"You might have hit me," Elizabeth said hotly.

Thomas brushed his straight brown hair back from his forehead and still smiling said, "Awful sorry. I sure didn't mean to frighten you." He walked over to the girls with his musket over his right shoulder and his powder horn and ball dangling over the other one.

Elizabeth's frown relaxed as she smiled back. "We've come to pick flowers from your woods, Thomas."

"I'm afraid it's a little early. But next month there'll be plenty." He turned to Laura. "See anything of Red?" he mumbled.

"No . . . not since he left."

"Who's Red?" asked Elizabeth, stepping between Laura and Thomas.

"A friend of Laura's, from out of town." Thomas smirked at Laura.

Elizabeth, staring at Thomas, missed Laura's glare. She just turned to Laura and said, "You never told me about your beau."

"He's not a beau. He's just a . . . " Laura was furious with Thomas, for he knew how curious Elizabeth would be and that Laura couldn't explain about Red. She could see that Thomas was enjoying himself immensely. She had to stop him from saying more. "Would you like . . . to join us for lunch?" she stammered. Bett had packed more than enough.

"Don't mind if I do," Thomas answered speedily. He was familiar with Bett's picnic baskets.

Thomas and Elizabeth walked ahead together through the grass and underbrush, back toward the woods. Laura held on to Mira, who said she needed Laura to protect her from snakes. In a few minutes, they stopped at the spot where Laura had dropped the picnic basket, but it was nowhere in sight.

"I thought we left it right here." Elizabeth gazed down at the trampled grass.

"I thought it was here, too, but maybe it was a little over there," Laura said, stepping a few feet nearer to the trees. A trail was leading to the woods.

"Maybe Levi is playing a joke on us. Maybe he took it," Laura responded.

Elizabeth looked up surprised. "I didn't see Levi. Was he hunting rabbits too?"

"No. He was still cleaning out the stables, the last I saw of him," Thomas offered. "But you never know. He could have started out later. The land's not quite dry enough to work up yet. Maybe Dad let him go." Laura knew that Mr. Mayo had been keeping close watch on his sons lately.

"I can't think of anywhere else the picnic basket could have gone," said Laura, "and I don't think it's very nice of Levi to steal our food."

"Oh, for crying out loud, Laura, if Levi took it, he'll bring it back any minute now. And I don't really think he did. You two stupid girls probably just lost your own picnic basket."

Laura's eyes narrowed into slits. "Thomas Mayo! You have no right to talk to us that way."

Mira ran over and gave him a kick in the shin.

Elizabeth's head shot up in the air as she looked down her nose at Thomas. "That was a horrible thing for you to say, Thomas."

"Well, I can see I'm not wanted here." Thomas turned away, his powder horn banging against his side. The three girls watched him disappear into the woods.

The sun was high now as the girls looked back across the meadow. "I was planning on eating down by the river bank," said Elizabeth. "But let's go and sit a while anyway."

"I'm hungry," shouted Mira.

"We'd better look some more," Laura said, as she wandered back to the place where she had last seen the basket. In the trampled grass, Laura spotted a piece of red cloth, the corner of a handkerchief she'd given Red. She knew now that Red had been there. Her pulse was starting to beat a little faster. It would be just like something that Red would do.

"Well if you're going to spend all our time looking for the stupid basket, I'm going home," said Elizabeth. "Grandpa is coming for me just after lunch."

Laura could barely hide her pleasure. If Red were in that woods, he would never come out with Elizabeth there. The sooner she left, the better. "How would you like to take Mira with you?" she asked. "She's hungry."

"No. I'm staying with you," said Mira, grabbing Laura's hand.

"I don't want you anyway, Mira," Elizabeth grumbled. "Good-bye, Laura." She turned and marched sedately back to the main path.

When Laura saw Elizabeth's flat straw hat disappear behind a knoll, she walked over to the woods and shouted, "Hello there." She twirled around with her hands grasped tightly behind her back, their signal that all was safe.

The sun, now at high noon, was warm, and Mira was happily picking violets and dandelions, so Laura ran on into the edge of the woods. Was Red really there? She stood still in the shadows of the trees, listening for the scampering sounds of small animals.

"Not so loud," said a raspy voice behind her. She spun around and saw an unshaven man standing a few inches away.

"Who are you?" Laura shot back. The man was carrying a musket in one hand with a powder horn slung over his right shoulder, and in his other hand, he had their food basket. At the sound of movement between the trees, Laura turned again. Another man with scraggly brown hair was coming towards her. Laura thought of running home, but she did not want to leave Mira. She could not outrun these men if she carried her sister. Besides, they had her basket, which she was not going to give up without an explanation.

Just as the second shaggy-haired man approached her, Red came running up behind them. "This is Laura," he said. "She'll not give you away."

Laura was relieved to see Red, but she backed away from the men a little. "Why did you take our food, and why didn't you answer my signal?" Laura stared furiously at Red. She wouldn't mind feeding Red but she didn't want to feed two strange men, who might even harm her and Mira.

"I went to the other side of the woods to look aroun'. I just got back."

"But your friends took our food." Her voice trembled. Who did they think they were anyway? The first man settled himself down on a tree trunk, tore the white linen cloth from the top of the basket, and threw it on the ground.

"There's lots of food there," said Laura. "Help yourself. But you'd better leave the basket for me to take home or my father will be asking questions. I'll be back for it soon." She stood staring at the men for a few more seconds.

The first man was eating a turkey drumstick with one hand and one of Bett's delicious buns with the other. The other man was chewing with his mouth wide open on a huge piece of white meat and a sandwich—both at the same time.

Laura glared at Red and motioned him over to a beech tree a few feet away from his rude companions. "You'd better explain yourself and those men fast, Red."

"I just found them there—honest," Red began.

"I don't believe you, Red."

"Well, they *are* my friends. I sorta told them you'd help us get food. They hadn't eaten for three days."

"Are they Shay's men?"

"I'll not be tellin' on my friends."

"They are, aren't they!"

"If you promise you won't tell about 'em, they'll leave tonight and no one'll be the wiser. I need your promise, though. I'll vouch for you."

"Do they know who my father is? He'd go after anyone who harmed his daughters."

"No, they don't know who your father is, and I certainly wouldn't want them to find out."

"Why? They say the fugitives are afraid of my father."

"You'd be in even more danger if they knew. There's a lot of them bitter toward your father. And remember both those men are armed. It's best they don't know."

"I want to leave as soon as they'll let us. I suppose we're being watched."

"You are that. Do you promise me you'll not reveal their identity?"

"I promise."

"Cross your heart and hope to die?"

"I didn't tell on you before, did I? And I won't tell on them if they'll just go and leave us alone."

Red scanned the fields and glanced back at the men. "Come dark, they'll be away from here, but I'd like to stay in the barn overnight."

As Red walked over to tell the men his plans, Laura wondered what part he was playing in the rebellion now and why he had to hide out alone. The less she knew, the better, she thought, looking across the tall grass to where Mira was playing. She felt a little better as she looked at her younger sister and thought about the day. The picnic had turned out not badly after all. She had managed to get rid of Elizabeth without even trying and she had found Red again. It was strange how bad beginnings turned into happy endings at times. She sighed and smiled.

"Well, milady, shall we be off?" Red had walked up behind her. "I've set the lads straight and now I'm after a lodging place. Do you know of one hereabouts?"

"For the likes of you? I wouldn't count on it!"

"Hah-hah, too late. I already have a reservation, you know. One night's lodging in the finest cow stall in the county. It says right here." Red pulled a blue handkerchief out of his right pocket and started waving it in the air.

"Oh, your handkerchief, the red one I gave you . . . it's lying in the grass, just a bit past Mira. Mira, go pick up the red handkerchief in the grass over there and bring it back to me." As Laura watched Mira run, she noticed that someone else was in the field. She was disappointed to see Thomas Mayo. He was probably on his way to find out what Red was doing here. It wasn't as if Red was her beau, but it would have been nice just to talk with him alone for a bit.

"Well, hello there," Thomas called as he ambled towards them. "If it isn't my old potato hole companion!" He walked up to Red and clapped a hand on his shoulder. The two looked at each other in silence.

"I still don't forget what you did for me, you know," Red said after a few seconds. "I mean, it's not every host that lays on such a spread of spuds."

"Oh, it was nothing. We treat all our guests well."

"Laura, Laura, I found the handkerchief! Here it is," Mira yelled, running over to where Laura and the boys were standing. "Can I keep it?"

"No, Mira, it's Red's."

"No, it's mine! I found it! You're wrong and I'm right. It's mine!"

"Mira, it belongs to Red. Just give it to me and I'll give it to him."

"No, no! You'll have to catch me first!" Mira started running at full speed across the grass and onto the muddy pathway by the river's edge.

"Mira come back! Come back right now! It's dang. . . . " But Mira heard nothing. She just kept running, right into the clump of pussywillows on the riverbank.

Laura ran after her as fast as she could, but when she got to the pussywillows, Mira was nowhere in sight. Laura looked down to the river and saw what had happened. Mira had lost her footing and was now rolling down the bank and into the river. Laura screamed, but when she started for the water, her knees suddenly gave out, and she sank to the ground. Then she heard a splash and saw Red jumping into the river.

Everything was a bit blurry, but Laura thought she saw Mira surfacing and Red grabbing her. Mira was choking, sputtering and hitting at Red. Laura could not believe her eyes. While Red held Mira, still struggling, they both soon disappeared under the splashing water. When they came up, Mira had stopped struggling. Red swam back to the riverbank, holding Mira's head above the water.

Now Red was out of the water, slapping Mira on the back. He was wet and shivering, but he didn't seem to notice. He was gazing intently into Mira's face, the crease between his eyebrows getting deeper and deeper. Finally, Mira started breathing between coughs.

"Here, put my coat on her," said Thomas, who had set his gun, horn and bag down on the ground and was standing above Red. "Turn her over and hit her again."

Red did that, and Mira spit up some more water. Then she started to breathe normally.

"What is it? What are you two ruffians. . . . " It was Father's voice. He had returned home the middle of the morning, and when Elizabeth had come to the house with a strange tale about a missing food basket, he had decided to investigate. He was only a few hundred feet away when he heard Laura's screams and raced ahead to the meadow.

Red and Thomas were not listening. Red was lying on his back, breathing heavily. Thomas was picking Mira up and wrapping her more tightly in his coat.

"Here, Mr. Ingersoll. My friend just saved your daughter's life."

"Why . . . it's Mira. What happened? Well, never mind. We can lose no time. Let's just get her inside." Father took Mira, and started running with her. He was headed back to the house.

From the woods, Red's two companions watched Father take the child. They were only a hundred feet from the riverbank but they could not recognize him. The older one took out a small telescope and looked through it.

"Do you know him?" asked the younger man.

He nodded, and without a word, handed the other fugitive the telescope and started to load his musket. "It's him all right," the young one said as he lowered the telescope. "We'll need to get closer to fire. When they pass the far end of the woods, the trail is almost within touching distance, and we'll be there ahead of them."

Laura couldn't keep up to Red, who was running with unusual speed towards her father. He had saved her sister, but why was he so determined to run at her father's heels? He had always tried to avoid her father before now. Panting and shaking, she sped along, hoping to catch up to her father and this crazy boy with the red hair.

As they reached the east end of the woods, she had almost caught up to them when she looked up to see Red, running between her father and the woods. Then she remembered those men. Now she knew that Red was running beside Father to protect him from his would-be assassins. Red was directly between Father and those men. But who was to say they wouldn't shoot anyway?

Laura circled out into the wet fields away from the path and away from the woods. She was too far away to call to her father, and she didn't want to be captured by the men. She started running. All she could hear was her own beating heart and pounding feet and the sounds of birds chirping. She braced herself for the shattering sound of a musket.

She kept on running and running—it seemed almost forever—until she almost bumped into Red and Thomas.

"How's Mira?" Laura gasped as they ran side by side. For the moment she had forgotten Red was the enemy.

"She seems fine.... Your father's... taking her... to the house."

Laura gave Red a sideways glance. "Come on up yourself for dry clothes." Her father could decide about this boy. Maybe she *should* tell her father about the men. She'd have to think about it.

Thomas added, "Yeah, Red,... you just saved the man's daughter. He'll not turn on you now!"

They all stopped running a hundred feet from the back door. "I better not go in." Red stared at the ground. "Please don't tell on us, Laura. We didn't harm you none 'cept for eatin' your victuals."

"That's true," she said and grabbed his hand and started to pull him along toward the house. "C'mon. You've got to get dry or you'll catch your death."

"Oh, all right." He did not take much persuading, for he was starting to shake from the cold. "Those men will be gone come dark."

"I hope so."

Laura left him and Thomas in the back shed while she went into the kitchen. Already Bett had removed Mira's wet clothes and wrapped her in a dry blanket. The fire blazed brightly in the hearth. Bett handed Laura some dry clothes and kept drying Mira's curls.

"It's mine! It's mine!" Mira whimpered as Bett set her down on the couch near the fire.

Laura slipped into the side pantry, where she changed into the dry clothes. Then she hurried back to the kitchen. Father was standing by the fire, looking down at Mira. "Don't you ever go down by the river again, young lady," he said sternly. "And whatever were you thinking of—letting her go there, Laura? I thought you were responsible enough to watch Mira. I see I was wrong."

Laura cringed and she swallowed before she said, "I need dry clothes for the boy." Then her legs gave way and she sank to the couch beside Mira. She put her head in her hands and started to cry.

Father's face suddenly changed. "There, there, Laura. Don't cry. Mira's fine, now. I didn't mean to be harsh. Where is the boy?"

"In the shed, and Thomas is with him."

"Bett, have Sam get the boy a change of clothing," Father called back as he opened the door into the shed. In the far corner, Father saw a boy not much bigger than Laura, shaking from the cold. Even in this wet condition, it was obvious that the boy's clothes were in shreds.

"Come in, you two. What is your name, boy?" Father had a feeling he had seen Thomas' companion before.

"Red." But the name couldn't have been less appropriate at this moment. The only colour on his face was the blue of his lips.

Sam appeared just behind Father and winked at Red, "I have clothes, sir," he said. Red was thankful to see Sam, who had been secretly giving him food for the past month. Sam smiled as he handed Red a pair of his own large trousers and a homespun shirt.

"Thank you, Mister," the boy said to Father and Sam. It didn't take him long to slip out of his own wet clothes and into the huge dry ones.

"Come in and get warm. And let's get some tea into all of you," Father said. "Thomas too."

"Well, sir, I can't stay. There's chores I'm to do. So I have to get back. But thank you." Thomas went out the back door, turning to wave goodbye to Red.

Inside the kitchen, Father handed Red a towel to dry his hair. "Come over to the fire and sit right here. I don't know how to thank you for what you did."

"Laura would have got her if I hadn't, Mister."

"I'm a weak swimmer. I doubt I could have saved her." Laura did not admit that she hated the water and had feared it ever since a boy had drowned at a town picnic the year before.

Before long, Mira was chatting away as usual and Laura's father did not look quite so stern, so Red got up to leave, "I must go now," he said.

"Where do you live?" asked Father. Laura glanced quickly at Red, who was staring straight back at her. Father saw the worried expression that passed between them. Then he remembered the red-headed boy in Shay's rebellion, who was following behind the others carrying their gear in the battle—the boy who had never been found. But this couldn't possibly be the same one. After all, it was obvious that he and Laura were friends. Mind you, he was a strange-looking one.

Laura almost held her breath as she waited for her father to demand an answer from Red. He kept staring at the boy, who was looking down and mumbling in an unintelligible manner, "I used to live with my uncle, but he was killed in a battle. And now, Mister, I'm searching everywhere for work."

Did her father know what battle that was? Laura could not be sure but couldn't think of any excuse and was too weak to try.

Red was almost hidden in the loose-fitting shirt and big twill breeches. His eyes looked even larger and his face thinner as he peered up at Laura's father and waited.

Father's eyes softened, and then he said, "You saved my daughter. So I'll find you a job if you're willing to work hard. Nobody wants an idle boy."

The boy's whole face lit up as he gave Laura and her father a wide smile. "I'm not afraid of hard work. I've grown up on hard work," he said. "It's like mother's milk to me, 'tis."

"You can help Sam around here for now," said Father. "Come and I'll show you where there's an extra bed in the servants' quarters. If you've warmed up, I could take you over there now."

"I'm fine, Mister." Red was still shivering a little as he followed Father, but he turned back towards Laura just as he was going out the door, and winked.

With great relief, Laura lay down on the couch beside Mira, who was wiggling out of her blanket. Mira jumped onto the woven mat in her bare feet and ran over to the window. Rain was coming down in torrents. She pouted at the sight for a few minutes, then trotted back to the couch. Laura sat up and lifted Mira onto her lap. She pulled the blanket tightly around her, and they sat there enjoying the soothing warmth and smell of the fireplace.

EIGHT

Thud! Thud! Father was lifting the heavy knocker on Judge Whiting's door and letting it fall against the oak panels. He and Laura were standing on the front verandah. It was not long before the door creaked open and the tallest butler Laura had ever seen appeared. He looked over the top of Laura's head to her father.

"The Judge is expecting me." Laura's father announced.

The butler motioned for them to step into the cold, dark hallway. The house was built of fieldstone, which kept the place cool in summer, but it was cold and damp at almost any other time of year. Laura shivered as she looked down the long, carpeted hallway. It stretched beyond the butler towards an arched doorway that led into what looked like a throne room with carved wooden chairs and couches covered in velvet.

That morning, when Laura had found out that Father was going to visit Judge Whiting, she had asked to come along to see Red, who was now working as a groom and handyman for the Judge. Father was reluctant at first, but in the end he gave Laura permission to come. He seemed to be kinder these days, now that the rebellion was put down.

"Come with me," said the butler. Laura decided he looked like Sam, only a lot broader and taller. "The Judge has urgent out-of-town business, but he is waiting to see you before he leaves." He led the way to a room at the far right end of the hallway, just before the throne room.

"Judge Ingersoll to see you, sir," the butler announced.

Father walked into Judge Whiting's office, leaving Laura standing outside in the hallway. Laura could hear screechy-scratchy sounds coming from a violin behind one of the closed doors in the hall. She thought that must be Elizabeth practising, for she had often told Laura how well she played the instrument. Laura almost laughed aloud at the sound.

Just then the butler returned."And you're here to see Red," the butler smiled. "Well, he's just outside in the back raking up the old fall leaves that are clogging up the tulip beds. So you just follow me now, and I'll point him out to you."

Laura fell in step behind the giant butler, who seemed a lot gentler now. She found herself standing on the back stoop, looking out into a yard full of forsythia and tulips. And there, in the middle of it all, was Red, busily stuffing old leaves into a barrel. Laura nodded to the butler (she thought that was what you were supposed to do) and walked down the steps.

Would she clap her hands over his eyes and say, "It's robbers!" or would she just say "Guess who?" in her own voice. The last idea would probably be the best, since Red would be surprised when she spoke. In any case she didn't sound like a robber. She moved slowly out around a few leaves that he had left behind so there wouldn't be any rustling sounds to alert him. She tiptoed across the stone pathway that ran straight to the back gate so her hard leather shoes with their heavy, brass buckles would not make a sound.

Unsuspecting, Red finished pushing some more leaves into the barrel, grabbed his rake from the ground, and without looking toward the house, started to work again. As Laura continued on her way towards him, he bent onto his knees to rake under the fence. Laura was only three feet away from him. For once Red would be the scared one.

"Stop this minute!" A shrill voice broke through the silence. Laura and Red both jumped at the same time and saw a young woman in a dark blue silk gown standing at the back door of the house. "Why are you sneaking around in our yard?"

"She's come to see me, Missus," sputtered Red when he saw Laura just behind him.

"He's right. I've come to see him." Laura knew she was probably looking at Sally Whiting Backus, Elizabeth's mother. She was a pretty lady with long dark hair, but her eyes were flashing as she looked at Laura now.

"Red, return to your work," she said. "And you, young lady, march right over here and tell me what you are doing in our back yard, and how you got here."

Laura stared back at her. Perhaps having a sick mother in bed all the time was better than having one like this. Poor Elizabeth! With her head high, Laura walked as sedately as possible along the pathway.

Laura came to a stop just before the back door. Whoever this woman was, she had no business interrupting her visit with Red. "Please, Missus, I would like to talk to Red for a few minutes."

"Who are you?" The woman was younger than Laura had though, but she was obviously used to giving orders.

Laura was surprised she did no know that she and her father were visiting. "Why I'm. . . ."

"She's my daughter," interrupted Father, who had appeared on the back stoop. "Sally, I'd like you to meet my daughter, and, Laura, meet Mrs. Backus."

Sally turned then from Laura to Father and with a gracious smile, she said, "Why, Thomas Ingersoll, I haven't seen you in years. What a pleasant surprise!" She spoke softly now and was smiling at Laura too. "I'm pleased to meet you, Laura. Red is just over there working. You run along now and have that visit you were talking about."

Laura stared at her for a few seconds. She could not believe it was the same person talking.

"Well, Laura," Father said, "I thought you wanted to visit Red. Here's your chance."

Without a word, Laura turned and ran across the grass. This time Red heard her coming but kept raking as she approached.

"We can talk now, Red." Laura stopped right beside him.

"How'd you change the missus' mind?" Red stood leaning against his rake with one eye on the back door. Just then they saw Sally step back into the house with Laura's father following, and the door closed.

"I guess she knows Father. So how do you like it here?"

"It's great! There lots to eat, and the Judge is very kind. He even told me he felt sorry for some of those men in the rebellion. My Uncle. . . ."

Laura saw tears come to his eyes. "Well, are you going to stay here then?"

"If they'll have me. They have their slaves, and I don't know how long they'll want to keep me on. I hope I can stay until I earn enough to go back home to Ireland."

"To Ireland? What do you want to go back there for?"

"Wouldn't you go back if you were a complete orphan? I have no family left, no land. My folks are back home, and even if I'm going to be poor all my life, at least I won't be lonely."

"Oh, Red, I have a brilliant idea. Why don't I go with you? We can both run off to sea just the way we planned. And maybe we don't even have to go back to Ireland. We could go wherever we felt like going."

"But we were just pretending, Laura. This is for real. And real ships are a lot different than what you dream about. On my way over from Ireland, I was stuck down in the bottom hold with a bunch of whining children and sick women and I was bringing up in my boots all the time."

"That wouldn't bother me. Please let me go with you, Red. I can't imagine anything more exciting."

"Laura!" It was her father calling. Her had come out onto the back stoop again and was motioning Laura over to the house.

"I have to go, Red. But don't forget what I said."

"I wish you could come, but I don't know if they take girls." His mouth opened into his old lopsided smile, and his eyes twinkled.

As Laura came into the house, she heard her father's hearty laugh coming from farther down the hall. Laura had not heard her father laugh in a long time, and she wondered what Sally could have said that was so funny. Laura didn't think she was nice enough to make anyone laugh. In fact, she had been downright nasty until her father had appeared.

Sally turned to Laura with her face wreathed in smiles."Did you have a good visit, Laura?" Sally asked.

"Yes, finally. I hope the few minutes that Red took from his work did not bother you too much," Laura said a bit too cleverly.

"Of course not," Sally smiled. "He's a good worker."

"So why didn't you want me to see him?"

The smile left Sally's face. "I'm sorry, but I didn't know you. We can't be too careful these days. Ever since those men from Shay's rebellion came tramping through the town, we've all been in shock."

Thomas gave Laura a stern look, and then turning to Sally, he asked, "And did they stop by here?"

"Oh, yes. They took Papa's best wine and most of the victuals from the kitchen. I was scared to death."

"But did they hurt anyone?" asked Laura.

"No, but they might have if your father hadn't stopped them down near South Egremont. I hear that you are going to receive a promotion, Thomas."

"Yes, I believe so."

"I'm happy for you. It must have. . . ."

"Goodbye, Mrs. Backus," Laura interrupted. "We must get home to Mother. She's not well, you know."

Sally was quick to respond. "Yes, I've heard. I am so sorry."

"Mercy has a bad cold. When the warmer weather comes, it'll clear up," explained Father.

"She's very sick, Father," Laura said pointedly. "Bett thinks it's consumption."

Father looked awkwardly at Sally. "Laura has been a worrier ever since her mother died. . . . "

"You've certainly had it hard with your first wife passing away so suddenly, and now your second wife sick all the time. And it certainly can't be easy for you to care for two daughters."

He doesn't take care of us, thought Laura. He's too busy most of the time to know what we're doing. But her father seemed to be liking Sally's sympathy, for he smiled back at her as he said, "We must go now. . . . Thank you for helping the boy. Goodbye, Sally."

"Goodbye, Thomas. Goodbye, Laura. Come again any time to see Red."

Laura nodded and wondered if she really meant it. She and her father walked down the front steps of the house and along the stone pathway to the road where Sam was waiting with their horse and buggy. Just as they reached it, Red jumped off the other side, where he'd been talking with Sam. He rushed away before Laura or her father had a chance to speak to him. Laura hopped up onto the side step and landed in the front seat beside Sam, while her father sat down silently beside her.

"I didn't know you knew Mrs. Backus," said Laura questioningly.

"I don't know her that well. I knew her husband, though. He was a good soldier and a fine captain, quite a few years older than Sally, who was only a slip of a girl when she married him. She can't be any more than twenty-seven now."

"And how old are you now, Father?"

This old father of yours is now thirty-eight years of age," Father chuckled. "I thought you knew that, Laura."

"And how old would Mother have been if she had lived?"

"She would have turned thirty next January," Father said quietly.

Laura was pleased that he sounded sad. Laura liked her stepmother, but she would always remember her real mother even if Mira couldn't. Surely Father would always remember her too.

Thomas looked into his daughter's questioning eyes and saw the longing there for her own mother. He reached out and put his large hand over Laura's small one and tightened his hold with a gentle squeeze. "Don't worry, Laura," he said. "I'll never forget your mother."

Laura looked up with relief, her large brown eyes intent upon him.

"When I look at you, Laura, I always remember. You're growing to look more like her with every passing day."

Laura smiled back. It was good to have Father home.

NINE

Laura and her sisters sat quietly in the front pew of the Episcopal church. Laura looked straight ahead. Father had been wrong again. Mother Mercy had died two weeks after their visit to the Whitings'.

Now four months later, the light of the early September evening fell across the front of the church where Father stood beside Sally Whiting Backus. Sally's parents, the big white-haired judge and the little bent lady, sat on the other side of the aisle. Elizabeth, sitting beside her grandma, was wearing a beautifully made pink silk gown with a tightly boned upper part and a contrasting full petticoat. Her stylish straw hat was highly decorated with fresh flowers and was tied under her chin with a pink ribbon. Her curled blonde hair fell out below her hat and around her neck.

On Laura's left side in the pew sat Mira, and on her right were Aunt Nash and Uncle Samuel with Abigail, the sister that Father had given away right after Mother died. She was sitting between them and kept asking Aunt Nash when the minister would be all done. Aunt Nash kept shaking her head at Abigail so hard that the large orange feather on the top of her hat almost fell off.

Mira was gazing up at Sally. "I never thought we'd get such a beautiful mom," she had said to Father the day he'd announced the marriage.

Later Laura had scolded her. "Do you think mothers just come like things you buy at the general store? You're supposed to have one mother all your life, and that's our first mother, who was more beautiful than Sally and much kinder!"

In the hot August days before the wedding, whenever she could get away from chores, Laura had spent a lot of time lying on the riverbank, thinking of Mother. She remembered the time she and Mother had been picking raspberries out behind the house and a big stringy garter snake had come up beside her. She had jumped, but Mother had said, "He's quite harmless. He's more scared of you than you are of him." Laura saw her calm smile, but then it would fade and all that would be left were the raspberries and the meadowlarks flying and singing overhead.

Reverend Bostwick just kept droning on. Laura gazed past the minister to the spot before the altar where her stepmother had lain just four months before. She remembered Reverend Bostwick's words to her and her sisters after the funeral service. "She's in a better land, where there is no sickness," he had said, but Laura did not respond. She just stared at the stony face in the coffin.

Finally she had looked up at the minister. "She's with Mother now." Then she explained in case the minister had forgotten. "My real mother, I mean."

Laura's thoughts were broken now by the wedding vows she had heard her father say just two years before. Finally, the minister said, "I now pronounce you man and wife. What therefore God hath joined together, let not man put asunder." Laura did not have high hopes for this marriage. The way Father picked wives, Sally would probably die in a couple of years too. But Laura would be prepared this time. She vowed she would never become attached to another mother.

She looked at her father. But he was looking only at Sally, his new wife, who was smiling radiantly up at him.She's too young for Father, Laura thought. Why did he ever want to marry again so soon? He's never home much anyway. She'll just interfere with Bett and me and our work. She'll want to boss us all.

The newly married couple were bending over the Bible at the front of the church where they were signing their names. Laura remembered the day they had visited Red at the Whitings and how bossy Sally had been. She is not as she seems now, Father, she thought. But she will be in for a surprise. I obeyed her at her home, but now she is coming into mine, it will be a different matter. I will never call her "Mother," and I will not do what she says, and I'll see that Mira doesn't either, that is, when you aren't home. Laura knew that she would have to obey Sally when her father was home.

The couple were starting down the aisle now, and Laura noticed Mira wiping her eyes. Laura didn't know if she was crying because she liked Sally or because she was remembering Mother and

Mercy. Whatever it was, she decided she must try to look happy for Mira, so she squeezed the little girl's hand and attempted a wan smile. Mira looked up through her tears and Laura saw how sad she really was.

Laura slid her arm around Mira's shoulders. "Don't cry," she whispered. "We still have each other, and I think Sally will stay at her parents' house a lot when Father isn't home. It won't be so different."

Silently, Mira shook her head while the tears streamed down her face. Laura drew her sister back into the pew, where Mira dropped her head onto her older sister's lap and sobbed aloud. The wedding party was outside the church now, making a lot of noise. Laura handed Mira her big lace handkerchief.

"Just think! We'll have a great time at the party over at the Whitings," she whispered.

Mira's sobbing started to grow weaker and she mumbled, "Will there be candy?"

"Yes, and all kinds of cake," said Laura, "and Red will be there."

That made Mira stop sniffling; Red had already taken her for pony-back rides around the dooryard and she was quite fond of him.

"Are you ready to go now?" Laura asked her sister, who was wiping her face and blowing her nose on Laura's best handkerchief.

Mira nodded her head.

Laura stood up, straightened Mira's hat, and pressed out a few wrinkles in the snug bodice of her own gown. She pulled her hat a little tighter and checked its silky red velvet bow at the front and back. By the time the two sisters emerged from the church, the only vehicles left were a covered buggy and an open democrat.

Red was perched jauntily on the top of the uncovered two-seater, and when he saw them, he began to wave."They've got a great meal waitin' back at the Whitings. Let's go!"

Laura and Mira clambered into the wagon and squashed themselves in beside Red, who slapped the mare's reins across her back. The horse moved ahead.

Laura gave him a frown. "Don't hurry that horse! I don't care if we never get there." With her elbows on her knees and her chin in her hands, Laura hunched forward, apparently examining the road beneath the horse's feet. When the other buggy pulled up on their right, Red reined the mare in to a halt.

The driver was Thomas Mayo, who did look splendid in his fine woolen breeches and formal black coat. Sally must have asked him to escort Elizabeth, Laura decided. She hadn't paid any attention to the few rows of Whiting guests who'd been sitting on the opposite side of the church. She guessed Elizabeth had gotten over the quarrel they'd both had with Thomas the day their lunch was stolen.

"Good day, Laura . . . Mira," beamed Elizabeth. She did not acknowledge Red's presence. Laura couldn't help wondering how Elizabeth felt about the marriage. Then she caught the full force of Elizabeth's cold, green eyes and unfriendly smile, and she knew.

Thomas was trying to give Red and Laura the same cold look. It was obvious that he was proud to be escorting Elizabeth to the wedding reception and would do almost anything to please her. Laura was disgusted. She knew Thomas admired Red and here he was pretending Red didn't matter—all because of Elizabeth. Turning to check his prancing horse, Thomas pulled the reins a little tighter. "Whoa, Duke."

Red looked enviously at the sleek animal. His coat was a shining chestnut, and his lighter-coloured mane had been fully combed. Red's eyes travelled down to the slim, strong legs of the race-horse. He knew the horse would be fast. "Is he a racer?" he asked.

"The best!" Thomas smirked at Red. "Where'd you get that old nag?" He motioned to the Ingersoll's mare Red was driving. "She looks like an old. . . ." Elizabeth let out a high pitched giggle.

"Molly used to be a racer too," Laura interrupted. "She's half blood-horse, still has lots of spirit, and she's as fast as any blood horse of yours." Her brown eyes were snapping now.

Elizabeth poked her head around Thomas. "Prove it. Race us home."

Red rose to the bait and without a reply, he hit the reins across Molly's back. Startled by the sudden whack, the mare shot out onto the dirt road ahead of the other buggy. Red's infectious merry laughter filled the air.

It was Laura's turn to look smugly back at a shocked Elizabeth, who was sitting bolt upright beside Thomas as he hit his horse with the whip. "Hang on, Mira," Laura yelled.

"If we can just keep them behind us till the bend," Red mumbled almost to himself, "then we'll have them beat. They can't pass us on a single lane road." He kept a firm hold of the reins as Molly raced ahead."They could still pass us on some of those flat stretches, where the ditch is almost level with the road."

Laura glanced back to see how far behind they were. "They're catching up. Hurry, Red."

Laughing with excitement, Red tapped Mollie lightly with his whip. Unused to this treatment, she broke into a running trot that jolted the buggy unevenly.

"Help," screamed Mira. Some mud from the horse's hoofs had hit her. Her hat was hanging loosely around her neck, and her brown curls were blowing out in the wind. She wiggled out from between Red and Laura and dropped onto the buggy floor at their feet. Giggling with delight, she clung to her sister's legs and skirt with both arms.

Laura turned back to Red, whose long hair was flying out in all directions. He was perched on the very edge of the seat with the reins loose. Molly was taking the road in great striding leaps, jolting the buggy rapidly ahead. The single lane was no more than thirty feet ahead when Duke nosed his way up along beside Red. Red struck Molly a harsh blow with the whip, and she shot ahead of the other buggy onto the single lane. With a ditch on either side, the other horse could only fall back behind them. Molly's back was wet with sweat as she kept up the fast pace.

"We've got them now." Red turned to Laura, his big lopsided smile spreading across his freckled face. He pulled the reins a little to get Molly to slow down, for he didn't want to wear out the mare unnecessarily.

"I'm not so sure. There's a long flat stretch beyond our laneway turnoff and just before the Whitings." Laura was pleased, though, that they were ahead for now. She settled back on the seat alongside Red, who was sitting back, more relaxed.

"They won't try to pass us there. It's in sight of the house and folks don't race at weddings."

"Who's going to notice?"

"They'll have someone out looking for you."

"I doubt it. Father doesn't care about us anymore."

"Well, Judge Whiting cares about horses—even your horse, and so does Sam. I had to coax Sam into letting me come for you."

Molly wasn't slowing her speed now, but they could hear Duke snorting behind them. With a deep ditch on each side, he had no room to pass, and he was a racehorse, trained to pass. Red let Molly slow her pace even more.

"I can see the house," said Laura when they broke over the top of the hill. Red hit the mare lightly with the whip; she picked up speed and broke into a fast trot again as they reached the flat stretch.

"He'll not dare go faster here," Red explained, "that is unless he loses control. His horse does sound mighty restless."

They could hear the steel rims of the other buggy pounding on the ground behind them. Red kept to the middle of the road, and then just before they reached the bridge over the Housatonic River, he turned left, to enter the Whiting property by the back laneway. Red was turning off just before the main entrance on the other side of the narrow bridge ahead. He didn't want to drive up to the house at this speed.

"Don't let them pass us, now. It's the front entrance that counts. Only servants use the back lane!" Laura screamed at Red. In that split second, Red pulled his horse back to the middle of the road in an effort to cross the bridge and reach the front entrance first.

But Thomas and his eager horse had already seen the space, and they shot by on the right. The distance between the bridge abutment and the wagon, now back in the middle of the road, was narrow. The racing horse slipped between, but would the wobbling buggy, not yet ahead of the wagon, make it safely through the space and onto the bridge?

Red pulled his horse sharply to the left to avoid a clash, and the buggy just barely cleared their vehicle, but it scraped the abutment to the right. There was a crash of splintering wood as the racehorse shot down the road, dragging the reins and a single whippletree behind him.

Meanwhile, the buggy was teetering backwards off the road onto the grassy slope, and tilting from side to side, it careened down the knoll to the stream. First, Elizabeth came flying over the right side of the buggy as she jumped for the grassy side hill with her full silk petticoat blowing out like a flag in the wind. Then Thomas jumped from the other side just in time. In seconds, the buggy had crashed into the stream, where it travelled a full fifteen feet before it came to a stop.

Elizabeth was stumbling and gasping as she struggled out of the mud just below the grassy slope. Her hair hung in clumps down the back of her silk gown and her petticoat had a big rip in the front. She started to limp up the hill.

Laura covered her mouth with her hand to stifle a giggle. Red jumped out over the side of their wagon and raced down the knoll towards Elizabeth, but before he could help her, Thomas was by her side taking her arm. Together the two bedraggled wedding guests walked up the knoll to the road.

"This is all your fault!" Elizabeth hissed at Red and Laura.

"Can I help?" Laura asked.

"No! And I'm telling Mother," Elizabeth screamed.

Laura glanced over at Red whose smile was starting to spread from ear to ear. She couldn't help giggling out loud as she held out her hand to help Mira step down from the wagon. They too would walk over the bridge.

"Thanks for the ride, Red," she said as he grabbed the reins to drive the horse down the back laneway.

Laura smoothed the wrinkles out of her sister's fine linen dress, and pulled a small comb from the pocket under her petticoat. She combed Mira's thick curls and quickly whisked the comb through her own hair. Then she adjusted her petticoat and hat, and took Mira by the hand.

With every hair in place and heads held high, the sisters marched towards the house.

TEN

"I've decided to move us to Upper Canada next month." Father had called the family together into the study for an important meeting, but no one was prepared for the shock of what he had just announced. He was sitting behind his desk; the rest of the family was clustered onto the leather chairs and horsehair loveseat on the other side of the room.

"To Upper Canada? And why so soon?" asked Laura.

"I've been considering this move for two years."

"You knew about it, and you didn't mention a word to us!" Mira burst out. Father gave her a hard stare. It was bad enough to have his oldest daughter questioning his decision, but he was not going to let Mira object so strongly. She wouldn't be fifteen for two months yet. Then, he looked across to the other side of the couch, where Elizabeth sat beside her mother. She was blowing her nose with a limp lace handkerchief.

"I went to Upper Canada two years ago to look into their land offer for settlers and made application then. I didn't see any need to tell the family because I didn't know if we'd be accepted. And I hoped that affairs here might improve so we could stay." As he looked straight into the glowing flames of the fireplace, Laura saw pain on her father's face that she had never noticed before.

Thomas put his chin in his hands as he continued. "I just can't go on here. The court decisions that have been forced on some people have been so unfair. I can't stand to watch it any more."

In the years since Father's marriage to Sally, times had grown worse and Father had been away more than ever. Two new babies had arrived: Charles, born in 1791, was four years old now, and Baby Appy was a year old. Laura and Elizabeth had finished at the local school and were busy at home helping Sally. Father could not afford to buy more slaves, and Bett was growing too old now to keep up with another baby.

"The farmers have suffered terribly," Father went on. "They've worked hard all their lives. They're honest, God-fearing, hard-working people, yet they've seen their family farms taken away to pay debts. It's not their fault they can't sell their produce for a fair price and pay their taxes." Thomas Ingersoll talked on, still staring into the fire. Laura had never heard him say so much in one conversation. She had not realized that his work had been so hard or that times had been so difficult. "These are the men who are willing to go to Upper Canada with me. They have already lost their land here and their hope along with it. I must persuade them they can still have hope . . . in Canada. Rugged it may be, but there is law and order there, and a man will receive justice. The British seem to have learned from their mistakes with these colonies."

"Was the revolution for nothing, then?" Laura asked. "Didn't the colonies fight to stop the harsh taxation?"

"No, the war was not in vain," Father spoke more evenly now. "Freedom and justice will come, but it will take time. A new country always has growing pains. But I'm too old to go through those pains. I want more security for my family."

"But Canada is still under British rule," Mira objected. She had been only three years old at the end of the Revolutionary War, but she had learned about it in school and from her father.

Father's face brightened now. "They are offering settlers a good deal. Two years ago I travelled to Newark—that's the capital of Upper Canada near Niagara Falls—I made a petition to Lieutenant Governor Simcoe for a land grant there. I agreed to take forty settlers over a seven year period. Each family will receive two hundred acres for a nominal fee. My friend, Captain Brant, the Mohawk Chief, has agreed to help me choose a stretch of fertile land for my settlement."

Father had first met the great Mohawk chief before the war on a visit to Moor's school in Connecticut, and Captain Brant had visited the family at Great Barrington three years ago. He was on his way home from a meeting with General Washington, with whom he had discussed the Muskingum River boundary for the dissenting tribes still on American soil. The chief had told Father then of the great opportunities in Upper Canada. But Laura had never once thought that the family would actually settle there.

Sally handed the baby to Elizabeth and went over to sit in the chair beside Father. She was frowning. "But the land grant is just the beginning, isn't it?" she said. "The settlers will have to break up the land and build houses and barns and start from scratch just like our great-grandfathers did. It will not be easy."

"No, it will not be easy," said Father. "But life never is. It hasn't been easy here either. In fact, it is impossible now, for my own resources have dwindled and I have just enough left to take us to Upper Canada. We'll have to sell almost everything before we go . . . I simply can't afford to transport more. We must go. We have no other choice."

"We do have a choice. Papa will take us in." Sally suddenly turned away from Father, grabbed the baby from Elizabeth, and rushed out of the room.

"Never!" Father boomed as he stared at his wife's retreating figure.

Elizabeth blinked back her tears.

"I know this is not easy," Father said, "but we must be brave. I have to get to work now. I have so much to do before we go." He turned to Laura, "Please try to reason with Sally." Laura nodded and hurried the girls out of the study. She hadn't accepted the idea herself yet, but had promised her father, so she would have to try.

"Well, I still don't like it," Mira grumbled.

"Father has been planning for two years. So it's not a sudden decision. We'll manage fine." Laura hoped her voice sounded more confident than she felt.

"I don't know," Mira began. Her deep, brown eyes were brimming over with tears.

"Well, I don't like it," said Elizabeth, "and I don't know why you do, Laura, unless maybe you hope to find a beau up there."

"Yes," said Mira, "I've heard there are lots of unmarried men up in Canada."

Laura blushed. She would be twenty in September, only five months away, and it was true that she had no beau. Elizabeth already had a beau. Now that she was seventeen, Thomas was calling on her every week. But Laura had little time to attend social events. As the oldest of the family, she was always busy.

Laura smiled mischievously and responded. "I hadn't thought

about that, Elizabeth, but perhaps you're right. I may just marry a Canadian and leave you two to do the work without me."

Mira looked even more distressed, and Laura regretted her joke, but she was pleased by Elizabeth's deflated expression. "Stop worrying about Canada. You may just be surprised. You may like it there." Walking out of the room, she smiled across at Mira's shocked face. And maybe it was true. Maybe she would like it. Since there wasn't really any other choice for any of them, they had better make the best of it.

As she passed the hall mirror, she stopped for a moment. Her fine, straight features and long, thick, wavy hair told her that she was not unattractive. But she had hardly ever gone to a party escorted by a young man. Many girls younger than herself were married, and quite a few were already mothers. But Mercy and Sally had both been past twenty-five when they had married Father, so there would be time yet.

Then she thought of Red, the boy who had come and gone that horrible year when her stepmother had died and Father had married so soon afterwards. She had hoped he wouldn't go back to Ireland, but a year later, he did. Laura had made many a trip down to the Whiting residence to see if there might be a letter for her, but there was never anything. He had not even written to Judge Whiting, except for one letter thanking him for passage money. As the days dragged into months, she had finally gone to Judge Whiting to ask for Red's address but was surprised to find out that he had never given it to the Whitings. In fact, they didn't even know his real name. Laura knew that Red must still fear being tracked down for his part in Shay's rebellion.

Busy now with her thoughts as she hurried into the kitchen, she almost bumped into Sally, who was perched on a stool at the long utility table, peeling potatoes. Sally brushed the back of her hand across her eyes to hide the tears, but kept her head down, intent upon her work.

Laura grabbed a paring knife and started to peel a potato. "You don't need to help, Laura," she said. "You spend too much time helping us all."

"Are you complaining?"

"Why no! Whatever would I complain for, Laura? I couldn't

have managed these last few years without you, but sometimes I feel that the household . . . is taking too much of your time." She wiped a hand across an eye again. "Every girl needs a life of her own." They continued to peel potatoes in silence.

"About moving to Canada," Laura said finally, "you know we'll manage fine with the children. They're strong. And we can come back on visits too. It's not like it was at first after the war. Please say you'll go with us."

Sally took her hands out of the potato pan and sat down on the couch beside the fireplace. She sobbed harder than ever into her apron.

"Please don't cry," Laura said, sitting down beside Sally and putting her arm around Sally's shoulder.

"Why . . . should I . . . leave?" Sally gasped out between sobs.

"Because I need you, Sally. First I lost Mother, then Mother Mercy. I can't lose you too." Laura's voice trembled and her eyes too were misted with tears. At that moment, she realized how important Sally was to her. Though she had never thought of Sally as a mother, she had become like a very close sister.

Sally looked up through her tears, pulled back the long, dark hair that had fallen across her face, and stared with surprise at Laura. The afternoon sun shone through the window across Laura's face, and Sally could see the sadness that Laura had covered up for so many years.

"You won't lose me, Laura," she promised.

They clasped each other tightly as tears fell down their cheeks.

*****

Laura watched Thomas and Levi helping Father load the family's belongings onto their wagon. She spotted her own small horsehair trunk near the top of the load. They would be going by wagon to the Hudson River, where they would take a sloop upriver to Schenectady. From there they would travel by boat up the Mohawk River and portage to the Oswego River, ending up at Oswego on Lake Ontario, where they would board a ship for Newark.

Charles was tagging along behind the men trying to help, but Father almost stumbled over him while he was carrying a trunk.

Sally stepped out onto the verandah with the baby in her arms. Elizabeth and Mira, close behind, were wearing their warm winter cloaks, for there was a raw wind this early April morning.

Laura knew the loading was almost finished, so she slipped back silently into the house and ran through the empty kitchen and hallway to the stairs. She rushed back up to her room and looked around it once again. Already it didn't seem the same, for all the furniture was gone, but she looked over to the window and remembered her mother rocking Mira there as she talked with Laura. She could almost hear her mother's soft voice singing, "Hush! the rain sweeps o'er the knolls. . . ."

Then the chatter of the family below and the snorting of the horses eager to be on their way broke through Laura's memories. She turned away and ran down the stairs and out the front door. Walking along the verandah, she almost bumped into Elizabeth and Thomas, who did not notice her. Thomas was holding both of Elizabeth's hands in his. "I'll come to Upper Canada one day," he was saying, "but I can't leave my folks right now. They need me now that Levi has his own farm and a family to support. But sometime I'll come, Elizabeth." Laura stepped off the verandah and slipped quietly around the south side of the house.

As Laura walked around the white frame house, she remembered saying goodbye to Red under that very apple tree the day he had come up to tell her he was leaving. Judge Whiting was going to take him to Boston, where he was to book passage back to Ireland. Laura stood and looked at the bare branches of the gnarled apple tree. It looked half-dead today, but the day Red had left, it had been full of white blossoms.

"I'll never forget you, Laura." Red had smiled his lopsided smile and his red hair looked bronze in the sunlight.

Laura had stood there hardly believing that he was really going, for he had become the happiest part of her life the year Mercy had died.

"Why can't you wait just a few more years and I could go with you, Red?" Laura had pleaded.

"There's no future for me here, Laura," he'd said. "Back home, I at least have family."

"But there are things you can do here that you won't be able to do in Ireland. You've already learned to read and write, and the Judge could teach you lots of other things . . . and I could. . . ."

"Don't be daft, Laura. It's all settled and it'll be the best thing in the end. I'll see you again, too. You just wait."

The tears started to stream down her face then and he leaned over and kissed her gently on the mouth. She had never been kissed by a boy that way before and she looked up shyly into Red's twinkling eyes. He smiled then and left her standing there leaning against the apple tree. At the end of the lane, he turned and waved. She waved back and watched him disappear down along the highway. And she had never seen nor heard from him again.

"Laura!" Father's voice broke through her thoughts. She hurried around the side of the house. The whole family was all ready to go. Charles was sitting on the back of the wagon, swinging his short legs back and forth over the edge.

"Come sit here, Laura," shouted Charles. He was patting an empty spot beside him. Sally and the baby were sitting on the front bench with Father, and Mira and Elizabeth were just behind them. Laura put her hands on the flat of the wagon and shunted herself up beside Charles.

"Ready to go?" Father shouted.

"Yes, all ready!"

"Get up!" The reins fell lightly on the horses' backs and the wagon started moving slowly down the lane.

Laura looked over to the field beside the lane at the gravesites of her own mother and her first stepmother. They were on top of a small knoll where red roses grew from June to August. Laura would not be seeing those roses this year. Nor would she see the blossoms come out on the apple tree at the side of the house.

"I don't want to go," Charles whimpered, staring up at Laura with his big hazel eyes so like his father's. His lips were starting to quiver.

Laura blinked back her tears and smiled at Charles as she put her right arm around him. "And miss that boat ride? You'll love the boat ride, Charles."

Reassured, he nodded and leaned his head against his sister.

Laura drew him in closer. The only home she had ever known was growing smaller now as the long lane stretched behind them.

PART TWO

JAMES

ELEVEN

"Hard 'a starboard, hard 'a starboard. There's a shoal to port. I've seen ships wrecked in gales like this in Superior and I'll be blessed if this isn't. . . . Starboard, I said, starboard."

Laura woke up startled. There was a lot of noise up on deck but she knew it couldn't be that the ship had docked. The cabin was pitch-black so it must still be the middle of the night.

A flash of lightning streaked through the porthole and illuminated the figures of Elizabeth and Mira, who were sleeping in quilts on the floor on either side of her. Sally was sleeping beside the wall, with Appy snuggled into the crook of her arm and Charles beside the baby.

Just as Laura was propping herself up on one elbow, trying not to disturb her sisters, the floor suddenly went on a tilt. She and Elizabeth and Mira slid all the way over to where Sally was lying and Laura bumped against Charles. A minute later, the floor slanted in the opposite direction, and the three girls and Charles slid over to the other wall.

Laura looked at her sister's faces. They didn't seem to have noticed a thing, and Charles was still sound asleep.

"Elizabeth, Mira . . . are you awake?" Laura whispered.

"We're awake," grumbled Mira. "You don't think we could sleep through this, do you?"

"Elizabeth, are you all right?"

"No," Elizabeth replied weakly. "I think I'm going to throw up." They could hear her gagging into the pail that had rolled down on top of her.

Laura started to make her way up the moving floor. "I'm going to see what's happening," she mumbled.

"You'd better stay here, Laura," Sally said in a trembling voice, holding Appy tight. "Your father will come for us if there's any danger."

"But what if he can't?" Laura asked quietly. A moment of silence hung heavy between them in the dark. The time between the lightning and the thunder was growing, and with relief they heard the rain, both signals that there was less danger from the lightning now. But the rain was heavy, pelting against the boat in gusts. Deafening waves hit the small schooner broadside, tossing it back and forth.

In the darkness, Laura started to edge towards the doorway. The rain and wind half-drowned the sound of Elizabeth being sick again. Laura hoped fervently that the skipper had kept the southern shore of Lake Ontario in sight. As the swaying boat tipped more and more from side to side, Laura knew they would need to land soon or the schooner would capsize.

She felt along a wall until her hand touched the little knob on the door. She turned it and pushed, but at first the door would not budge. When she managed to open it a crack, a cold gust of wet wind cut across her face.

"Shut that door," screamed Mira.

"All right, all right. I just have to get out to see what's happening!" Laura said as she took in a gulp of cold air. She needed all her strength to hold the door open against the wind. Gradually she pushed it out far enough to squeeze into the small stairway that led to the deck.

"Be careful," Sally gasped as the wind hit her.

Laura crept on into the stairway. But she was not prepared for the next wave that hit the schooner. She found herself slammed against the other side of the narrow hallway with such force that she fell back, stunned, onto the steps.

She sat still for a few minutes on the stairs. Then she was abruptly aroused by the sound of the Captain shouting, "Quarter the wave," and then heard the crew moving about on deck. It was a welcome sound, for she had not heard them for a while, and feared they might have been washed overboard.

She started again to stumble up the steps one at a time. Her whole body was shaking with cold. The raw wind swept down on her, and her heavy flannel gown was soaked. She had lost her cap and her thick hair clung in wet clumps to her back. Finally she got hold of the side railing, stuck her head above the top step, and shouted, "Father!" But the storm drowned out all sound of her voice.

Just as she was deciding to turn back, she saw a figure coming towards her. "Father," she screamed again. She started to stagger towards him.

"Go back!" he shouted. "Go back."

Laura hesitated, then turned and grabbed the side railing at the top of the stairs. As her father hurried towards her, an engulfing wave washed against the boat and across the deck. Father fell backwards with the force of the wind, his feet slid out from under him, and he was swept to the side of the deck. Two crew hands rushed to help him, but they became a big blur in the darkness as Laura strained to see if they had got there in time.

Laura clung helplessly to the railing, straining to see. All she could make out was the crew shouting and figures dashing across the deck.

She waited. The rain was still heavy, but the wind was letting up a little, and the schooner seemed to be rocking less violently.

Finally she saw a figure coming towards her again, and a minute later she recognized her father.

"Thank heavens . . . we're . . . near shore," he gasped. "We've got to land . . . somewhere. Go back and keep inside, all of you."

"Can't I help?"

"Yes, keep the family inside and calm. We may hit the shore with a sudden jolt. Be ready for it. Then when we are still, get out."

"How will I know?"

"You'll know! Anyway, I'll try to get down there. The water's not deep here. Hurry back now."

Laura grasped the railing as she hurried down the stairs. Then she stumbled against the cabin door and finally squeezed inside. "We're landing . . . soon," she choked out.

Mira wrapped a blanket around her shoulders. "You're soaked, Laura."

"It's blowing and wet even in the stairway."

"You'd better change," Sally suggested.

"There's no use." Laura shook from the cold. "We'll all be wet in a few minutes unless this rain lets up. Father said to get ready to leave the ship. We'd better get our bags together."

"Get the children's cloaks, please, Laura," Sally said halfheartedly.

Laura reached into a bag and pulled out the children's cloaks. Mira handed Elizabeth hers and then helped Laura finish packing. Laura rolled the quilts together with the other bedding and wrapped canvas around them with a piece of heavy twine.

Charles snuggled over next to Laura. "Can I help?" he asked. Laura drew his arms into his heavy cloak and gave him a big hug.

"Just stay close to me, Charles," she said.

Suddenly the schooner lurched again, and the whole floor spun around beneath them as they rolled together to one side of the room. Then the floor stayed on a slant, though the boat still rocked lightly. Charles had clutched one of Laura's legs with both arms.

"We're okay now," Laura told the frightened boy. "You can let go, Charles. We've landed."

But Charles still clung to her. Carefully she pulled his arms loose and picked him up. He clasped her around the neck in a bear hug. "I have to open the door, Charles," she said. "Here, can you carry this bag of food for me like a big man?" Laura picked up the bedding.

Charles slowly released his hold. By now, Mira and even Elizabeth had their bags, and the whole family headed for the door. Laura and Charles reached it first, but when Laura grabbed the door, it held firmly. "The door's jammed," she exclaimed. Even with repeated efforts, she could not pry it open.

A sickening feeling came over Laura as she sat back on the roll of bedding. "We're trapped," she thought. Charles snuggled up next to her.

It wasn't long before they heard pounding on the door and Father shouting, "Stand back. I'll have to break the door."

A dim light came through the porthole now and they could see a crowbar wedged between the doorpost and the door. In no time at all, the door came loose and swung open freely.

Father reached out to help his wife, who had been struggling to hold Appy.

"Where are we?" Sally asked as they all crowded around him.

"We've landed on the southern side of Lake Ontario," Father explained as he motioned them ahead of him up the stairs. "It's okay now. . . . We're not in very deep water and the wind's letting up."

Huddled together, they pushed across the open deck. With relief, Laura saw the flat shoreline. The crew had set down a ladder into the water, for the dry shore was too far away for the gangplank to reach. Father took Sally first while Laura and her sisters held the small children. Then Father came for the children, carrying them through the water one by one. Two sailors carried Elizabeth and Mira across, but Laura plunged into the water herself and waded across to the dry land. Though she still feared the water, she was glad to see that it was not deep, and she thought she couldn't get much colder than she already was. On the shore, Laura grabbed Charles' hand and headed up the slope.

Father walked toward two of the crew members who were trying to put a tent together. He grabbed the corner of the canvas and held it down while they braced it at the far corner with a sturdy stake they had cut from a nearby maple sapling.

Laura gazed along the shoreline, which was barely visible now in the dawn, and could see no sign of habitation. About two hundred feet straight ahead was a dense forest, heavy with what smelled like cedar and spruce. Farther along the shore, there was open space but not even one flickering light to show that someone lived there.

Now, the four crew members were spreading large sections of canvas across the top of a framework of poplar poles and closing in the sides as the family watched. Ominous clouds hung darkly in the sky, and Laura knew the storm might strike again at any moment.

"C'mon, Laura," Charles was shouting. "It's not so cold in here." He came running up to her, grabbed her hand and started to pull her towards the tent that the men had already erected. Already the crew were busy unloading their supplies from the boat. It wasn't long before they had set up cots, and Sally started handing out quilts to the girls. Laura took hers and walked over to a nearby cot with water squishing out of her moccasins.

"At least it's solid ground," Sally sighed as she pulled a wet, wool stocking off Appy's chubby little leg, "but I don't believe we'll be able to settle here. When we do reach civilization, though, I'm staying, Thomas, I vow."

Laura noticed Father's jaw muscles tighten, but he silently

pulled a blanket up over Elizabeth, who had already fallen asleep. Then he turned to Laura, just inside the door, "I have to help the crew," he said. "I'll be back before too long." He strode out the open doorway with a piece of canvas and tacked it back over the entrance. He had no sooner gone than the wind and rain started to pelt down onto the tent.

Half an hour later, they were all still huddled under the quilts. Laura wished she could go out and help the men, but she was so tired she could hardly move. She lay down now beside Mira, who was already asleep, and finally fell asleep too, dreaming of the apple orchard that would soon be blossoming at home. In the dream, she was running through the trees to her mother, who was planting the vegetable garden behind the house. Then she saw her mother walking down the long lane that led to the highway, and Laura was running after her, shouting "Mama." She struggled to grab her mother's skirt but couldn't quite reach her no matter how fast she ran.

TWELVE

The schooner completed its turn from the lake into the mouth of the Niagara River, plunging between the steep shale and limestone cliffs that rose up on either side of the water. Scrubby bushes and many trees jutted out from the steep banks. Beyond the riverbanks were huge stands of oak, maple, ash, chestnut, and pine. The current in the river was so strong the ship was travelling very slowly.

The whole landscape was at once gentle and wild. The trees and grass looked almost like the ones that grew at home, but here they were not contained in neat woodlots and meadows. They had grown up together in a wild majesty that no one had yet disturbed. And everything seemed larger and deeper here than at home. A booming sound was coming from up the river.

"What is that sound?" asked Laura, who was looking over the side railing with her father.

"Ah, that is the sound of Niagara Falls. I travelled down here when I visited Newark two years ago. It sounded as loud then as now. And look, the spray from the falls is just over that rise. Can you see it?"

"Oh, yes, I thought it was a low cloud."

"No, that just shows you how powerful the Falls are . . . to send up a spray like that. I've heard you can see the spray from forty miles away on a clear day."

What a strange country we are coming to, thought Laura.

Mira walked up beside them. A robust girl, she had taken on the appearance of a farm worker. Her cheeks looked all the more ruddy from the windy, sunny days on deck, and she was almost Laura's height—five feet four inches. Laura was paler than Mira, which made her eyes look even darker.

"When are we going to see Niagara Falls, Father?" Mira asked.

"Oh, not today," Father gave Mira a big broad smile. "But isn't this a grand country? This is where we're going to make a new life and where we're going to stay. Right here in Upper Canada."

"But Father, we're so near the Falls. Couldn't we just go around the bend and take a look?"

"No, Mira, first we need to get settled at the Landing—or Queenston I guess it's called now, then I'll be going out to clear the land site on the La Tranche River."

"Queenston," boomed out the schooner's Captain. He must have been as relieved to see the landing point as anyone on board. After the shipwreck, he and the crew had spent a week repairing the schooner before they were able to continue their voyage, and the vessel was still in rough shape. They would have to take another look at her once they landed. The schooner turned in towards the riverbank. The bank came closer and closer, and finally the gang-plank was lowered.

Father was among the first to go ashore. To find temporary accommodation for the whole family would not be easy, and he needed a head start.

Queenston did not appear big enough to be even a small village. Only a few houses stood within their sight at the top of the hill above the shore. Along the shoreline stood a row of rundown huts that looked like part of a decayed military base. Laura wished for Sally's sake that they could have stayed at Newark by the mouth of the Niagara River, where almost one hundred families were settled. This didn't look like the kind of place where Sally would want to live.

The ship's captain approached them, his long bright scarf blowing in the wind. "We've unloaded your things now, Missus." He spoke directly to Sally. "You'll be just as comfortable on shore. It's a balmy day." He was smiling as they left him. He did not usually take passengers on his cargo ships, and Laura guessed that he was happy to see them go. It had not been as easy voyage for any of them.

With the help of the crew, the whole family and Sam and Bett were soon standing on the shore beside their belongings.

"Look," Mira shouted. "There's a big shade tree over there. Let's go sit on the grass." The sun was shining down hotly now.

"And leave our things here?" Sally sounded alarmed.

"We can take almost everything except the biggest trunk. No one's going to walk away with it without our noticing. But I could stay and guard it."

"That won't be necessary, Laura. We can see it from there," said Sally. "Now everyone take a piece of luggage and let's head up that hill."

Sally sounded relieved now that she was on land and that made everyone happier to help. Even Charles proudly struggled along with a large canvas bag over his shoulder.

Once all the luggage had been carried up the hill, everyone except Sam sat under the oak tree. He had insisted on going back to guard the large trunk. Leaning against one side of her own trunk, Laura watched the sailors unloading barrels and taking cargo from the teamsters onto the ships. One waggoner had a huge pile of furs on his wagon. When he reached the ship, the skipper counted them and motioned to his men, who set out several barrels and a few crates. With firm, fast strides, the waggoner walked from the dock to his wagon and back, loading his produce. When he finished, he grabbed the horses' reins and walked beside the creaking and groaning wagon, urging his team up the steep path, towards the oak tree.

Now he was coming closer to where the family was sitting. Laura guessed he wasn't a farmer because his clothes were too neat and fresh. Yet he was not wearing the uniform of a soldier or the powdered wig of an English gentleman.

To everyone's surprise, he drew his horses to a halt right in front of the oak tree. As the horses rested, he looked over at them. His deep blue eyes were bright against his dark hair and thick side-burns, and his nod of welcome was accompanied by a kind smile that lit up his whole face. His eyes rested on Sally, who was struggling to get Appy to go to sleep.

Quietly, he stepped toward them. "May I help, Madam?" he said, and his friendly smile broke out again.

"We're expecting my husband shortly." Sally eyed him cautiously. "We'll manage, but . . . thank you."

He noticed her hesitation. "Are you folks planning to settle around here?" He pulled his horses' reins more tightly, for they were ready to go now.

Sally nervously shifted Appy to her other arm. "Yes . . . but not in this area . . . farther inland. We'll be stopping at Queenston for a while, though."

"Well, in that case, we'll be neighbours for a while. I'm James Secord, and I've just opened a general store in St. David's five miles away. Perhaps you'll come by one day."

Sally nodded and smiled, "Yes, we'll be needing supplies."

"Well, just ask anyone in Queenston the way to my store. I'd be honoured by your visit."

James lifted the horses' reins to get ready to leave, and gave the nearest one a light slap on the rump.

Then, before she knew what she was saying, Laura blurted out, "Excuse me, but . . . you could help us with a trunk. It was too heavy for us to bring up with the others."

He pulled the reins taut and turned to Laura. "I'd be glad to." He drove the team ahead a few feet and looped the horses' reins around the branch of a sturdy maple sapling.

Laura stepped along beside him as he headed down the slope. She had to walk quickly to keep pace with him.

"There it is." Laura pointed to the only trunk set in among barrels and crates. Sam was leaning on it.

James took one look at the big trunk and the tired elderly man. Then he saw a waggoner coming down the hill with a teenaged boy sitting beside him, and James called out, "Hey, Josh, could you give my a hand?"

The boy was thin, but he had a big smile and was willing. So Laura didn't tell James that she figured she could have helped him and Sam better than the boy. It was obvious they knew each other and Josh liked being helpful.

James took the heavy lower position of the trunk, and Sam and Josh took the other end and carried it up the hill to the oak tree, where they set it down beside the smaller trunks.

"Thank you," Laura said, as the men stood for a moment to catch their breath. As James turned to her and smiled, Laura realized he was about her own age.

"I'm pleased to help," he said, looking at her intently. "Are you folks from the States?"

Laura hesitated and then said, "Yes. A friend of my father has picked out a land site for us near the La Tranche River."

"I guess you won't be at Queenston very long then?"

Laura thought he looked disappointed but could not be sure. "I don't know," she said. "My stepmother would like to stay here or at Newark."

"Well, if you have any trouble finding accommodation, try Fairbank's Tavern. Tell them James Secord sent you. It's a good inn. You'll be treated well there. Goodbye now."

His horses had become restless. He loosened their reins, slapped them lightly against their backs, and said in a low voice, "Get up . . . haw."

The rear of the wagon was not yet over the hill before Mira sat down with a sharp thud onto Laura's trunk and exclaimed,"My. Is he ever handsome! I sure hope he's a sample of the young men around here."

Laura smiled at her sister, "His name is Josh." She guessed he would be only a couple of years older than Mira.

"I'm not talking about that *boy*. I mean James."

"He seemed pleasant enough," admitted Sally, "but I don't like to see you speaking so much to strangers." She was looking straight at Mira with a slight frown.

"That won't leave us many people to speak to," Mira muttered.

The sound of another wagon coming along the pathway interrupted them. Another man had stopped, allowing his horses to get their second wind.

"Just arrived from the American States, have you?" he said gruffly. He was about Father's age and a farmer, for he was dressed in a homespun smock.

Sally hesitated before she answered; the question was so abrupt. Then she replied directly, "Yes. We've come to settle here."

"Loyalists? Driven off your lands?"

"No, we're settlers."

"Settlers, eh?" The man frowned, cracked the reins over his horses' backs, and briskly pushed along up the hill.

Somewhat surprised, Laura was still staring in the direction where the man had disappeared when she spotted her father. He strode over the crest of the hill and hurried down along the path towards them.

When Father reached them, he mumbled somewhat apologetically to Sally, "The village isn't as large as I thought. There are only two or three good stone houses in the whole place."

"Well, we can't worry about that now, Thomas," said Sally. "Just get us into the inn. Charles is getting so restless."

Father looked at the grass beneath his feet. He couldn't face Sally's anxious eyes. "There is only one inn and it's full. I figure we can stay in one of those empty soldier's huts we passed along the way."

The silence hung heavy between them all for a few minutes. Then Laura remembered what James had said.

"Father, a man helped us with our largest trunk, and he said to ask at Fairbank's Tavern and to tell them James Secord sent us."

"That's the place. They have no rooms left."

"Let's ask again and give them the message."

"I don't see what good that'll do."

"Why don't you try, Thomas," Sally interrupted. "This man did seem sincere."

"I'll go with you. I'd like to see the village." Laura turned to walk up the hill.

Father reluctantly started up the hill behind her. They had walked not more than a few hundred feet beyond the top of the slope when they saw the inn on the right side of the path. It was a grey clapboard building with a verandah all across the front. At once, Laura recognized the horses hitched up outside. "That's James' team and wagon," she said excitedly. Father was only slightly moved by her enthusiasm, for he was very tired and not too hopeful about this second attempt to find rooms at the inn. He had come only to please Sally.

Attached to the north side of the inn was a shed over fifty feet long, where horses were eating in their stalls. Behind them was a forest of unhitched wagons and buggies. The inn must really be full. Laura's heart sank but she and her father kept walking up to the main entrance of the inn. Father hesitated just inside the doorway. "It's no use, Laura. The man at the desk is the same one who refused me before." He turned and trudged back out the door.

Laura stood alone in the entrance and looked around the room. Behind the man at the desk was an open doorway to a larger room, where several men were sitting around a table. Voices drifted out to her, but she could not hear any distinct words. Still, only a single voice could be heard at any one time. A meeting of some sort must be in progress.

"Laura," her father was calling. She turned to go, but just then, she felt a hand on her shoulder. Startled, she whipped around and looked up directly into the eyes of James Secord.

"Miss Ingersoll? Are you looking for rooms for your family?"

"Yes, but Father tried here already and they said there was nothing left."

"Oh, I see. Well, I'll ask for you if you wish."

"Oh, yes, would you?" Laura said hopefully.

James Secord walked over to the desk while Laura stayed back in the doorway. James spoke in a low voice to the man there, who put down his fine quill pen as he talked. Laura saw the man shake his head, but when James muttered something back, he nodded. Meanwhile, Father had come back inside to find out why Laura was lingering behind.

James came toward them before father had a chance to speak. "Mr. Ingersoll, I'm James Secord. Welcome to Queenston." He extended his hand and smiled a welcome.

Father shook the extended hand. "Thank you, James. Just call me Thomas, and I want to thank you for moving the trunk for my family."

"I was glad to help. Now I understand you're looking for accommodation. Two rooms are available with two large bedsteads and they'll set up cots for the rest of the children. Will that be enough accommodation for tonight?"

"Why, yes," Father replied in amazement. As long as there were beds ready for them all to collapse onto, he didn't care how small the quarters. "We're mighty obliged to you for getting us a dry roof over our heads."

"I'm afraid it's just for tonight. The inn is full, but the owner is doubling up his own family to give you a couple of their rooms. Now tomorrow, I can bring you a tent and set it up on some property I have on the edge of town. I'm sorry I can't offer anything better."

"It's the best offer we've had yet and I thank you. Sally will be so relieved. She and our youngest are very tired from the trip."

"What part of the states are you from?"

"Great Barrington, Massachusetts, and I've come to set up a farm in Upper Canada."

"You daughter told me about the farm. I hope you like it here. We have good fertile land just waiting to be cleared."

"My good friend Captain Brant has already picked a site for us, but I haven't seen it yet. I have to get the family settled at Queenston first. Now, we should be getting back. They've been waiting a long time." Father stepped out onto the verandah with James and Laura following.

"Let me help you bring your load up here to the inn," said James.

Father hesitated. "That would really help, but your team is already loaded down." James' horses were shifting restlessly and ready to be on their way home.

"I have to take my supplies to St. David's about five miles away, but then I'll come back and help you. I'll hurry. I won't be long."

"We would appreciate your help, and I'll gladly pay for your services." Father was reaching into his pocket.

"No, that won't be necessary, and I hope the wait won't be too hard for the women." He looked at Laura again as he spoke. "Just a minute; wait here." James turned and strode back into the inn before they had a chance to answer.

Laura noticed the relief in her father's face, but he looked very tired as he leaned against the railing on the verandah of the inn. His hair seemed more grey than brown now.

James returned about five minutes later with a round basket covered with a bright cloth. "This will help pass the time until I return," he said with a broad smile as he handed it to Laura.

Laura could smell fresh-baked bread and, peeping under the cover, she saw huge slices of cheese, a large, spicy apple pie, and some oatmeal cookies. "Thank you," she called out. He was already off the verandah and busy unhitching his horses from the post where they were tied.

Laura walked slowly behind her father down the pathway to where the family was waiting. Only once did she stop and turn, and look back along the road to St. David's but James had already disappeared. All she could see was the hard, rutted road and miles of budding trees stretching on towards the horizon.

*****

"It's surprisingly comfortable, Thomas," Sally admitted. While still returning to the inn for meals, they had worked for three days putting everything in order in their two canvas houses, which stood side by side on a green stretch of land at the edge of town, just below the Heights.

"Well, if a canvas house is good enough for the Lieutenant-Governor of Upper Canada, it should be good enough for us," Father said with some satisfaction. James had told them about Governor Simcoe bringing Captain Cook's canvas house from England, and when the Simcoes found it too crowded in Navy Hall, the Government House at Newark, his wife had insisted he have it set up immediately for their private use.

Laura sat on a stump beside the front door to the big tent and looked out with wonder at the beauty of the steep, wide escarpment just to the south of them. The local people called it the "Heights."

Laura turned toward the roadway when she heard sounds of an approaching team of horses. Charles rushed out past her, for he too had heard, and they both knew that James Secord was going to be delivering fresh supplies that their father had ordered from his store in St. David's.

James drove his team right up beside the tent, and when he jumped down from the wagon, he grabbed the excited Charles and sat him on the back of one of the horses. "Giddy up," shouted Charles, digging his feet into the mare's side.

The team lunged forward, but James had been watching and he pulled the reins back tight. The now-petrified Charles grabbed the horse's mane and clung to its neck to keep his balance. After he had settled his team, James lifted Charles down and smiled at Laura, who had walked over to take the squirming boy.

"You'll make a good rider some day," said James as he put the boy on the ground beside his sister.

"I'd like to ride him now!" Charles shouted back.

"Charles, go in the house," said Father, who had come out just in time to see the boy being put down. "Thanks for delivering these supplies, James. I'm hoping to buy a team and wagon today, and then we can pick up our own supplies."

"I'm glad to have your business, Thomas. St. David's is not on the main mercantile route and it's overlooked sometimes. The Queenston stores have an advantage."

"Well, we'll be going to St. David's to buy our supplies," Father promised. "It's not that far away."

James started to hand down the bags of flour, salt, and other household items to Father, and when they had finished stacking them, Father pulled out his money to pay James.

"Are you sure you want to pay in cash?"

"How else?" Thomas asked.

"Trading at the Landing is mostly in produce or labour."

"Well, I've nothing to exchange and I'm not free to work yet," Father explained.

Laura sat down on the stump again as she watched her father and James shake hands at the front door of the tent. James saw her there and came over but stood in silence.

Laura looked up shyly, "Do come again, and thank you for all your help, Mr. Secord."

"It was nothing," he replied, somewhat embarrassed as he continued to stare at her. Then he shifted his cap to his other hand, and said, "Please call me James, Miss Ingersoll."

"And I'm Laura," she said looking up into his deep blue eyes.

Just then the horses made a snorting sound and wrenched their bridles. James turned and saw the reins had become tangled in the branches of the tree, where he had tied them.

"Laura. . . ." The horses pounded their feet more. "They're hungry. I have to get them home. Good night, Laura!"

"Good night, James."

Then James jumped into the wagon and snapped the lines lightly on the horses' backs. They needed no urging to pull the empty wagon and were off at a great speed.

THIRTEEN

"Thomas, I can't believe you are going to do this!" Sally exclaimed.

The family were quite comfortably settled into their canvas house and were sitting on benches around the table after breakfast. On the left side of the room was Sally and Father's bedstead, and under it was the little trundle bed, where Charles slept. Appy's large cradle was nearby. The rest of the tent was filled with the family's everyday needs—a cupboard with cooking utensils and bags and barrels of supplies. The girls' cots and trunks were housed in a smaller attached tent. A third small adjoining tent had been erected for Bett and Sam's sleeping quarters. On sunny days, Sally and the girls cooked outside at a campfire that Father had set up, and on rainy days, the family ate sandwiches inside.

Fresh milk was delivered each day by a neighbour boy, Josh. He was the same boy who had helped James move the large trunk, and his father's farm touched the part of James' land on which their tent stood.

Father was trying to reason with Sally. "But you are getting to know people in the area now, and you have Sam and Bett to help."

Laura felt sorry for her father, for their settling here in Queenston was only supposed to be temporary to appease Sally until their new home was ready. Laura too was eager to see the site, and though she sympathized with Sally, she couldn't help wondering if Sally really had to complain so much. If he listened to her, they'd be sitting here forever in a tent instead of building a great home on an estate of their own.

Sally stared back at Thomas. "What do you mean by saying we are getting to know people in the area? Who? Tell me. The only one I see stopping to visit is James Secord, and sometimes that boy Josh takes time to visit with the girls. James has been a great help and so has Josh, but his parents haven't visited, and no women have come to call."

"They're busy. May is seeding time for the farmers, and most wives do their share too with the crops and the cattle. There are only a few families right inside Queenston, and they have large gardens. The farm women nearby are just too busy at this time of year. Anyway, what time have *you* had for visiting?"

"I would have had more free time if we'd had more help. Back in Great Barrington, the women often helped a new neighbour settle in."

"You had three grown girls and Bett and Sam and me. Not many women around here are that lucky, but I am taking one of the girls or Bett with me to the site to cook meals. It'll save time for building."

"I hope it's not me." Mira was starting to look forward to Josh's visits, and lately he had dropped by quite often—even after he had finished delivering his milk. He and Mira would sit on the stumps in front of their tent and talk for ages. Father said that one day his father would show up to drag him home to his work.

"I suppose I could go," offered Elizabeth, "but you know I wouldn't be much help if I get my usual spring attack of bronchitis."

Laura did want to see the site, but she certainly didn't want to leave right now to be gone for a whole month. She'd been hoping every day that James would come calling again. He had been so helpful, and she was almost certain that he really liked her. Or was he friendly to everyone who came to Queenston? She wasn't going to act silly, like Mira, and show her feelings, but she did want to be here when he came by. If only he had a store in Queenston, she could casually drop in to see him. This waiting was bothering her. It had been a week now since he had brought the last load of supplies and stayed to chat with the family for the whole evening. He had talked with her more than Father, but then the whole family had been there.

"And what about you, Laura?" Father was staring at her with his head tilted sideways, "Will you go with me?"

Laura had been thinking so hard about James that she had lost track of the conversation. "If I must," she stammered, "but we just got here."

"Why, Laura, that's a switch. I thought you were anxious to see the site." Father's shoulders were drooping and his eyes looked tired. Laura felt a small twinge of guilt, but ignored the feeling and looked away from her father's questioning eyes.

Sally was blinking back tears now. "You see, no one wants to go."

Mira was still pouting and Elizabeth was teary-eyed.

"Oh, all right," said Laura. "If you need me, I'll go, but are there any close neighbours?"

"I don't believe so. That's one of the things I'm going ahead to check out."

"How long will you be gone?" asked Sally.

"Two to three weeks—no longer. A portion of the land is already cleared. Joseph and the Mohawks used to camp there in the summer."

Laura knew it might take longer than her father said and started to feel very disappointed that she wouldn't be able to see James for so long. Noticing her downcast face, Father said, "I think I'll take Bett along to cook for me, since none of you girls seems up to the job."

Maybe that was the answer, Laura decided , and maybe Sam could go too, but then that would leave the women folk alone in an unfamiliar place. She didn't suppose Father would approve of that.

Father got up from the bench and walked slowly to the doorway. "I'm headed over to St. David's now to pick up supplies for my trip. I don't suppose any of you are interested in going along."

"I'll go," Laura volunteered, trying to sound reluctant. Her father raised his eyebrows, surprised at Laura's sudden interest.

A few minutes later Father was driving his new team over the dirt road to St. David's. It was a warm, sunny morning, and blotches of sun and shade fell over the road and the wagon as Laura and her father rode along.

They could see a clearing ahead with a few buildings when Laura finally broke the silence. "So you're really going this week—to the site?"

"Yes, Laura. You'll all be fine, and Bett said she'd be glad to go and cook for me." He stared straight ahead as he steered the horses a bit to the left, ready to turn as they approached the buildings.

Laura was somewhat hesitant. "I think she'll need Sam along to help her. He could fetch the water from the river and help a lot. She's too old now to go without him." Her father looked sideways at Laura as she continued, "And we'll be fine in Queenston, but I was thinking that you could ask James Secord to stop in more to check on us while you're gone . . . in case we need help or something." Father stared at her in silence. "You know how Sally is," she stammered.

"Are you speaking for Sally or yourself?" he muttered just before he turned the horses toward the hitching posts in front of James' store.

In a few minutes, Laura and her father were walking up the wooden steps to the frame building that even had a second floor and two windows at the front. When they stepped inside onto the wide pine floor boards, Laura could still smell the freshness of the new wooden building.

Inside, James smiled broadly and strode out from behind the counter over to the doorway. "Good morning, Thomas . . . Laura."

The room was large and bright; light came in through windows in the front and north walls. Shelves filled with merchandise covered the other walls, and long wooden counters across each side held pails and bags of things to sell. A table along the back wall also served as a counter. At the far back corner a door led to a storeroom.

Smiling proudly James proceeded to show them around. He stepped around the fireplace built into the front corner and pointed to his shelves. He sold not only basic supplies like salt and sugar, but also bolts of cloth by the yard. The prices were very reasonable. Salt sold for twelve shillings per bushel, and maple sugar was only a shilling a pound—but loaf sugar cost three times as much.

"I'd like to look around a bit first," said Father, who was acquainting himself with prices in a new country and trying to plan for his trip by pricing the items he needed most.

"Go right ahead," said James. Laura was pleased at his quick response, for she felt he must surely want to spend some time alone with her. Then James turned and motioned towards his shelves of yard goods. "Would you like to see some of the materials?"

"Yes, I would, but I'm afraid I can't buy anything just now." She was looking up shyly at him. He was certainly as handsome as she had thought a little over a month ago when she had first seen him at the Landing. But it wasn't his good looks that made him so attractive. It was the kind way he had with people that made them feel important.

"You must have lots of customers in this store."

"Not yet, I'm afraid. It takes time to build a business."

"How long have you had the store?"

"A little over two months now. My sister Magdalen and her husband, Richard Cartwright, are coming up from Kingston one of these days to advise me. He's a very successful businessman."

"Families can be helpful," Laura said.

"Yes, and since I'm the youngest in the family, I always get lots of advice from the rest of them. . . . Sometimes too much!" He smiled.

Laura laughed. "You sound like my little brother Charles. He thinks his three big sisters are always bossing him around."

"He's sure a lively boy. I promised him a ride on my horse one of these days."

"He would love that. Come any time, James."

"Thank you. Tell him I'll be over soon."

Father came over to the counter then. "Do you have any panes of glass?"

"Yes. I have building supplies out back. Come along and see. There may be other items there that you'd like. Please excuse me, Laura, and you feel free to take any materials out of their shelves to look at them. Just make yourself at home."

Laura stared longingly at some of the expensive items for women. Most of the materials were in dark shades, but side by side they made a colourful display. There were bolts and bolts of linen and cambric—even a bolt of imported silk showed at the top of the pile. And there were fine ladies' slippers and hose. Who would be able to buy them? Stockings were nine shillings a pair, and printed calico and flannel were priced at five shillings a yard. Laura looked again at the bolt of pale blue silk. She tried to imagine what she would look like on a dance floor in that shade of blue.

"May I help you?" asked a young girl behind the counter. Laura was staring directly into the eyes of the most beautiful young woman she had ever seen. Her shiny black hair curled out from under her cap around her rosy cheeks and flowed onto her shoulders. She was poised and confident as she came toward Laura, and her dimples made her smile even more welcoming.

"I'm Phoebe Secord," she said in a friendly voice. "I've heard all about you folks. James tells me you've settled in Queenston."

"Yes . . . for now, but our permanent site is some distance away," Laura replied. She noticed Phoebe's large brown eyes, long, thick lashes, and rosy complexion. She knew that James had no younger sisters and so Phoebe couldn't be his sister. She certainly didn't fit the description of the nagging older sisters he had mentioned once when he had visited them at their tent house.

"Too bad. Well, can I help you? We have all kinds of merchandise for ladies. I'll show you anything you want to see. It's no trouble. Just point it out and I'll bring it down to the counter."

"Yes, I see you have a nice assortment of goods, but I'm just looking while my father buys supplies for his trip."

"His trip? How nice."

"Yes, he's looking forward to travelling to our site in a few days."

"Well, we'll have to delay our visit then. James promised to take me over to meet you folks."

"Some of us will still be there," Laura said. She looked across for her father, but he had disappeared with James into the back of the store. She pretended to be interested in some pieces of lustre china. So James is married after all, she thought. It was strange he hadn't mentioned his beautiful wife.

As Phoebe set the bolts of calico and linen on the counter, Laura studied her more closely. Her purse, a large pocket, hung outside her skirt the way a young girl would wear it. Then Laura saw her reach into her pocket for a small note showing the prices of articles. No doubt she wore the pocket outside for convenience until she had memorized all the prices.

Now Phoebe was showing her a special lustre plate. Laura could clearly see Phoebe's hand through it. There was no ring on her finger, but in these times, young couples could not always afford rings.

"I see you two have met," James said.

"Yes," Laura replied and smiled back. Then she abruptly walked over to her father. "Are you ready to go yet, Father?"

"Yes. All set. We loaded the wagon out back." Then he turned to James, shook his hand, and said, "Thank you, James. I am deeply grateful for all your help."

"Have a good trip, Thomas. Goodbye, Laura."

Laura nodded and smiled weakly at Phoebe, who was replacing the china.

"Come again," Phoebe called after them.

Laura sat quietly as they rode along the trail to Queenston. She was still wondering about Phoebe's identity when her father broke the silence.

"James certainly has a beautiful wife to help him."

"Yes," Laura replied numbly. That settled the matter. She had finally met someone she could really care about, and it was too late. He was already married. It had been silly to imagine that he might be interested in her. Well, she hoped that some day she would meet someone just like James.

FOURTEEN

The path beneath the chestnut mare's feet was knotted with tree roots and covered with old leaves from the previous autumn. Laura was getting a good look at them when the occasional shaft of light filtered through the oaks and maples onto the forest floor. The day was hot, even for early June and Laura was tired. She did not feel very confident either, sitting on the back of the saddle. Behind her were two of Captain Brant's sons, Joseph and Jacob, leading two horses that were carrying supplies. Ahead she could make out the forms of her father and Captain Brant. Father was wearing dark woolen breeches and a light linen shirt and waistcoat over his slightly stooped shoulders. Captain Brant sat tall in his saddle, wearing an open yellow-beaded shirt, tied at the waist with a wide red sash that hung over his brown leather breeches.

After discovering that James was already married, Laura had not felt much like staying at Queenston, and she had volunteered once more to accompany Father to the site of their new home on the La Tranche River. They had been away for a little less than a month and were finally returning to their canvas house in Queenston.

Father and Captain Brant had built a large one-room log cabin about twenty feet long and sixteen feet wide. And Captain Brant's Mohawk friends had come for a day to add some finishing touches. They split oak logs for the floor and built in bunk beds in three corners of the big cabin. Then, with Father's help, Captain Brant built the large fireplace in the opening on the north wall. The hearth of flat stones was backed by large field stones piled vertically and stuck together with hardened clay as high as the wall. The cabin even had one small window beside the door on the south wall, made from glass and putty that Father had bought at James' store.

All the while the men were building the cabin, Laura had been busy preparing meals on the outside hearth set up beside the canvas tent where they kept their supplies. The tent was also Laura's bedroom. At the end of each day, it felt good to lie there, for even the ground seemed restful, and she could hear the gurgling of the river flowing along.

At first Laura had been very lonely, but then Captain Brant's sons, Joseph and Jacob, had come to help. They had both graduated recently from Dartmouth College in Connecticut and spoke English well. They had all become good friends, and the brothers had taught Laura how to trap small animals and how to use herbs for medicine. She was no longer lonely and she had enjoyed the last week so much that she wasn't eager to return to Queenston, where she was certain that she would now feel hemmed in.

But this afternoon, they were headed back and already things were starting to change, for the Brant boys were talking together in their own language, and Father and Captain Brant were discussing political matters. She felt very alone again, just like a piece of excess baggage.

Suddenly, Laura felt branches brushing across her face. She knew she was being pushed backward. She let the reins go and grabbed for the horse's mane, but by now she was too far back to reach it. The deerskin saddle slipped away as she slid farther down the horse's back and over the wiry hair of his tail. She landed with a thud on some knobby roots and lay in a heap on the ground as the horse trotted on ahead. The boys behind drew their horses sharply to a halt on each side. She looked up into the tawny face of Jacob.

In her shock, she yelled, "Father, wait for me!" Not far ahead, her father and Joseph Brant turned, and seeing her sprawled on the ground, started back.

Thomas helped his daughter get on the mare again, and Captain Brant looked back at the shaken young woman. "Are you hurt, Laura?"

"I'm fine," she lied. Now that she was out of danger, she was embarrassed about her accident.

"You'll need to watch for low branches . . . and duck. If you had watched, you could easily have avoided falling," Captain Brant said a bit gruffly but with a kindly glimmer in his eye.

"I think it best I ride behind Laura," said Thomas.

Laura did not object, and they all mounted again. This time she was directly behind Captain Brant, but his horse moved swiftly, and she found it hard to keep track of him and watch for low branches at the same time. So she rode in an uncomfortable position, crouched over the horse and ready for any branches she might fail to see.

Dusk fell and still they travelled along. Laura felt tired and ill at ease, especially when strange hooting sounds started coming out of the trees along with the noise of breaking twigs on either side of the narrow trail .

Just as it was getting nearly too dark to see, they came out of the woods and into a clearing where a small frame house stood. It was Captain Brant's home, where they had stayed on their way out to the site. Joseph Brant led them beyond the house and down the path to the Grand River, where he dismounted. Laura wanted to get off her horse, but she felt too bruised to jump down. Fortunately, Father noticed she wasn't moving and helped her. Joseph and Jacob led all the horses to the water's edge. The tired animals dipped their noses eagerly into the water.

Sore from her long ride and bruised from her fall, Laura left the men at the river and limped along up the knoll to the house, where she knew Captain Brant's wife Catherine would have made up fresh beds and set out hot tea.

* * * * *

The next morning Father wanted to get back on the trail as soon as possible, but Captain Brant insisted on showing him and Laura around the little settlement, where he had brought the Mohawks, who had fought with him for the British. The whole village consisted of only seven houses, a log schoolhouse, and a chapel, and Laura wondered why Captain Brant was so eager to show them the place. But then they came to the chapel. The high spire above its bell tower had round-arched openings in its sides, which matched the arches above the four windows on each side of the building and over the entranceway.

"Those arches would not be easy to build from planked logs," Father remarked.

"That's true," Brant smiled, "but we had help for the design from two Loyalists, Wilson, and Smith, who came to live in our Mohawk valley. And we worked very hard together to erect it. Our men squared the logs, boarded, and painted it. Then they fashioned the pews out of sawn logs joined by wooden pegs. We put our best effort into God's house."

Inside, the chapel was as spacious as a meadow. An aisle ran down the middle with pews on either side. At the front in the centre was a wide pulpit, divided for a speaker and an interpreter.

"The pulpit was built in the centre so that all could hear God's message equally," Joseph Brant explained.

Behind the pulpit on the wall were large black tablets with gold print. In front of the pulpit was the communion table. As they went closer, Laura spotted a carved walnut box. Brant opened the box and showed them its contents.

"This is the Bible and part of the communion silver that Queen Anne of England sent to my people at the Queen Anne Chapel in New York in 1712. During the Revolutionary War, the Bible and the silver were buried for safekeeping. They were preserved, and we were able to bring them to our new chapel ."

Laura looked more closely at the communion silver and saw that each bore the inscription:

"*The gift of her Majesty Ann by the Grace of God, of Great Britain, France, and of Her plantations in North America, Queen to her Indian Chappel of the Mohawks.*"

"Do you have your own minister now?" Thomas asked.

"We conduct our own services. I have translated the gospels and a prayer book into our language."

"And how are your people adjusting to the new life here?"

"Well, it helps that we are together and that we have kept our own language, but our life is different here. The land on the Grand River is good for planting corn and other farming, but we cannot forget our great farms in the Mohawk Valley. Our farms were fruitful and plenteous with large apple orchards and flowing fields of corn. Many of these farms were burnt out by the Rebels in the Revolutionary War."

"But now you are settled on your own land on the Grand River. Why can't you farm your new land in the same way?"

"With what? We were not provided with farming tools and supplies for three years like the white Loyalists! So I tried to sell some of our land to get money to buy tools for our people to begin farming. They loathed selling any of our land, but when a man is starving. . . ." Joseph Brant stared ahead in silence.

Father said softly, "But when you sold the land, then did you buy the necessary tools?"

"Then I found out that we had not been given clear title to our land as the white men were! We could not sell any of it to buy tools or anything else. We continued to struggle on with only limited resources from our hunting. Game is just not plentiful, for the animals are being driven north by the settlers who inhabit all the area around us. My people are still in great need and some are rebelling. Even my own son, Isaac . . ." Captain Brant turned away then and quietly walked to the door.

Laura's father followed, but Laura stayed behind to get a closer look at the stone carvings on the wall behind the pulpit. On the black background, there was gold printing in a language she could not understand, but she supposed they were the Ten Commandments because she recognized the Roman numerals I to X.

When Laura turned from studying the carvings, the heavy front door was closing behind her father and Captain Brant, and she knew that her father would be wanting to start travelling again. It was then that she looked down behind the pulpit and froze in fear.

Crouched there was a young man, the exact image of Joseph Brant. She stared at him, her heart beating loudly, and her first impulse was to run. She started to back away a safe distance.

"Well, what are you doing there? Repairing the pulpit?" she babbled. As he stood up, the rips in his dirty beige breeches and buckskin shirt gaped open, showing his bronze skin. Laura continued, "And don't tell me that you can't speak English. You're another one of Joseph Brant's sons, aren't you?"

He glared back coldly, his bleary eyes filled with hate, but Laura stood her ground. He drew his right hand from behind his back, and his fist clenched the carved handle of a sharp bladed hunting knife. Laura froze at the sight before she turned to run, but in two quick leaps, he reached her and wrapped his free arm around her waist. Her scream filled the air.

Instantly, Father and Captain Brant rushed back into the church. They stood staring at the man with the knife, waiting for his next move.

The young man had pinned Laura in front of him with his arm around her in an iron grip. Captain Brant stared at his son in disbelief. "Isaac, let her go!"

"Why? She's my way out of here." Like his brothers, he spoke perfect English. "Don't come a step closer." But Captain Brant started to walk very slowly towards his son.

"Give yourself up, Isaac, and I will help you. I'll speak on your behalf to our judges."

Laura felt the point of the knife cut into the waistband of her petticoat. The pounding of her heart filled her ears and she started to tremble.

"For the love of God, do what Isaac says," Father gasped.

Captain Brant hesitated and Isaac spoke again. "Now stand back both of you. I'm going out that door and leaving on this horse with the girl. I see that you have supplies that will last me for days. If you touch me, I'll kill her." Turning to his father, he snarled, "You know it won't be the first person I've killed. Now stand back!"

"Don't take my daughter," said Father, "and we won't follow. Take my horse and supplies but leave my daughter."

Isaac turned to his father. "Do you promise also?"

Captain Brant's face was drawn in anguish. "I won't follow you today, my son. But tomorrow I will, and I'll find you too."

His son's laugh filled the air as he flung Laura roughly to the floor and strode past the men.

"Please, Isaac. I'll go with you to the authorities. I know it was only an accident, and you did not intend to kill the man. I'll help you. We'll go together. Please, listen."

The young man turned and spat at his father. Then the heavy door slammed behind him. Captain Brant rushed outside while Father helped the shaking Laura to her feet.

Outside the chapel, Laura and her father found Captain Brant sitting on a bench, staring at the trail leading up the knoll from Brant's Ford. Both their horses were still there but their supplies were gone, and so was Captain Brant's magnificent stallion. Laura sat down with relief on the bench between her father and Brant. She was still trembling.

"He didn't kill a man. It was an accident," said Captain Brant. "The man was stabbed by his own knife. It was a drunken brawl.

They were both drunk, and no one knows how it happened. But Isaac's had a problem with drinking ever since the Revolutionary War."

"I'm sorry, Joseph," said Father.

"He was too young to be in the war, and I was away so much. He turned to the rum, and he's been having spells like this ever since."

They sat in silence for a moment. Then Captain Brant turned to Laura. "I apologize for my son. Are you all right now, Laura?"

"Yes, I'm better now, thank you."

"Good. Thomas, I'll get you more supplies. You'll be fully paid for what my son has taken. Come to the house now. My wife will have a meal ready for you before you continue on to Burlington Bay. And I will travel with you, so you will not be attacked again. I will see you safely on board the ship."

* * * * *

In the early evening of the same day, Laura and Father sat on the deck of a schooner sailing from Burlington Bay to Queenston.

"How are you, Laura?" Father said, looking at her intently.

"I'm fine, now. But I can't help wondering about Captain Brant and his son Isaac. He was so different from his brothers. Did he ever attend school like they did?"

"Locally, yes."

"Then why didn't he turn out like his brothers? They were so friendly and helpful."

"Sometimes, Laura, parents can provide the best for their child in education and training, and still the child doesn't benefit. . . ."

"Perhaps his father was not able to be with Isaac as much in his earlier years."

"That's true, for Isaac is the oldest, and his father was completely involved in the Revolutionary War when Isaac was reaching manhood. I too was away from my family so much during the war years. But I've always been proud of my daughters and thankful for them. Perhaps sons without their father would have turned out differently."

"We missed you. Even after the war was over," Laura said quietly.

"I know . . . it was a hard time . . . to make ends meet. Many men went under with the taxes. I saw what happened to their families when they were thrown in jail for debts. It would be better to follow the way of the Mohawks—no jails."

"That's right. There was no jail at Brant's Ford."

"Captain Brant had harsh words to describe our jails and the white man's cruel "justice" that is handed out to people who cannot pay their debts. He feels the Mohawk way is better. They do deal with offenders, but they help those who cannot pay up when misfortune strikes." Father's face looked grim as he remembered such incidents at Great Barrington. Then he continued, "I pledged I'd keep a roof over your heads. And I did."

"Yes, we were well provided for, and I am grateful." Laura looked away from her father's sad face.

"Sally still blames me for coming to Canada, but I couldn't live off her father."

"I know. And Sally will be fine. I bet she's missing you right now.

"Sometimes I wonder if she'll be gone when we get back. I left the savings with her. She can afford to go back in better style than we came." Father was staring back behind the boat. The dampness of the evening air was bringing mosquitoes now, but he didn't seem to notice.

Laura sighed to see her father's concern. "Sally would never do that and neither would Mira and Elizabeth!"

"Oh, she wouldn't take Mira. She'd leave her with Bett and Sam. But I'm afraid she'll be gone with Elizabeth and the younger children."

"She'll still be there, Father. I'm sure, she will." Laura was remembering the promise that Sally had made to her back in Great Barrington.

"I hope you're right," Thomas mumbled in a scarcely audible voice and sat with bent head, looking across the water swirling out behind the boat.

Laura knew her father's thoughts were back with Sally, and she felt a sudden surge of sympathy for him, and impatience with Sally for not trying harder to adjust to their new life. They sat there in silence for a long time until the growing dusk brought the mosquitoes in hordes, and they took shelter down below the deck.

FIFTEEN

"I never thought I'd hear you say it, Thomas." Sally was staring out the doorway of their canvas home into the pouring rain. A waggoner was going past, coaxing his bedraggled team through the mud. "It's a wonderful idea! And if your business here at the inn is a success, maybe you'll give up clearing land for a farm." Father and Laura had arrived back from the site two weeks before.

Father, who was sitting across the table from Sally, shook his head.

"No, Sally, this is just temporary, but for now it seems best. The Inn is selling at a price I can afford. So we'll be warm there for the winter, and sell it for more in the spring when we'll head out to our farm with more cash to buy supplies."

"I'll be so glad to move," Sally sighed. It had not been easy living in such crowded quarters with two small children an it would be another difficult day with the rain pouring down so heavily and the children both inside. "How soon will we be moving?"

"Sooner than you think. I found out that Fairbank's Inn was empty and up for sale the day I came back, and the next day I asked about buying it. My offer was accepted just this morning." Thomas avoided his wife's surprised eyes. "We can pack now and move when it stops raining. And that's not all. There are separate living quarters for the family. I think you'll like it, Sally."

"Really! Oh, Thomas, I'm so delighted." Sally came around the table and gave him a kiss on the cheek.

Laura and Elizabeth stepped into the large tent just then and shook the rain out of their capes. They were getting along much better now. In fact, Laura noticed how hard Elizabeth was trying to keep up with her share of the housework. Still, Elizabeth had confided in Laura that she didn't like Queenston at all.

"Did I hear correctly?" Laura asked. "Are we really going to be running Queenston's one and only Inn and Tavern?"

Elizabeth was excited too, "Maybe we'll make some new friends." Laura guessed she meant men friends. When they first came, Elizabeth had gone to the Landing every day to see if the incoming mail might have a letter from Thomas Mayo. But none had come, and Laura knew how hard that was! She would always remember how disappointed she'd been when Red hadn't written.

Father was looking at Laura now. "I'm counting on you to help me with the books. You always have been good with figures."

"I'd like to do that," Laura said. Back no more than a week and already she was bored. The only visitor they had seen was Josh who delivered the milk every day, but he spent most of the time with Mira. Laura could not believe how grown-up her sister had looked as she left for the ball with Josh the previous Saturday. Josh, whose full name was Julius Hitchcock, had taken Mira to Lady Simcoe's ball at Newark to represent his family, who were well established in the area.

As for James he seemed to be nowhere in sight. Father did ask him to help move the family's belongings from the tents to the inn, but between sorting clothes and lifting bags there was not much opportunity to speak.

Then came the business of setting up operations at the inn. Laura became so involved with balancing the books and keeping track of supplics that shc hardly had a moment to herself.

Late one afternoon, a month after they had moved into the inn, Laura was sitting at thc little oak desk just inside the main entrance. She had totalled the two columns for profits and expenditures, and she was worried.

As she had feared, the expense column was much higher even though they had been busy. In fact, everyone had remarked on how business was booming.

Because Queenston was the beginning of the portage route around to Chippawa and connected the great Lakes, many people passed this way, both overnight settlers and those who frequented the tavern. Her father and Sam handled that part of the business, but all the accounts came through her books. The problem was the credit that her father gave to a number of newcomers. The business just couldn't afford it.

"Laura, you've been pouring over those books all day," said Thomas as he stepped into the office in the inn.

"I just totalled the month's income and expenses. The expenses were much higher."

"Were they?" Father looked surprised.

"It's the credit you give. We just don't have the capital to last long that way." Laura handed him the open book and, leaning over, pointed out the number of unpaid bills already on their account.

"Whoo!" Father whistled through his teeth. "I had no idea."

"We cannot afford this," Laura said, raising her voice. She was annoyed that her father never could seem to make ends meet.

At that moment, James Secord walked in the door. "Excuse me if I'm meddling, but I couldn't help overhearing your conversation. You don't need to worry, Laura. Credit's always extended in these parts. Folks will pay. It just takes a little time. They're honest folk."

Laura turned around and looked directly at James. She saw he was alone and wondered why he never brought Phoebe when he came to visit. She blurted out, "Hello, James. Why didn't you bring Phoebe? I'm sure your wife would like to visit too sometimes."

"My wife!" laughed James. "Phoebe is my niece, David's daughter."

Laura knew that David Secord was the magistrate of St. David's and the founder of the village. She stared quietly back at James, who continued, "She's far too busy to go anywhere with me. She has so many beaux."

Laura was annoyed to feel her cheeks flaming red. Blustering with embarrassment, she said, "I didn't know. Now back to these accounts. . . ."

"I assure you I wasn't eavesdropping. . . . I just didn't want you to worry for no reason."

"It's quite all right," said Father. "Here, have a chair. You've come at just the right time." James sat down with a confident smile.

"Now, Laura," Father said, "what were you about to say?"

"I . . . I suggest we give credit at the inn only in emergency situations. The tavern should not have any credit accounts." She wondered if James really was the great businessman her father thought he was.

James interrupted, "As I was saying, you'll find folks around here are an honourable lot. They'll settle their accounts." James spoke calmly as he tapped a tune on Laura's desk with his fingers.

"He's right, Laura. I've always said you worry too much," Father continued. He gave her a pat on the shoulder and abruptly changed the subject. "James, would you like to join us for supper?"

Laura was furious. How could her father take her advice so lightly? If he had worried sooner, his family would be in better circumstances today. His motto had always been never to cross a bridge before he came to it, so he was never prepared when they did reach the bridge. And who suffered? The family. They always had to take a detour. Well, this time she'd just have to see to it that they didn't need to go around in circles. She could run this business successfully if her father would give her a free hand. And here was James, her ideal man, giving bad business advice. Well, maybe James wasn't so great, after all.

Laura slammed the accounts book shut and took a long look at the men.

"I'm going to see if Sally needs any help with supper. It's a good job women don't wait till folks are at the table before they prepare the meal."

She marched quickly out of the room with her head held high. Surprised, James turned to watch Laura until she disappeared down the hall.

* * * * *

A week later, Laura was taking time out from her duties at the inn to pick wild raspberries. Sally was bent on making jam, even though business continued to be brisk at the inn, and Laura had been chosen to do the picking. She had to hold her petticoats up to keep them from brushing against the ox-eyed daisies and devil's paint-brush that dotted the land at the foot of thc Heights. It was almost exactly midsummer. A grilling sun was beating down on her back. She didn't know whether it was worse to take her hat off and risk a burn or to leave it on and feel even hotter. She resigned herself to leaving it on.

She turned along the road that led west to St. David's. In order not to lose her way, she planned to keep the road in sight. Josh had told Mira there were lots of berries in plain view along the sides of the road and up the hillside on land owned by the Hitchcocks—and she was welcome to any pickings there.

"He was right," she said aloud as she spotted a thick patch not far from the road. The red berries hung heavily from the canes, and she dropped them easily into the small pail she had tied around her waist. She thought about picking berries in Great Barrington with her Mother when she was a little girl back home. "Maybe I can pick enough for Sally and Bett to make a pie too," she thought with some satisfaction. She pulled a few leaves from her berries in the pail.

As she picked and ate, the sun became stronger and she rubbed her hand across her forehead to wipe away the beads of sweat. Three small pails would be enough to get a start on the preserves and it wouldn't take long to pick that many.

With her pail half full, she sighed and reached for more branches, only to find that she had picked most of the near ones clean. She would need to go on farther in, where there might be snakes. Then Laura remembered the time a snake had surprised her when she was picking berries with her mother in Great Barrington. "That snake is quite harmless; he's more scared of you than you are of him," her mother had said. She smiled and stepped ahead.

"Can I help you?" A man's voice came from the direction of the road.

Laura jumped with surprise, but she recognized the voice. It was James. He was tethering his team of horses to a tree by the roadway. Then in long fast strides, he hurried over to her.

Laura felt the hot sun burn more deeply as she looked up at him. She could not imagine how terrible she must look with berry stains all around her mouth and sweat dripping from her forehead.

"I thought that was you, Laura," James said as he came closer. He reached out and grabbed both of her berry-stained hands. "You look like you've been through a war."

"Watch out, James, or you'll be covered with berry juice," Laura laughed as she looked down to her pail between them. Then she added, "Help yourself."

He took a few. "These are good, sweet berries. It must be a fine year for them. . . . Let me help you pick."

"Don't you have to meet a boat?" Laura asked, thinking once

more that James couldn't be that good a businessman if he could take time off in the middle of the day to pick raspberries.

"It'll be docked for a while. Anyhow, it isn't due until this afternoon."

"Well, if you really have the time, I'd love your help. I have to pick three pails full."

The two worked away as the heat of the day grew, and the silence was broken only by the drone of the cicadas and the creaking of the berry pails. Before long, the three pails were filled to the brim with the bright red berries.

"Well, I guess that's it," Laura declared, untying her berry pail from around her waist. She smiled at James, whose eyes looked bluer than ever. "Thank you for helping me out. That's a hot job, and. . . ."

"Laura, what would you say if we went up the Heights for a bite to eat. I brought lunch in my wagon. You'll love it up there. You can see a long way back along the Niagara River."

Laura didn't know what to think. Was James just asking her to be nice, or was he really interested in being with her? She couldn't help thinking how different James was. Red would have been cracking jokes and they'd both be laughing by now. But James. . . . there was something reassuring about him.

"Well," she said, coming back to herself, "I don't . . . I guess . . . I can't think of anything nicer to do."

Laura blushed and James turned and ran back to the wagon with the berries. Laura stifled a laugh as she watched him get his linen breeches caught on all the raspberry canes. The same thing happened on the way back, only it was worse because James was carrying a basket of sandwiches, a jug of water, and a smaller berry pail. He didn't have a free hand to pry himself away from the clutching bushes. Laura could stay still no longer, and when she raced over to help him, she caught her petticoats on the bushes.

"Here, you hold these." James handed her the food, disentangled himself, and reached down to free Laura's petticoat from the canes. Laura watched with fascination as his big gentle hands pulled off each burr—one at a time. In a few minutes, he had them all and was taking the food from her and motioning her to follow him.

James held back the thick, scratching canes as she edged her way out to the clearing. From there they clambered up the steep, grassy hillside away from the road. Weaving through the young undergrowth of oak, fir and maple, they hurried along side by side until they reached a small, stony plateau.

Looking on up the hill, Laura could see that they were far from the top. A steep path wound ahead between the trees. James led the way up the narrow winding path to the summit, where they emerged onto a larger plateau.

"Turn around the other way, Laura, and you'll see the view." James placed a gentle hand on her shoulder, and with his other hand pointed to the view below.

Laura realized then how far they had come up the Heights. There lay the Niagara River far below and beyond, and the densely wooded slopes hid Queenston completely from view.

"Oh, can't we stay right here and eat?" Laura blurted out, turning around, then stopping abruptly as she was confronted by James' sapphire eyes. "We . . . we can see the river from the shade of this elm tree."

"Well, I guess there's no reason to look farther. This is a superb spot. Here, you undo the sandwiches, while I get the place ready." He pulled the weeds and trampled the long grass, then motioned Laura to sit down across from him. Before they ate, Laura waited until James bowed his head and prayed briefly for their meal. Then she opened her eyes shyly, only to see that James still had his head bowed. He was still praying—but silently.

In a moment he looked up, and Laura looked away, embarrassed.

"It always helps to know He hears and cares," James said as if answering her unasked questions. "Life is not always easy."

She did not answer.

A bushy-tailed grey squirrel hung from a nearby branch and jumped down onto the grass in front of them.

Then James broke the silence. "How does your family like Queenston?"

Laura turned to answer. "Mira is really happy. She makes friends easily and Josh visits a lot."

"I've heard he's courting Mira."

"She's only fifteen. He's just a friend. But he's a good friend to all of us. He came by one day, just last week, after his morning milk delivery and offered to help with chores at the inn. Mira had him baking in the kitchen."

"Josh! In the kitchen! I can't believe that!" And James burst into hearty laughter.

Laura started to giggle. "It was a funny sight! He couldn't have caused more problems. First, he upset the fresh berry pie that Mira asked him to take out of the oven. It spilled out of his hands and landed face down on the floor."

James' laughter filled the air again. "I can see it," he responded.

"Next, he ran into the utensil rack that hung over the table, where all the other fresh pies were spread out, and all the ladling spoons and sharp knives fell down onto the fresh pies. The raspberries splattered all over the wall and floor. That's when Sally came in and sent them both out."

"I bet she wasn't too happy."

"I assure you she wasn't, but she didn't say too much to Josh. He was apologizing and looking so distressed. It's hard to be angry with Josh. I feel guilty even telling you about it. He's such a nice, young man, but such a. . . ."

"I know Josh," said James still chuckling, "and don't worry. I won't mention a word to him. I'm surprised, though, that he was free from the farm work in the middle of the day. It's such a busy time for farmers just now. . . . And how's Sally? Is she liking it better now at the inn?"

Laura paused, then responded. "Sally's still not too happy and neither is Elizabeth."

"It's hard at first. They're probably homesick."

"No, it's more than that, James. Sally can't understand why they haven't been invited to the teas or quilting bees. She'd love to get acquainted with the women in Queenston."

James looked away. The squirrel was running now to the trunk of a large willow. It scampered up the trunk and disappeared under the low-hanging branches. James turned back to Laura.

"Well, the farm women around Queenston are very busy this time of the year. They have quilting and sewing bees only in the winter. Now they're working in their gardens and helping with crops and farm work."

"Is that the only reason?" Laura asked, noticing a certain hesitation in his voice.

"No. There is some resentment towards settlers," James replied honestly.

"Why? The war is over."

"It will pass, Laura. They are kind women. They'll soon forget when they come to know you."

"I wasn't even old enough to understand what was going on in the war. I was born just after it began."

James hesitated a moment. "I was three years old at the beginning of the war when my mother escaped with us to Niagara. There were five women with thirty-one children. I was the youngest. We made it to a shelter at Fort Niagara in November of '76. A terrible winter. It was a nightmare. We nearly froze to death and arrived half-starved. Mother says we almost died—the lot of us."

"Couldn't your father help?"

"No, he was away fighting the Rebels. He was a lieutenant in Butler's Rangers. My older brothers fought with his troops too."

Laura looked out over the Niagara River. "Did you say you arrived in November of '76?" That was well into the war. "Why didn't your mother leave sooner?"

"Well, they thought they might not be in danger. My father and brothers had fled for their lives from our home in New Rochelle, but at that time, the Americans didn't bother women and children. So they stayed with the hope that the whole rebellion would soon be stopped and their men would be allowed to come home again. That didn't happen, unfortunately, so they fled across country to Fort Niagara. It was farther than they thought."

"We lived at Great Barrington, not far from New Rochelle."

"I don't really remember New Rochelle, since I was so young when we left. Mother told me it was named after La Rochelle in France. Father's ancestors came from there in 1681 and founded the town in 1689. It used to be a French settlement."

"Is your mother French too?"

"Yes. She was Madelaine Badeau before her marriage. One of her ancestors fled from France to Bristol in England and from there he sailed to America. His name was Elias—Elias Badeau. Now my mother lives in St. David's with my brother, David. Father would be there too, but he died in '84 just a year after the war ended."

"I'm sorry."

"It was an old war wound. It just became infected and that . . . that's what killed him. He's buried in Colonel Butler's private burying ground."

"How old were you when he died?"

"I was eleven. . . . He was never home much until that last year, but I was glad I came to know him before he died. He was worn out and disheartened. He had hoped to return to the French settlement at New Rochelle after the war."

They sat silently for a minute.

"Pardon me for talking about myself so much, Laura. I'm sure both sides suffer during wars."

"That's true, but we had more trouble after the war. Scavengers kept raiding and the authorities couldn't stop it, but when they did catch the guilty ones, they were very cruel. People were hanged for stealing, and many who were in debt had all their property taken away. Some were even thrown in jail." Laura couldn't help thinking of Joseph Brant's anger at the white man's jails.

"It wasn't that bad here, except for one year, the hungry year of '88. We nearly starved. Some people did starve to death. And it could have been prevented. For the first three years after the war, the government provided food for the people. Then, just as a bad drought hit the land, the government claimed they had fulfilled their obligations and stopped sending supplies."

"What did people eat, then?"

"Pigeons, rabbits, anything. People even died from eating poisonous roots. Not that many, but some. Most people found out what was poisonous by asking the Indians or watching the animals. Instinctively, cattle rarely eat poisonous plants."

"Really! It's good to know that's all in the past, though."

"Well, folks are more prosperous now, but they can't forget the suffering."

"So that's why they haven't welcomed us?"

"Yes. And there were rumblings, again last fall, of war with the

States. Simcoe sent his wife and children to Quebec for the winter. They say he was afraid of an outbreak, I'm thankful the crisis is past, and he's brought his family back again. I suppose folks won't trust Americans for a while, but soon they'll come to know and accept you."

"I hope so. We can't go back now." Laura looked out over the Niagara River to the distant horizon where the deep blue of the water met the light blue of the sky.

"I hope not," he replied.

Laura felt the emotion in his voice. She looked up then and realized that he was looking at her with a tenderness she had not seen in a man's eyes before. Suddenly she felt uneasy.

"I think we'd best be heading back. My family will be expecting me."

"I hope we can see each other again soon," he said.

"Yes, I'm sure we can. I'd like that."

James chucked the water jug into the picnic basket and pushing it along his arm, he managed to carry the berry pail over the same arm.

With his free hand, James reached out to Laura, and clasping her hand securely in his, they climbed down the steep hillside in silence.

SIXTEEN

Laura hurried to the office of her father's inn. He would have quite a few questions to ask her today, since he had been to the site at La Tranche River for over a month. It was October now and Laura had been running Ingersoll's Inn & Tavern at Queenston since he left. Business was good. James was right about one thing. A great deal of traffic did pass through the village.

The evening before he left, Father had told Laura that James had come to him one day to confide that he was having financial problems in his new store in St. David's. Since Laura had not talked to James about his business after that day at the inn, she suspected that he was having trouble because he was giving too much credit.

"He could lose everything if he's not careful," she thought as she remembered such cases in Great Barrington. She wondered if some people took advantage of James' attitude to credit and his easygoing ways.

Business aside, Laura wished James would come by the inn more often. In fact, she was puzzled that he hadn't called on her since that wonderful hot afternoon on the Heights. Maybe he felt too poor just now to plan for a future with a wife. Was that the reason he hesitated to ask for Father's permission to call on her regularly? Or perhaps she had only imagined that he cared for her in a special way. She knew now that James was kind to many newcomers to Niagara. But why the intense look in those deep blue eyes, and why had he held her hand so tightly going down the mountain?

Laura had come to the door of her father's office and saw that he was sitting at his desk.

Father looked up from his account book and smiled. His inn was doing well in spite of his hasty decision to start the business, and the tavern had flourished. There was a lot of money to be made in selling to thirsty men along the business route. Now he would be able to save money to help buy tools and seed for his land in the spring. He thought it would not be long before he would be able to take his family to their site.

"How was your trip?" Laura asked, taking a seat in the captain's chair opposite the desk.

"Very good, Laura."

"Did you see Captain Brant?"

Father frowned and hesitated before he answered, "Yes."

"Did he find his son?"

"I'm afraid so."

"Well?"

"Actually, his son found Captain Brant one evening when he was leaving an inn at Burlington Heights, where the Grand River tribes were meeting. Isaac was drunk and lunged at his father with a knife, and when Joseph tried to get the knife, Isaac was wounded. Four other men jumped in to restrain the young man and they took him to a doctor to dress the wound. It was not a serious wound and needed no sewing, just a dressing. But he tore off the bandage and spat at them as he left."

"Poor Captain Brant."

"That's not the end of the story. In a few weeks, Isaac's wound became infected and he died."

"Captain Brant must be heartbroken."

"Devastated, yes, and that's not all. He blamed himself and gave himself up to the English authorities for the murder of his son. Fortunately, the court decided it was his son's fault for not caring for his wound. They declared the wound itself to be an accident, and the result of a fight caused by the son. So they freed Captain Brant."

Laura felt tears of fury and sorrow coming to her eyes as she remembered the man who had held the knife to her not so many months before. "Surely he cannot blame himself for Isaac's death anymore."

"It isn't that easy, Laura. He felt he was responsible—so he went to the Mohawk chiefs and declared his guilt."

"What did they do?"

"Much the same as the British authorities. They tried him and freed him."

"How is he now?" Laura asked.

"Very sad, but he has finally accepted that it was not his fault. He spends a lot of time in the chapel. He'll get over it. His people need him still."

"I would like to visit the Brants again."

"You will," her father assured her. "We'll be moving to our cabin in less than a year. . . . Now, Laura, would you add up this week's receipts while I go and attend to the tavern?"

Laura took her father's place and started adding up the columns of figures. Halfway down the second one, she heard a familiar voice.

"Good morning, Laura." James looked down over the counter.

"James! How nice to see you again!" She put her quill pen down and smiled up at James.

"How have you been, Laura?"

"Busy. But Father's back now."

"I see. Would you be too busy to go for a ride today? I have to pick up supplies from a boat later this morning, but I'll be free till then."

"I'll check with Father and be right back. I'd really like to go."

Laura found her father serving a drummer in the far corner of the dining room. He raised his grey eyebrows when he turned around and saw her standing behind him.

"Laura! Is something the matter?"

"Uh . . . n—no," she stammered. "I just, well, James is here. "

"Yes, yes, well show him in. I haven't had a good chat with him for a long time."

"No, Father, he wants to take me out for a ride. We won't be long. Can you let me go for a few hours?"

"A few hours! That's . . . well, I guess you must have a lot to talk about." Father noticed Laura's heightened colour and shining eyes. "Go on, then. I'll get Elizabeth to look after the counter."

Laura raced out of the dining room, not slowing down until just before she got to the doorway of her father's office. She stopped a minute, took off her apron, and smoothed her outer petticoat.

"Father says he can manage without me," Laura smiled, as she entered the office. "Where do you want to ride?" She dropped her apron on a chair and pulled out her white fichu from under the counter. She wrapped it loosely around her neck and fastened it at the front with a pretty yellow ribbon.

"Well, I thought we'd just ride to the bottom of the Heights and then walk up where we did before. Come on, let's go! We don't want to waste the day."

James led her out to the wagon and closed his hand over hers as he lifted her up to the seat in front. Laura felt like an important lady, even though she was still wearing the same brown petticoat and beige jacket that she wore almost every day.

James swung up into the seat beside her. He smelled of fresh soft soap and cedar. Laura knew he must have just taken his fall clothes out of cedar shavings, where they'd been kept all summer. James slapped the reins on the horses' backs and gave Laura his big, blue-eyed smile. "Well, where to, my girl?" he grinned.

"To the Heights, of course!" she commanded. At that, James made the horses move faster and before long they had come to the tree where James had tethered the team that day in July.

*****

"I have never seen anything so beautiful," Laura gasped. "It's like a different country." Laura and James had come to the top plateau again and were looking out over the Niagara River, but now the landscape was a massive expanse of yellow elm and oak, red maples, and a few evergreens standing brilliant in between. The smell of woodsmoke drifted through the air and a blue jay screamed overhead from time to time.

"It *is* a different country, Laura, and it's our country now. God has brought you through a lot, and he has done the same for me, and now it seems he has brought us out into a spacious place."

Laura wanted to understand what James was saying, but she was getting a bit lost. Or maybe she was a bit afraid to hear what she'd been wanting to hear for so long.

James slipped his arm around Laura's waist, and Laura felt her cheeks reddening as she felt the warmth of his body sheltering her from the brisk October air. He too was conscious of her nearness, but as he looked down, he dropped his arm to his side with a sad smile. As his eyes searched her face, Laura saw concern there and wondered what the reason was.

James broke the stillness. "Let's find a flat stone to sit on and rest a while."

Laura found a stone that was warm from the morning sun, but the thick shrubs around them were still damp from early dew. "How is your store coming along, James?" Laura said awkwardly, once they were seated on their perch.

James hesitated and then replied, "Any new business takes time to prosper." His mouth settled into a firm line, and Laura wished she hadn't asked the question. She knew full well he was having problems. Why did she have to pick that topic? James looked up then and continued, "Financing is hard at first, and my sister's husband, Richard Cartwright, has urged me not to extend credit. He says no young business can survive that way and that it's better to have produce on the shelves to be claimed by creditors if cash is not available."

Laura stopped herself from pointing out that that was what she had been talking about the day James had taken Father's part against her.

"I will always extend credit to some. They are hard-working folk who are in need, and some day they will pay me. I think it's what God wants me to do."

Laura was puzzled again by James' talk of God. It was true that many folks were religious and went to church whenever there was a visiting minister. Some local people even led meetings themselves, but they didn't talk about God that way. He wasn't part of their business and their everyday lives.

"I hope they do pay you back, James, and your store prospers, but sometimes God doesn't answer prayer." Sheresponded as she remembered her mother and stepmother lying in their graves back in Great Barrington.

"Sometimes he answers differently than we expect," said James.

They sat in silence then, happy to be together. It no longer seemed necessary to talk, but James looked thoughtful as he gazed out over the water. As Laura sat there quietly beside him, she knew that she loved this man—no matter what the state of his business. And besides, she could get his business in order in no time—if she were in charge. Yes, it would take her no time at all to have James on the road to prosperity. Life ahead was looking very good.

"Laura," James interrupted her daydream. "I have to go on a trip to Kingston where my sister and her husband live and then on to Montreal and perhaps farther."

"Farther? Montreal is a long distance."

"New York, maybe. It's a business trip. I'm leaving in the morning. Right now, I have to pick up my supplies at the Landing and have things in shape so I can leave very early tomorrow. I'll be riding up to Newark and catching a boat there."

"Oh, why . . . I wasn't . . . I was hoping I'd see you again soon."

He looked at her and smiled then. "I'd like that too, Laura, but I have no choice. I have to make the trip. I'm afraid too that we must go back now. My supplies will be waiting at the Landing."

They stood up, and James reached out and clasped her hand, which she tightened around his. Why did this man always seem to disappear as soon as he started showing a real interest in her? Was this the way God was answering her prayers? She said nothing to James, but she just held his big hand a bit tighter and braced herself against the wind.

At the bottom of the incline, the horses were switching their tails and snorting as if they were impatient to take James away.

"Laura," James said softly as they approached Queenston. He was letting the horses travel at a slower pace now.

"Yes, James."

"I'd like to come to visit you as soon as I return."

"I'll, I'll look forward to seeing you," Laura mumbled. She could think of nothing else to say.

"I'm not sure just when that will be." He appeared anxious and spoke with hesitation, looking straight ahead.

"I'll be waiting, James," Laura quietly promised.

He turned toward her with a smile.

Laura smiled back.

James drove the horses with one hand, holding the reins tightly. With the other, he reached out, clasped Laura's hand, and held it next to him all the way home.

*****

Laura sat in her small bedroom under the eaves. She was reading from her mother's Bible by the light of a candle. Mira had gone to a party with Josh, and her stepmother and Elizabeth were away at an evening ladies' meeting.

Time had brought such changes. She wondered how God could have taken both her mother and her first stepmother away. Life had not been easy, but she'd tried to smile for Mira, and gradually the pain had eased. James had not had an easy life either, but she knew now that he always asked God for help to face the problems.

Laura knelt down beside her bed, and by the flickering light, with her head bowed over her mother's Bible, she prayed. Her prayer was short, but Laura felt a great relief when she finished. She left the Bible open on the table, and reached across for the candle. As she blew the flame out, it left a small trail of smoke. Then Laura climbed into her four-poster bedstead. It felt good to lie down on the straw mattress.

As Laura looked out the window at the harvest moon, her thoughts drifted off to James. She felt warm inside when she remembered how he had held her hand and finally put his arm around her waist as they climbed the Heights. She couldn't help wondering if he would be safe on this long trip going to the distant city of Montreal—at least seven days away from Queenston. If only she could be with him. She knew he was a good man and she wanted to share her life with him. Though he would soon be far away, she felt closer to him than she had ever felt to anyone.

SEVENTEEN

"Mira, if you don't tuck that robe in, you're going to freeze," said Laura, standing beside the sleigh in front of the inn, pushing the hairy buffalo robe in under Mira's legs.

"Oh, Laura, you still think I'm the baby of the family," Mira chuckled. For a minute, Laura felt offended, but when she looked into Mira's laughing brown eyes, she started laughing too. She never had been able to stay angry with Mira for long.

"I'm sorry, Mira. I'm so tired, I guess I don't know what I'm thinking. If you can drive this sleigh, you should be able to take care of yourself by now!"

Laura really was having trouble thinking straight this morning. She had stayed up most of the night taking care of Elizabeth, who had come down with a ravaging flu. Now she had to head to James' store in St. David's to buy more supplies to make up some medicines and a mustard plaster. Since Josh was working in the store during the winter months, Mira was eager to go too. She had volunteered to drive because Laura was tired, and Sam and Father could afford little time away from the inn. It was mid-February, but the traffic passing through Queenston had not decreased much since the fall.

As Laura swung herself into the sleigh and tucked an end of the big buffalo robe around her, she could still see in her mind's eye Elizabeth's face, flushed red with fever. Time after time Laura had cooled her forehead with a wet cloth, but Elizabeth just kept getting hotter and hotter. As she stroked her step-sister's brow, Laura remembered all the times they had fought over the years. She was really just so different that Laura sometimes thought how strange it was for them to have ended up in the same family.

Just before sunrise, Elizabeth had roused enough to notice someone there, and Laura saw that tears were running down her face.

"Laura, is that you?"

"Yes, Elizabeth, I'm right here. Don't try to talk. You need to sleep."

"No, I'm all right. I just thought for a minute . . . I thought you looked so much like Mother. I thought she was still here."

"No, Sally's asleep. She stayed with you all last night. And she had such a busy day, she couldn't sit up with you."

"Laura. . . . " her voice trailed off and Laura stroked her forehead with the damp cloth again. "Do you remember the flower garden back at Great Barrington? I dreamt I was there with Grandma and Grandpa Whiting. Do you remember, Laura?"

"Yes, Elizabeth, I remember." Laura stroked Elizabeth's blonde locks back over her pillow and smiled at her. Elizabeth tried a smile, but it faded before she began, and her eyes closed. As Laura watched, she realized how much Elizabeth needed her now.

"Goodbye, Laura! Goodbye, Mira!" Father was waving to them from the front entrance of the inn. "You be careful now and don't go too fast or you'll tip over! We'll see you back here in the afternoon." As Mira touched the whip to the horses, he turned and went back inside, shutting the big oak door behind him.

The trail was easy to follow, for it was the route all the sleighs took between Queenston and St. David's. On either side, the trees that had looked so brilliant the previous fall now stood naked and black against a lowering, grey-blue sky. It looked to Laura as if a storm was going to blow up at any moment, but Father had reassured them that it would wait until they got back home. Anyway, there were two of them in the sleigh. If they did get stuck, they could unhitch the horses and ride together for help.

Now they were passing the windswept Heights, where the snow had drifted deeply in places. Toward the top, the swirling snow blew out across an open space, and Laura remembered the wonderful hours she had spent there with James. She wondered if she would spend time with him there again next summer. The bleakness of the howling wind pierced like a knife and she felt an overwhelming longing to be with him, wherever he was. She remembered James telling her about an older brother John, who went away and was never heard from again. Maybe that's what had happened to James. She hadn't heard a single word from him since he had left last October. She shuddered at the thought of never seeing him again. Then she recalled James' quiet reassurance that God would show him the way, and she felt somewhat comforted.

"Have you heard from James yet, Laura?" Mira asked, as if reading her sister's mind.

"No, Mira, and I'm worried about it. It has been several months."

"Well, we can ask at the store and see if there's a letter there for you today. He may have sent you a message with his letters to the family. It is strange he hasn't written by now. Remember that boy Red? You were always looking for letters from him too, and none came."

Laura winced. It was true that Red had never written her back, but Mira didn't have to mention it. James was a different case. He had promised to write—or had he? Laura pursed her lips and turned to her sister.

"Oh, Laura, I am so clumsy. I didn't mean to say that. Of course, Red was just a boy—and I do believe James is madly in love with you. Not the way Josh is in love with me, maybe, but he has you somewhere in his heart."

"Mira, watch out!" Laura screamed. "You almost went into the ditch." The team had veered right off to one side of the main path and they were having a difficult time.

"Oh, dear, steering is the one thing I'm not good at with horses. They do tend to wander off, especially when I get talking and pull the wrong rein. Anyway, as I was saying, I don't think you need to worry about James, unless he falls for some lady in New York, of course."

"Mira, you do have a way of saying just the wrong thing. We don't even know if he's going to New York. Besides, he did say that he wanted to see me when he came home."

"I am sorry, Laura. My words just always get away on me. They're out before I know what I'm going to say."

"Yes, you always have been like that. It's just, well, I am a bit concerned that James might have forgotten me. It's not as if he promised to marry me. If he decided to court another woman, I would really have no claim on him. Just imagine if Josh went away for a long trip. Would you really know where you stood?"

Mira smiled and tossed back her fur-covered head. "Oh, I think

I would know. But then . . . well, I see what you mean." The two sisters rode on the rest of the way in silence.

The sound of tinkling bells drew their attention as an approaching team came closer. They were near St. David's now, and the traffic was getting heavier. Mira drove their horses as far as possible to the side of the road to let the larger team pass by, because the road had drifted in to almost a narrow trail.

"0ne of these days, St. David's will be cut off until spring," said Mira. "And look, the road into Phoebe's is drifted almost full." Mira pointed to the left, where the Secord's laneway was half-covered with freshly drifted snow from the wind that had blown up as they drove along. But the stone house at the end of the laneway was still clearly visible, and so were the nearby buildings and sheds, where they housed their horses and farm animals.

Next they came to the main intersection, where Mira steered the horses to the left, into the shed by James' store. They stepped out from under their buffalo robe and stamped their feet on the crisp snow. As they tied the reins to the hitching post, they noticed that the horses were unusually restless. Laura patted Bonnie reassuringly on the side of her neck and rubbed her vigorously, but she and the other horses still pranced about and snorted, their moist breath turning into icy clouds.

As she stood there calming the horses, Laura realized that she was almost afraid to go into the store. She was certain to hear some news of James and it might not be good. She couldn't help wondering if he had decided to set up business in Kingston with his brother-in-law. Perhaps he really had met someone else, and Phoebe would tell them of his marriage. After all, it was true that he hadn't made any promises.

"Are you coming, Laura?" Mira shouted as she held the door.

"Mira! Girls! It's great to see you." Josh came rushing over from the counter and vigorously shook their hands, then held onto Mira's without noticing Laura staring at them. He still had a ruddy complexion, and his robust appearance had not changed since he had been working in the store. But he somehow looked more mature than the thin youth they had met almost a year before. "Now what can I do for you?"

Laura pulled out the list of items from her pocket. Father and

Sally had both asked for supplies, in addition to the medicines Laura needed for Elizabeth. Laura called out each item, one at a time, while Josh hurried around to find them.

"When is James coming back to manage his store?" asked Mira, who was watching Josh with admiring eyes.

"We're not sure. We haven't heard from him for over a month now. His brother thought he'd certainly be back for Christmas. His mother's really worried . . . afraid something's happened to him. She's never really gotten over losing her son John so mysteriously. But David says he's probably having trouble lining up creditors for his business. If he doesn't get them, he'll be closing up his store come spring. His brother's sick of handling the business for him. He says he's busy enough with his own work as magistrate. Also, he doesn't feel it's fitting for his daughter to be working in the store all day. That's why he hired me. It's nice to be able to work off my debt this way and I enjoy the work." He went out back then to fetch the larger bags of flour, salt, and sugar.

"Well, we found out a lot from Josh in a short time," Mira laughed.

Laura was staring at Mira. "What debt is he talking about Mira? I thought the Hitchcocks were fairly well-to-do farmers or at least not debt-ridden so their son would have to work out to pay their bills."

"It's not his parents' bills. He's bought some things to set up his own place. He wants to start his own farm."

Josh had come from the back store-room with a large bag of flour over his shoulder. "If you girls watch the store for me, I'll carry these bags out to your sleigh."

Laura stood there and looked around. The store had a masculinity about it that reminded her of James, but she knew she could make it come alive with linen drapes at the windows instead of only shutters. And she'd rearrange the counters too.

Josh stamped the snow from his feet when he came inside. "I'm afraid there's a storm brewing. I don't like to rush you away, but the horses are restless. They feel it too."

Laura thanked him for his help and stepped out onto the stoop. Mira was lingering there beside the stove for a few last minute words with Josh. Laura knew Mira was inviting him over for Sunday dinner.

Suddenly the wind hit her with a gust that almost drove her back into the warm store, and Laura realized they would have to hurry before it hit with full force. Already there had been a few very bad storms this winter—much worse than they had ever had in Great Barrington.

Mira came running along just as Laura was tucking the heavy sleigh robe around herself. She jumped up onto the seat beside Laura, who had already taken the reins.

Laura had no trouble steering the horses back onto the main road. But before long, the wind had whipped up to the force of a gale, and they were surrounded by a blinding blanket of whiteness. There was no sign of a trail ahead of them. They might as well have been travelling in the dark.

"Shall we turn back?" Mira's words were blown away by the wind even though they were sitting close to each other.

"No," Laura said. "As long as the horses don't get stuck, we'll be fine. We know the trail is through the middle of this clearing. We'll just keep going straight ahead. The road is fairly straight." But the wind was beating hard against the horses and pushing them to the right, and it was swirling around the girls now huddled together.

Laura drove the horses at a slow but steady pace for some time, but it was impossible to tell how far they had come. She kept watching for the Hitchcock's grey barn just this side of Queenston. They must have come that far. She kept wondering why she didn't see it. Surely if the horses had wandered off the main road, they would have floundered in the soft snow at the side of the road. Yet they had been travelling for twice as long as normal, and still they couldn't see any buildings. There was only this blinding whiteness.

"Please God, guide us home," Laura prayed silently.

The horses slackened their pace, for the snow was becoming deeper and was almost to their stomachs. The flat sleigh rode slowly up and down on top of the deep snow drifts, and the girls tipped from side to side.

Laura looked back to check on the load and was thankful her father had insisted on sending an extra buffalo robe, which Josh had tucked in firmly around the supplies. Then, the horses stopped completely. In frustration and fear, she gasped out, "What do we do now?"

"Look!" Mira pointed ahead. "There's a blue patch in the sky and it's growing bigger. Perhaps we should just wait a bit." It seemed like a good idea, for as time passed, Laura was more and more worried about their exact location. They must have taken a detour around Queenston. They sat huddled together watching the sky, almost willing the blue patch to increase in size, and Mira was right. The blue patch was growing larger, so they waited and watched, slapping their faces with their mittened hands and stomping their feet to keep themselves warm.

It seemed that they had sat there huddled together under the thick buffalo robe for an eternity when finally, there were visible signs that the storm was dying down. The wind had dropped and the snow was falling more gently.

Laura urged the horses ahead again, and this time they slowly started forward. They wound their way around between the snow-laden trees. Laura knew that they were off the trail, but in the light now, surely they were not going to fall off suddenly into the river. The horses struggled along through the snow that reached right up to their flanks.

At last, they came suddenly to Queenston's main street. They must have wandered away from the St. David's road and were now coming into the village from the south instead of the west. Laura shuddered to think how close they had come to the river on the east side of town. They had gone in a half-circle without knowing it.

The snow on the main road was deep, but not nearly as deep as near the field hedges where they had wandered. Only one sleigh met them as they rode along and it turned in at a house by the way. The other streets were completely deserted, overhung with snow-laden tree branches.

It took some time for the sleigh to make its way to the inn, as the horses were panting and moving very slowly now. Finally, they drew up to the back door. Before they even came to a full stop, Father ran out from the tavern. He grabbed the horses' reins and tied them to the hitching post. Then he helped the girls down, and Laura could feel the warmth of his hug even through her thick clothing. It was good to know her father really did care. Then

Father led the exhausted, sweating horses to the warm barn. In spite of her relief at being home, Laura felt stiff and cold as they went inside.

Sally rushed over to them and threw her arms around Mira and Laura. "Thank God you're back. I was worried about you. Now come and sit by the fireside. I've got hot soup ready. You must be frozen." She made them sit in the armchairs beside the fire and ladled out the soup and slices of fresh bread, still warm from the bake-oven.

"Well, Laura," said Father once they had taken a few sips, "I guess I was wrong to send you off in that weather. It's a good thing you and Mira kept your heads. I'm very proud of you."

"For a while I thought we were heading straight for the river's edge. I'm sure glad the storm stopped when it did," said Laura.

"I wish I coulda gone," grumbled Charles, who was now five and game for any adventure.

Her soup finished, Laura tiptoed down the long hall to Elizabeth's room. She was tired to exhaustion, but Sally had told her that Elizabeth had been asking for her all day.

"Elizabeth," Laura whispered, knocking lightly on the door. "Are you awake?" There was no response. Laura pushed the door open and saw Elizabeth lying there, her face drawn and her blonde hair still damp with sweat around her forehead.

"I'm home, Elizabeth. We're all back safe."

Elizabeth's eyes opened slowly. "Laura? You're home! I was afraid I would never see you again." The fevered girl stretched out her arm and took Laura's hand. Laura kept her hand there for a moment, then tucked her stepsister's arm back under the covers and brushed her hair from her face. Elizabeth was already asleep.

Laura crept out of the room and walked to her own room, where she changed into her nightclothes. As she snuggled down under the warm patchwork quilts in her bedstead, she couldn't help reliving the events of the day and her feeling of helplessness when she had realized they were lost. But now she felt so warm and secure that the scary feeling did not last for long. Then she thought of James. Where was he now? Surely he couldn't come to any harm at his sister's home, for her husband was an important man in the Kingston area. And it was not unusual for mail to be lost, especially in winter. The problem was maybe deeper than that, however. It was possible that James no longer thought about her and had forgotten their last conversation.

She began to pray, "Please, please bring him back safely," and then she added, "to me."

She always found the waiting hard.

EIGHTEEN

"Laura, we need to talk."

Laura looked up from the figures in her father's account book. Mira was standing in front of her. Her sister was quieter than usual and there was an urgency in her voice.

"I just have two columns to finish here, or should we talk first?"

"No. It's not that pressing, but I've been trying to find you alone and you hardly ever are." Mira sat down in the captain's chair and waited.

Laura rechecked her figures and continued with the next page. She was pleased to see that business was improving even more, now that spring had come. As many as sixty boats docked at the Landing every day to transfer their supplies to waggoners who travelled the portage route. Dozens of the sailors and business people stayed at the inn or stopped for a meal at the tavern. With the business doing so well, Father would be able to start up his farm that summer. Laura closed the book, satisfied to have completed her work. Then she turned to Mira.

"It's Josh, Laura," she said. "He wants to marry me in June."

"At fifteen!"

"Lots of girls marry at fifteen, and I'm almost sixteen."

"And how old is Josh?"

"Eighteen. Anyway, that's not the problem."

"Then what is?"

"Well, I haven't let him speak to Father yet. We're waiting for James to return. You know how Father'll want the oldest to marry first."

"I don't know if that matters. Besides, you know there's nothing definite between James and me. I was silly to think there even might be. Besides he said he would be back by now and he isn't!"

"We could wait, Laura."

"You don't need to wait for me, Mira, but you certainly do need to wait! I can't think of many girls who've married at fifteen."

"We don't want to wait, Laura. I love Josh and I want to be with him. He's built a cabin already at the back of his father's acreage. He hopes to buy more land next to it."

"Well, you and Josh had better tell Father and Sally your plans. Josh is a fine young man, but you're both much too young to think about marriage yet."

Mira left with a smile. It hardly seemed she'd heard a thing Laura had said. With a sigh, Laura turned her thoughts to Josh. He was a robust young farm lad who obviously cared deeply for Mira, but he was far from being the rich farmer Mira had hoped to meet. Still, they would have enough, and she was happy for her sister. She felt certain that Sally could easily talk her into waiting a couple more years.

Then she thought about herself. A young businessman passing through on the boats last week had invited her to dinner and she had refused. This week, he had come back on his return trip and asked her again, and she had agreed to have lunch with him. She was almost twenty-one now, and if she refused invitations from all men, she would soon stop being asked.

Still, she wasn't looking forward to lunch with a man who was almost a stranger. He would be coming in any minute now, and they would be having lunch right here in the inn, so at least the surroundings would be familiar, though a bit too close to the eyes of the family. Father was pleased that Laura had accepted the invitation because the man was one of his wealthiest business colleagues. Laura looked up just in time to see the man walk in, and hastily started adding up yet another column in the accounts book.

"Hard at work, I see," said Mr. Brown as he tapped Laura on the shoulder. "Our table is ready."

He was at least thirty, she was certain—maybe even thirty-five. His polished, self-assured manner did not appeal to her, but she could not let him know that. She stood up, quietly walked around from her desk, and followed him into the dining room. She consoled herself with the thought that it would be different to be waited on in her father's own inn.

"You must be a great asset to your father's business," he began, still smiling down at her. She noticed that his dark eyes, though alert and friendly, were not as kind as James'.

"I try to help."

"You would be an asset to any man." Laura stared back, surprised by the man's boldness. Since she barely knew him, he certainly couldn't be serious about her, or was he just judging her as he would a business asset or liability?

Fortunately, the meal arrived promptly and they were able to turn their attention to eating. Laura allowed time for him to give thanks for their food. He did not, nor did he wait for her. As she began to eat, she wished the meal were over.

After lunch, Mr. Brown continued to discuss his potash business in great detail and seemed about to drone on for the rest of the afternoon, when Laura noticed Elizabeth walking through the doorway towards their table. She still looked as pale as ever but was completely recovered from her winter's illness, which had lasted so long that the family had been afraid of losing her. She was dressed in a pale blue linen gown with a white fichu around her neck. Laura thought she looked almost beautiful.

"Oh, excuse me, Mr. Brown, I see my sister Elizabeth coming. I'd like to introduce her to you."

Mr. Brown stopped in mid-sentence and stood up to shake Elizabeth's hand. "Elizabeth Ingersoll. I'm charmed to meet you. My name's Brown, Hezekiah Brown. You don't look at all like your sister. You would never know you were related."

Laura was shocked to hear the businessman make such a personal statement, but then she noticed that he wasn't letting Elizabeth's hand go, and she said, "Why don't you join us for coffee. We were just about to have a second cup."

Elizabeth sat down. "Thank you. I'm sorry to bother you two, but I came to tell you, Laura, that there's a customer waiting for you in father's office. He says he's always dealt with you before and he won't deal with anyone else now."

"That's strange. I can't imagine who it could be. But I'd better go see." Laura got up from the table, relieved at getting rid of Mr. Brown but somewhat surprised at his sudden interest in Elizabeth. She was glad, though, for almost any distraction would be good for Elizabeth just now. A couple of weeks ago, Elizabeth had received a letter from Thomas Mayo telling her of his upcoming marriage this summer to a girl that the family didn't even know. It seemed she had moved to Great Barrington after they had left.

At least Thomas had had the nerve to write and tell Elizabeth. He didn't just leave her wondering, like Red and James had. And it was certainly clear how much Mr. Brown was attracted to Elizabeth and how fast he had lost all interest in her. Laura couldn't help feeling a little sorry for herself. Maybe she would never marry.

From the other side of the hall, Laura could see a man standing at he counter in her father's office. She couldn't imagine who would demand to deal only with her. Then she came closer and grabbed the side of the doorway, to steady herself. Her heart was pounding and her legs had gone weak. James Secord rushed over and took both her hands in his.

"Oh, Laura, I'm so happy to see you, so happy to be back."

"I'm pleased to see you too, James. But you were gone so long. Much longer than I expected."

"But I explained why in my letters. . . ."

"Letters? What letters?"

"Didn't you receive my letters?"

"No, I didn't!"

"But I sent them with two special deliveries of supplies to my store. . . . I suppose Josh or that other boy my brother hired unpacked the supplies and misplaced them."

"I received no letters and don't blame it on Josh." Laura's voice sounded angry.

"I suppose they're sitting under a bag of sugar on my shelves. I'm sorry, Laura." He still held her hands in his.

"Under a bag of sugar! That's likely the best excuse. . . . Oh, James, I was so worried about you. Phoebe said you were well, but then for so long there was no news."

"I can't believe this, Laura, I really can't. You mean, you've heard nothing from me all this time?"

"That's right! Nothing."

"Well, then I have all the more to tell you. I've just come off the boat and I came straight here. Could we go somewhere to talk? It's a little cool for a picnic yet." He gave her a big smile and hoped that she remembered.

"I guess so," said Laura. "No one will be in our parlour. It's at the far end of our living quarters."

"I have to check in a load of supplies at the Landing. I'll be back in half an hour. Will that be all right?"

"Yes." She smiled now, happy to see him, in spite of her surprise and anger over the lost letters.

"I'll hurry."

*****

James returned sooner than he had said.

Laura led him from Father's office down the narrow hall that led to the family quarters and then into a wider hallway to the parlour. It was used only for special occasions and there was no fire lit in the fireplace, but Laura did not notice the chill. She offered James a seat on the horsehair couch and sat down in a high-backed chair beside him. A blur of blue from the Niagara River showed through the heavy curtains that hung over the two tall, narrow windows. At the side of the room, a small table held Sally's best china, already laid out for tea. She always kept it set up that way.

"Laura, I couldn't forget our time together last fall. I wanted to speak to you at that time. . . ." He hesitated and cleared his throat. "But I felt I had no right to speak because my business was in such poor shape."

"And now?"

"I've received the backing to continue with my store. Richard has helped me raise the money from friends of his. I've borrowed £800 from Andrew and James McGill from Montreal, and with new ideas from Richard, I'm confident. I'll work hard and I feel God wants me to continue in the business."

"I'm happy for you, James."

"And I feel strongly . . . " He hesitated and, turning toward her, he searched her face with his eyes. She could feel the intensity in his voice and looked up hopefully as she waited for him to finish the sentence. "about you, Laura. I'd like to ask your father's permission to call regularly."

"I'd like that, James." Her heart was pounding with unexpected joy as she gave him a smile of encouragement.

James continued. "I thought about you all the time I was away, but I was determined to raise the capital for my store before I approached you. I'm afraid that's the reason I didn't write more often. But I missed you. How I missed you! And I love you, Laura. I know that now. Our time apart has only strengthened my feelings for you, and I've prayed a lot about us. I think that God will soon help me to know if we are meant to marry."

Laura's hopes were suddenly gone. So his intention of calling did not mean he necessarily planned to marry her, even though he had just said that he loved her. She suddenly felt a surge of energy and stood up abruptly.

James, surprised by her flashing eyes, rose to his feet.

"James Secord, when you and God decide to ask me to marry you, then I'll be able to tell you what God and I have decided to answer." She turned to leave but he grabbed her hand and pulled her back to him.

He held her closely, and all the loneliness and pain of the preceding months slowly left her. Softly he whispered, "I love you," and kissed her gently on the lips.

Laura gazed back into his deep blue eyes, but said nothing. Later, she would tell him how she had missed him after their last meeting and during the months he was away. She would also tell him how much she cared for him. For now, though, she just tightened her arms around him and hoped he knew.

NINETEEN

In June, the British soldiers gave a final gun salute before they left Fort Niagara and came across the river to Newark. Jay's Treaty between Britain and the United States had declared that the fort on the east side of the Niagara River should be given to the Americans.

Just as the last gun sounded, Laura Ingersoll came through the doorway of David Secord's home on her father's arm, dressed in her best clothes. The flowing skirt of her pale pink silk-taffeta gown rustled down the stone steps. Her large straw hat had matching pink ribbons that blew out around her thick brown hair resting on her white skin and curling over her shoulders. The sun glinted off the engraved silver brooch, fastened to the deep rose silk sash that circled her waist and was tied in a large bow at the back. She carried a small bouquet of wild roses, deep crimson ones surrounded by a thin border of small white roses.

Laura leaned a little nervously on her father's arm. James was standing in the shade of a flowering apple tree beside his older brother, Stephen. His other brother, David, was standing beside them wearing his magistrate's robe, a powdered wig, and oval spectacles tied behind the wig with a ribbon. He held his Bible open, ready to begin. Because there was no minister, he would perform the wedding ceremony as magistrate of St. David's.

Laura kept her eyes on James as her father walked her down the path to where the families were seated. James was a handsome figure standing so straight in his blue and ivory striped silk frock coat, which only partially covered his ivory double-breasted waistcoat and skin-tight breeches. His riding boots over his white stockings and his new round silk plush hat were the latest fashion.

"I love you, James Secord," Laura was thinking. "I'll love you forever." Soon she was standing beside him, repeating the words that would bind them together for life.

After the brief ceremony was over, Mira was the first to rush forward and embrace her older sister. Both sisters were dressed in their best cotton dresses, trimmed with bobbin lace. Mira's was pale pink and Elizabeth's blue. Both had fashionably high waistlines and full skirts.

"Remember," Mira smiled, "you throw your bouquet to me."

They all laughed, for everyone knew Mira and Josh planned to be married the next June. But Elizabeth had an escort today too, for Hezekiah Brown was calling on her regularly now.

Elizabeth, her blonde hair curled and shining, could not keep back the tears as she said, "I'll miss you so." She reached for Laura and they clasped each other.

"I won't be far away," Laura reminded her. "It's only a few miles to St. David's from Queenston."

Elizabeth managed to nod and smile as Sally, close behind her, stepped up. Her new high-waisted dress did not conceal the fact that she would soon be having another baby. Appy was two years old now.

"I'll miss you, Laura," Sally said, as she gave Laura a great hug.

"I'll be back to help you with the baby."

"I hope it'll be a brother for Charles."

"I hope so, Sally."

James' mother wore a wide-brimmed hat that shaded her face and covered the cap that held in her hair. Older than the other women, she was dressed in a deep blue silk dress. Its lines were straighter than the newer styles, and it was fitted at the waist. It had been her best dress for several years and was kept for these special occasions. The dress had seen many weddings, since James was her youngest.

She kissed her son and smiled happily at Laura before she kissed her too. "Welcome to our family, Laura," she said.

Next, Phoebe came rushing over. With eyes sparkling, she said, "Don't forget I could use that bouquet too."

"I'll remember," laughed Laura.

James' sister Magdalen hugged her brother, then clasped Laura's hand and said, "We want you to visit us soon in Kingston."

Her husband, Richard Cartwright, several years James' senior, came next and couldn't refrain from saying, "Remember my advice,

James, and your store will prosper." Then, looking at Laura, he added, "What a beautiful wife you are. I hear that you're very competent at keeping close accounts for your father. Maybe you'll be able to help even James!"

Just then Charles, his hands behind his back, came up to Laura with a solemn expression. "I've a gift for you, Laura," he said. "Want to guess what it is?"

"Charles, you wouldn't!" gasped Laura. She was remembering the many times he had surprised her with his captured pets, mostly frogs and garter snakes.

Charles smiled impishly, but extended a pair of empty hands in front of him. "I hope you'll be back often, Laura."

"I will, Charles, and you can come to visit us whenever you like."

The long line kept coming, until at the very end, her father reached Laura and tightly gripped both of her hands. He looked sad, Laura thought, and even older. "Be happy, Laura," he said simply. "It's a good land we've come to . . . and good people. James is a fine man, but I'll miss you."

Finally, after all the good wishes were expressed, the family slowly moved inside and sat at a long table for the wedding supper. Sally and James' mother had helped prepare the meal, and David Secord's wife had instructed the servants. The feast was a bountiful one, with roast turkey on the spit, lentils and mutton, creamed potatoes, and fresh buns, light and dark.

According to the tradition of her time, Laura cut the first piece of the wedding cake. Then, at the end of the wedding supper, the apple and berry pies appeared, along with tea, coffee, and herbal teas.

After the toasts, Laura left to change. She hesitated at the foot of the stairs, turned, and threw her bouquet. An enthusiastic Mira rushed ahead of the others and caught it.

Laura changed into a new gown of white silk with a powder blue overgown and a deep blue sash. The material was James' gift to her, but she had sewn the gown herself. It was edged with a piece of real plaited English lace. She placed her newly made cap on her head. It too had a frill of English lace around the front.

As Laura walked toward the front door, she saw James waiting outside. It was only a short way across his brother's backyard to his own store with the living quarters above. Laura felt content as James' hand closed over hers and they started to make their way across the yard toward their new home. The family had not planned a dance for so small a gathering.

"Don't forget we'll be along to take you to Niagara Falls tomorrow," Mira shouted as she stood beside her smiling Josh. Newlyweds were always driven to Niagara Falls by their young friends the day after the wedding.

Hand in hand, Laura and James walked away quietly. The chatter and laughter of their families became fainter as they approached their first home together.

PART THREE

LAURA

TWENTY

"You do look good in your sergeant's uniform, James. You're just as handsome as you were the day I married you. . . . But I hope you won't have to fight."

James smiled, but answered his wife in a serious tone. "The talk is not good, but I can't think we'll get pushed into war with the Americans over a battle that's not ours."

Laura reached for the supper dishes from the shelves above her bake table and carried them to the long, wooden table in the centre of the room. Her husband was standing in the doorway.

The Secords had built a home in Queenston eleven years before, just five years after they were married, on the site of the Ingersolls' first canvas tent. The Heights loomed up close beside them to the south. A green expanse of yard led eastward from the front door, down a sloped pathway of flat stones to the street of the town, and a few blocks farther on, the Niagara River wound its way past the Landing. The back door looked out toward the road to St. David's. Their grounds were spacious, and a small cabin and bake oven had been built behind the house.

The interior of the two-storey house was equally spacious, for James had prospered. The kitchen where Laura was standing ran the whole length of the house from front to back, as did the parlour on the other side of the downstairs hallway. A steep stairway at the back of the hallway led to the two bedrooms upstairs, which also ran the length of the house, directly above the parlour and kitchen.

James' prosperity was recent. The store in St. David's had continued to make only slim profits, so Laura convinced him to open another store in Queenston, and it had done very well. In the last few years business had increased, and James was able to support his wife, two daughters, and one son without difficulty. They were content.

"It certainly isn't our fault that the British are taking American sailors right off their sailing vessels and drafting them into the British navy to help them fight their war with Napoleon."

"I know that, Laura, and they know that, but the Americans can't strike back by sailing to Britain. The American fleet isn't even strong enough to protect their own ships."

"Why don't the British stop?" Laura asked, brushing back a strand of hair that had escaped from her mob cap. It was mid-June of 1812, and the day was sweltering hot.

"The British should stop, but they feel the new states aren't strong enough to fight back, and they need the men for their navy. The war with Napoleon has been going on for seven years now."

"Surely the Americans won't attack us to get even with the British."

"All reports say the American war hawks are pressing their new government to take action," James replied quietly.

Laura put the potatoes and asparagus down on the table and looked up at James as she spoke, "But surely they'll not take out their anger on Upper Canada. What good would that do them? Besides, over half of us are Americans who came long after the war. We had no fight with them. Their quarrel is with Britain."

"Sometimes countries fight their battles on foreign soil. It wouldn't be the first time . . . or the last."

"But isn't our Fort George entertaining the American soldiers at dinner tonight?"

"Yes."

"Well, then, you're worrying too much about rumours. Enjoy your dinner, James."

"I'll try."

At the door, he leaned over and kissed her. Then she watched him mount his horse and ride around the house, towards the main street. The backyard was still except for the smoke curling out of the bakehouse chimney. She turned then as Charlotte, her oldest daughter, came into the kitchen from the front hallway.

"Didn't your sister come back with you?" Laura asked.

"Yes, Harriet is on her way. She can't run as fast, and I had to run because I knew I was late to help you with supper."

"It's ready now. Put out the silver while I get Baby Charles."

Charles was already awake as Laura headed for the bedroom.

Her brown-haired baby, more than a year old now, smiled as his mother took him from the cradle.

Laura was grateful for her healthy children, but a great sadness came over her as she thought of her sister Elizabeth. She had not married until she was twenty-seven years old, although men were continually asking her out. In the end, Elizabeth had married Daniel Pickett, a Methodist circuit rider, who had come to the area near her father's farm. From the first, Elizabeth had been attracted to his quiet manner and kind ways. Laura thought he was a bit like James. Elizabeth was extremely devoted to Daniel. She even travelled with him on the circuit, which extended from Burlington Bay almost up to York. She planned to stop travelling once she had children, but the years passed and no baby came. She had come to help Laura with each of her new babies and had always told her how she longed for one of her own.

At last, a delighted Elizabeth came to tell Laura the news that she was expecting a baby. Laura made plans to leave her children in the charge of a neighbouring farmer's wife, Mrs. Clement, in order to go to Elizabeth before her time came. But her help was not required.

During her pregnancy, Elizabeth was infected with typhoid fever from water she had drunk in her travels. Elizabeth's weak body succumbed to the disease and she gave birth prematurely. Before Laura even knew her step-sister was ill, both Elizabeth and the baby had died.

Daniel Pickett brought them the sad news and told them how the baby daughter and her mother had been buried together. Laura often thought of Elizabeth. She remembered the Great Barrington days when they had disliked each other so intensely. How they had both changed since then! She could still see Elizabeth rocking the babies by the kitchen window. "I hope you're rocking your own baby girl now in that better land," she thought, as she held Charles closer and went down the stairs.

"Where's Papa?" Harriet asked when they were all seated.

"He's having dinner with the soldiers at Fort George tonight," Laura explained.

"Is he in the army now?" asked Charlotte.

"Only for a short time. He's a sergeant in the first militia regiment of Lincoln County, and his job is to train some local men for service in case there is a war."

"Are we really going to fight?" Charlotte's seriousness made her look older than her fourteen years.

"I don't think so, but we need to prepare. If the enemy knows we're ready, they'll think twice about coming."

"But the farm lads train for only three days a month and now with the summer crops, they'll be too busy even for that," Charlotte protested. "Besides, Papa's new store manager says there are more than seven million Americans and only around six hundred thousand Canadians."

"God will watch over us, Charlotte, and besides, I don't think there will be a war."

A loud knock on the back door interrupted them. Laura opened it to find her brother, Charles, standing there.

"Charles," Laura smiled, "you came at just the right time. Here, take James' place at the table. He's gone to Fort George."

Charles, a handsome young man of twenty-one now, was engaged to be married to James' niece, Elizabeth Secord. Her father, Stephen, had died four years before. She lived with her mother, Hannah, and her younger brothers and sisters in St. David's, where they continued to run the mill.

Laura's brother pulled young Charles' ear as he walked by. Charles shouted out but smiled at his favourite uncle. The girls were also happy to see this uncle, who usually had a knack for making them laugh. Laura soon noticed, however, that he was not himself tonight.

After the meal, he spoke quietly to her. "Can we talk . . . alone?"

Laura left the children in the kitchen while she and Charles went into the parlour. It was spotlessly clean, filled with Laura's best furnishings. She sat on the small sofa while Charles sat in James' large wooden armchair, stretching his legs out in front of him. His head was bent over and he was frowning.

"Laura, Father's sick," he said directly.

"How sick?"

"We can't be sure. He seems in less pain now, but it was his heart. He has asked for you, Laura."

"I'll get ready at once, but I can't leave the children until James comes home later tonight."

"Laura, he's never had the same strength since we left the farm, and that was more than six years ago. He took the loss of that farm and his dream of a settlement harder than any of us realized."

"But he's managed to provide well for the family at Government House Inn."

"But over on the River Credit, it's not like his own land. It's a leased business. It might not have been so bad if they hadn't cut him off right away when he couldn't meet the quota for settlers. Fighting and petitioning for an extension took so much out of him. And then the new governor had to go and take even the land he had cleared for himself. That was the last straw. That's what really broke him. You were so busy with your own family, Laura. You didn't see his grief the way we did. Some day I'll buy back that land, so help me God!" He hesitated and was silent a minute before he continued. "But I'm afraid it'll be too late for Father.... When I told him my vow, he didn't seem to care anymore. He just smiled sadly. He seems more at peace now, but he's anxious to see you, Laura, and I'd like to leave tonight."

"I'll pack now. I hope James isn't held up."

"We can travel by horseback to Newark and catch a boat in the morning and get to the inn tomorrow."

"Elizabeth's death was awfully hard on Father too. She was home longer than his other daughters."

"This has been a terrible year. Tragedies come in threes, they say. I wonder what's going to happen next."

"Don't think that way, Charles."

Laura left Charles in the study and called Charlotte aside to tell her about Grandpa Ingersoll. Then she hurried up the stairs with baby Charles to put him back to bed and to pack for the trip.

When she had finished, she left her bag on the bed and went back downstairs to help Charlotte and Harriet with the dishes. She gave Charlotte instructions for feeding the family for the next week and returned to her brother in the parlour.

Charles had drifted off to sleep. He still had a boyish look about him as he leaned his head against the back of James' chair, and she was reminded of the days when she used to care for him.

Laura went up to the bedroom that she shared with James and the baby, who was sleeping quietly now. Kneeling by her bed and leaning on the soft feather mattress, she prayed silently that God might heal her father.

*****

She was roused by the touch of James' hand on her shoulder. "Are you feeling well, Laura? You were asleep!"

She must have slept soundly because it took her a minute to remember why she was kneeling beside the bed. Then she told him about Charles' visit.

"I know. He's waiting for you downstairs," James told her. He hesitated before he continued. "There's no easy way to tell you this, Laura. War has been declared."

Laura looked up at James and felt her chest tighten.

"Word came just before we sat down to eat. The British officers didn't want to spoil our dinner with the American officers, so they held back the news until afterwards. We took the Americans down to their boats and shook hands as we parted. We know it will be far different when we meet again."

"Oh, James, I hate to leave you at a time like this, but I have to go to Father."

James knelt down beside her and put an arm around her as he spoke. "Our officers will not be acting too quickly on this news, and I don't think there will be any sudden attacks. Go to your father, Laura."

*****

As Charles and Laura entered the large front room on the main floor of their father's inn, Sally came rushing forward to meet them.

"Laura, I'm so glad you've come. Thomas keeps asking for you. He knows that Mira can't make it." Mira and Josh had moved to the United States several years before, and probably knew nothing of Father's condition.

"How is he?" Laura quickly asked.

"Not so well. The pain came again, but it's gone now. The local doctor was away, and when we finally got a doctor who was visiting from York, he couldn't do much. Your father's getting weaker all the time."

"Is he sleeping now?"

"No. He knew you were coming. He's waiting."

Sally led Laura to a small room at the back of the inn on the main floor.

"It's cooler here than in the bedrooms under the eaves where we usually sleep, and it's easier for me in the daytime when he's downstairs."

Laura opened the door and slipped into her father's room. He smiled up at her as she came over and kissed him gently on the cheek. Spotting a small wooden trunk beside the window, she pulled it over next to his bedstead and sat on it.

"Not feeling so well?" she asked.

Lying against large feather pillows, he reached out his hand toward her and she grasped it firmly in hers. She could not believe how much he had changed since she had last seen him. He was thin and pale and even his voice seemed hoarse and weak.

"I'm so glad you've come, Laura. It's been a while now . . . since we've had a good visit. How's . . . the family?"

"They're all fine, Father. They said to tell Grandpa to get better fast."

"And the baby?"

"He's fine too."

"Charles was really pleased when you named your baby after him."

"I know, and my baby loves Charles. They seem to have taken to each other."

Father smiled weakly.

"And how are things going at the inn?"

"Well, Sally and young Thomas can almost run the place without me now . . . and without Charles, I might add. He has this crazy notion we're going to have a war with the states."

"Well, Thomas is almost sixteen now," Laura softly replied. She had noticed the concern in her father's voice at the thought of war. He would have to know, but she planned to talk to the others about telling him. Perhaps Sally should be the one to do it.

"Yes, and Sam is a help too." Like most settlers, Father had freed Sam and Bett shortly after they had come to Upper Canada. They had moved a few miles away and had a cabin of their own on a small piece of land that Father still owned back near the La Tranche River. But Bett had died a few years ago, leaving Sam alone, so he had moved to Port Credit to be nearer the family. He helped them with the daily chores.

"How is Sam?"

"He has been . . . well. But last week . . . took sick. Could be the smallpox. Folks are afraid to go near him."

"Who's taking care of him?"

"The boys leave milk and food in front of his cabin. He keeps getting his food; so he's managing. I do have lots of help around here. Even young James is energetic. He'll be twelve soon."

"You must be proud of all your sons, Father."

"Yes, but my daughters, I'm proud of them too. They'll always mean as much to me, especially my firstborn." He squeezed her hand and added, "Our little Sarah is a handful. I think the older ones are spoiling her."

"I don't think Sally will let that happen."

"You look so much like your mother, Laura. So many years ago . . . but sometimes I remember her as if it were yesterday."

"Perhaps I look like her, but the family say I'm more like you."

Father chuckled. He seemed pleased to hear her say that. Feeling a little stronger, he sat up. Laura pushed more feather pillows behind him for support.

"This inn does keep busy," he said, brightening some more. "We have all types of people here, Laura. The governor stops here. The traders come on horseback from the north, and people sailing from the east come to this end of the lake. Most times, I enjoy their tales, but there's been talk of war lately. I can't see it happening though. We've all got relatives on the other side. At this job, I've learned not to pay too much attention to what I hear. I wish Charles would follow that advice." Father was becoming breathless now.

Laura tried to change the topic. "I hear you have a reputation as a fine host. People enjoy their stopover at this inn."

"The family have been carrying on very well without me lately, but I think I'll be up soon. Just talking to you like this is raising my spirits." Laura smiled and rubbed her warm hand over her father's thin one.

Father began to look tired again and rested heavily against the pillows. They sat there silently. Then he spoke. "It's getting late, Laura, and you must be tired. If you would just bring me a glass of water, I'll settle down for the night. We'll have a great long visit in the morning."

"I can stay a while, so we'll have lots of time to visit," Laura said. Actually, she wondered how long she could really stay with the threat of war over all of Upper Canada. James would have to defend Queenston if the Americans attacked, and she would have to go back to be with the children. Still, she could not worry her father with that news tonight. She would have to talk it over with Sally in the morning.

Laura made her father as comfortable as possible for the night and went for the water. When she returned, he was lying very still and she thought he was asleep. She set the water down on the night stand and tiptoed to the door.

"Laura. . . . " her father said softly in his raspy voice.

"Yes, Father."

"Thank you for coming. We'll have a good visit in the morning. I think I'll get up then. It's time I was getting about again."

"I'm looking forward to that. Good night, Father."

Laura went up to a small room under the eaves that Sally had prepared for her, and quickly got ready for bed. She was very tired from the hurried journey and from the strain of the war news. How could she possibly tell her father? And she worried about her children, so far from her. If Lake Ontario was blockaded, she would have to take the longer journey overland, and no one knew where the Americans would strike. James had said four main areas were possible targets: Amherstburg on the southern tip of Lake Erie, Kingston, Montreal, and their own Queenston. As a centre of the portage route, Queenston was in a strategic position.

At the side of the bed, she knelt to pray and asked God to help her father to face the news of war. Then she prayed for the safety of her children and James. After she knelt there a while, she thanked God for letting her see her father again. When at last she climbed into bed, she sank deep into the feather mattress and fresh sheets, and fell asleep almost at once.

*****

Laura awakened early as usual, to see beams of light streaming through the small open window across the foot of her bed. The morning air was much cooler than it had been the day before. She got up and dressed quickly, then walked into the hall, where she saw a pitcher of fresh water already sitting outside her door. Someone must have been up before sunrise. Feeling grateful that she did not have to go down to the pump, she took the water back to her room and washed up.

When Laura walked into the kitchen, Sally was already there, stirring porridge. She looked older now—wisps of grey hair hung loosely about her face. Laura wondered how she kept up so well at fifty-one, with five-year-old Sarah and all the work of the inn, now that her husband was too sick to help. Sally had certainly not had an easy time since they had come to Canada, but she had accepted the life here and grown to like it.

"How's Father?" Laura asked as Sally turned to greet her.

"I believe he had a good night. I looked in on him several times. I didn't want to disturb him. He was lying very still."

"He says he'll be getting up today."

"I hope he'll be careful if he does," Sally said as she sliced bread on her cutting board. Then she stopped and turned to her step-daughter, "Laura, please advise me. I don't know how long I can keep the news of the war from Thomas. People come by all the time. They'll be talking of nothing else. And Charles left early this morning. He's been called to active duty. How can I tell your father?"

Laura felt at a loss for words. "I don't know," she said finally.

"Well, I need to know now," Sally said even more anxiously. "I can make an excuse for Charles' going, but if Thomas gets up today, he's bound to hear the news. It'll be hard on him, Laura."

"It'll be harder if he learns that way instead of from us. Maybe we should both tell him."

"You're right, Laura."

Sally dished out two bowls of oatmeal porridge with maple sugar and they ate in silence. "May I help prepare breakfast for your guests?" Laura asked when they had finished.

"No, I'll wake up Appy. She'll take care of that. You could check on your father though. I haven't looked in on him since I got up quite early this morning."

Laura slipped into the narrow hallway and walked along to her father's room. His door was ajar and he was lying very still with his back to the door. She heard a gurgling sound just as she came into the room. She tiptoed across to the bed.

Her father's face was changing colour from pale to very, very white. His eyes were closed.

Suddenly Laura recognized the death-like whiteness that masked his face, and she spoke to him. "Father . . . Father." He did not answer.

Nor did he answer ever again.

Even in her grief, Laura was thankful that her father would never have to face the news of that day.

TWENTY-ONE

A day after the funeral, Sally and Laura were sitting in silence on the back steps of the inn. As the evening shadows fell across them, Sally turned to Laura, her eyes still red from crying, and said softly, "I have my children still with me, Laura, and I will manage. You must go now to yours."

Laura knew she was right, for the fear of war hung over all of them. "I will go tomorrow," she said, "but first I want to see Sam."

Just then, young Thomas came by and Laura felt a twinge of pain as he looked at his mother with his head tilted sideways. That was the way Father used to hold his head when he had something serious to say. "Sam did not pick up his food today," he said.

"I must go to him," Laura said. "He'll need help." They both knew that he must be very sick if he could not make it just outside his door for the food.

"But the smallpox!" Sally said. "Don't take Thomas. I can't have any more sickness just now." She started to sob into her apron.

"I'm not afraid," Laura said. "I know I'm immune and he may need care."

"How can you be sure you won't take the disease?" asked Thomas.

"I've had cowpox," said Laura.

"I know they say that cowpox protects you from smallpox, but I've known of some who'd had cowpox and took the disease anyway."

"Well, I won't. I've cared for many in our area with the smallpox when no one would go near them. Neither I nor my family have suffered. I'm careful, of course. I use lots of soft soap and hot water."

"You can't be too careful around smallpox."

"Has the doctor visited?"

"No, and I understand that he too is immune and unafraid to go into houses with the smallpox. But Thomas asked him to visit Sam, and he refused."

"Why?"

"Because Sam's black. The doctor was determined not to go, and Thomas was just too weak to argue."

"Well, I'm not," Laura said indignantly as she stood up and straightened out her long petticoat. She pushed back a few strands of loose hair behind her mob cap and left Sally and young Thomas sitting on the steps. She hastened along the pathway for the doctor's house, not far from the inn.

She had intended to pay this visit sooner, but she knew Sally would worry about her carrying the illness to the family. So she had planned to pack everything now and visit Sam on her way back home. But this sudden news about his food left her no choice.

The doctor's house was the largest in the small village, and Laura walked briskly up the front steps and knocked on the door. A middle-aged woman servant with a white apron over her petticoats opened the door and stared out silently.

Laura pushed back the open door and stepped inside. "I'm Thomas Ingersoll's daughter and I've come to see the doctor. Please tell him I'm here."

The woman nodded now with a look of recognition and respect, and motioned Laura to follow her down the hall to an open door. Laura entered and saw that the doctor was seated before his desk and was busy writing. He did not look up until he had finished the line. Then he started to speak even before his eyes left the page. "I am sorry about Thomas," he said. "He was a fine man, but I did all I could."

"I know that, thank you. I am not here about my father."

"Are you not well? I could give you some powders for sleep."

"It is not myself. I'm here about Sam. I understand that you are immune and do not hesitate to visit those with the smallpox."

The doctor's face hardened. "I was too busy to visit him when your father mentioned it. I'll drop by there tomorrow sometime."

"I fear that may be too late, for he did not pick up his food today," Laura continued. "Obviously he is too sick to go those few steps. He may even be unconscious."

The doctor lay his pen onto his writing paper and looked up impatiently. "Oh, very well. If I must, I'll go tonight."

Laura walked back to the inn, uneasy still about the doctor's tone. She realized she would have to go to Sam's this evening to make sure the doctor kept his promise. She would pack now, and her bags would be ready for Thomas to pick up, so she would not need to return to the inn.

Half an hour later, with only one small bag, she hurried in the moonlight along the grassy pathway to Sam's. She had changed into an old petticoat and jacket, which she would leave behind so that she would not carry the disease. Inside her small bag, she carried a complete change of clothing for her return trip and a bar of Sally's soft soap, heavy with lye.

As Laura reached the back of Sam's house, she recognized the doctor's horse and buggy tied to the back post. "Good!" she thought. "At least he's come promptly. His bark must be worse than his bite." With a sigh of relief, she quietly set down her bag on the stone stoop, lifted the latch on the back door and stepped inside.

She stood staring in silence at the sight before her. Across the room, the doctor was bent over Sam's small cot, holding a large feather pillow over Sam's face.

"Stop!" screamed Laura, rushing to the doctor.

The doctor turned in surprise and jerked the pillow away. "What good is he?" he snarled at Laura. "He's not of much account anyway and will only spread the disease. Not too many people are immune as we are. I'll finish him off now while he's unconscious and get someone here to bury him and his sores. Look! He's a mass of infestation."

Laura knew she did not have the physical strength to stop the doctor, but she would use the talent she did have, her sharp tongue. "As sure as you do, I will have you indicted for murder," she answered hotly.

The doctor looked up at her as she stood there unflinching. His eyes were beady lights in the dimness of the room. They stared at each other with the sound of Sam's heavy breathing between them. Finally the doctor put the pillow down beside Sam. Turning from the bed, he said, "Well, if we must save him, we'll have a heavy night ahead, for without help, he'll suffocate from the pneumonia before morning. First we need fresh water."

With relief, Laura lighted a candle and placed it on the small table beside the bed. Then she ran out to the well, which was only about ten feet away from the back door and let down the empty pail until she heard the splash as it hit the bottom. She lost no time rolling it up and pulling it out of the well. Would the doctor change his mind while she was gone and attack Sam again? In her hurry, as she ran along the pathway, the water splashed out of the pail against her petticoat and she was breathless when she stepped inside. She was glad to see the doctor busy mixing powders. He must have taken her threat seriously.

Laura started a small fire in the fireplace in the front room of the cabin, then filled two pans with water to boil. Peering under the mat in front of the hearth, she saw the trap door. In a moment, she had lit a candle from beside the fireplace, pulled up the door, and slipped down the ladder into the darkness. When she reached the dirt floor, she could see the piles of vegetables that Sam had stored there the fall before. When she came to the onions, she filled a large pan, and was about to climb up the ladder when she heard footsteps just above her. She heard the horses neighing outside and the doctor shouting. Was he leaving? Had he closed the door over the hole to the cellar? She stuck the candle into her pan of onions and hurried up the ladder, clutching the side with her free hand and hoping that her head would not bump against the dropped trap-door.

The entrance was the same as she had left it. Hurrying into Sam's room, she saw he was alone, his eyes still closed. She set the onions on the table and went to the door. The doctor was coming back inside.

"I've left more powders on the table," he said. "Mix them for him every few hours. If he regains consciousness, put them in his tea. They'll help the fever and pain. And get some rest yourself." He motioned to the other cot across the room. "I'll be back in the morning." He turned then and left without further explanation.

Laura went out on the back step to peel the onions. She was making a pack for Sam's chest to help relieve the congestion. She thought back to the days in Great Barrington when Sam and Bett had always been there when Mother and Mercy had been sick and Father was away. And she remembered too how Sam had made friends with Red and helped him. She was glad she could be here now, but she felt so alone and longed to go back to her children. What if the fighting started and she could not reach them?

After she finished her peeling, she rummaged around Sam's room for an old stocking, filled it with steaming onions, and placed it on Sam's chest. Then she went out to the back stoop to get some fresh air.

As she leaned against the corner post, she prayed, "Please God, may Sam soon be well enough to manage. And keep them safe back home."

*****

A week later Sam had recovered enough to care for himself, and Laura returned to Queenston. During the busy days caring for her family's former slave, she had not had much time to think of her father, and her grief for her loss was still fresh. Back in Queenston, though, she was comforted by her own children and by James, all active and healthy.

The summer days of 1812 were warm and mellow and the crops flourished, but Laura and James and everyone else who lived near Queenston thought of nothing but war. They wondered, at the beginning of each new day, whether it would be the one to bring disaster. James spent all his time at the Queenston barracks now, training local men for an emergency. However, most of the locals were farmers who were reluctant to leave their farms at this busy time of the year. James felt they were not taking the war seriously enough.

Then the unbelievable news began to arrive. An American brigadier-general, William Hull, had led troops across the Detroit River into Upper Canada. By the middle of July, he had sent men out to plunder the countryside, but he never did manage to attack Amherstburg's Fort Malden. British scouting parties took his supply trains and a British schooner seized even his campaign plans. In mid-August he retreated across the Detroit River.

Everyone gave the credit to the commander of the Upper Canada troops, Isaac Brock, who, with great daring, had chased the Americans to Fort Detroit and demanded their surrender. His boldness was rewarded, and he obtained a great supply of much needed weapons and stores for Canada. The news was not all good, however. It seemed obvious now that the next attack would occur farther east. Would it be at Queenston?

"The local fellows are taking this war more seriously now," James told Laura one day in September. Then he added thoughtfully, "We all are."

Laura stocked their cold cellar well. During the fall, she stored twice as many supplies of root vegetables and fruits. As usual she stored turnips, potatoes, russet apples, sugar pears, dried peaches, cherries, and berries. And then there were the plums—Blue, Damson, Green Gage, and Egg.

James had insisted that they keep Fan and Bob, the black servants he had hired while Laura was gone to see her father. They were a great help putting up the extra preserves. James had dug out an additional hidden back room behind and under the regular fruit cellar, disguising the entrance with a trap door hidden under the sod. Food could be scarce in war time, and he didn't want any of their supplies stolen.

In early October James returned from military duty one day with the news that Brock was expecting an attack along the Niagara River. Queenston seemed a likely place, since it was so close to the American side. Newark and Fort George, where Isaac Brock had stationed his men, were also on the alert.

James, a sergeant in the First Lincoln Militia, kept watch with his volunteers around the clock. With some anxiety, Laura watched him leave for duty day and night, and prayed for strength to face whatever lay ahead.

TWENTY-TWO

Laura woke up with a start. She was almost certain she had heard the sound of a cannon firing. So it had begun. The war they had all dreaded had come to Queenston and Niagara.

Laura jumped from her bed and hurried to the window to look out. She could see nothing but rain pelting against the window in the jet blackness of the October night.

James, where are you? she asked herself. Are you at the Landing to meet the enemy or have you gone to Fort George? Or maybe you're with General Brock. "Please God, protect him wherever he is."

"Mama, mama." The cry came from the cradle beside the bed as her son, Charles, woke up in fear.

Harriet and Charlotte stumbled into the room, almost tripping on their long, flannel nightgowns. "Is that gunfire, Mama?" asked Harriet, still rubbing her eyes.

Charlotte was fully awake and asking anxiously, "Is it a bad thunderstorm? Do you want us to go downstairs the way we usually do?" But Laura could see the fear in her eyes and realized that her oldest daughter was well aware of the danger ahead.

"You go back to sleep now . . . all of you," Laura said. "I'm keeping watch and if I need to, I'll call you." Reassured, they returned to their beds.

Laura sank to her knees and leaned against the bed until the thumping of her heart had eased and a quieter feeling came. After a short time, she got to her feet and dressed quietly, putting on her old short gown and petticoats. She lay back on the bed, fully dressed, and listened to the heavy rain.

It was still dark when Laura roused herself from a half-sleep. She looked down at Charles, who had kicked away his covering. His chubby, pink toes lay bare on the quilt. Laura got up and pulled the blanket back over him, for the chill of the storm had penetrated the house. The clock on the dresser struck five a.m. It was time to get the girls dressed and ready to leave the house.

In the girls' room across the hall, Charlotte was lying with her eyes wide open but Harriet was sleeping soundly in her bunk opposite the bedstead. Laura cautioned Charlotte with a finger to her lips and pointed to the clothes on the bedpost, then walked out of the room and went downstairs.

When Laura entered the kitchen, she was surprised to see Bob and Fan already moving around. Bob had a crackling fire going in the fireplace, and Laura stood by the hearth to warm herself. Fan was shaking as she stirred the porridge in the iron pot over the hearth. "Why can't them Americans just stay home, anyway? We don't want their laws here."

Bob and Fan came from the settlement of former slaves on the southwest side of St. David's. They and many others who lived there had been freed under a law passed by Governor Simcoe in 1793. The new legislation forbade the import of slaves into the province and freed the children of slaves when they reached the age of twenty-five. It was no wonder that Fan feared an American takeover. It could mean she and her husband would be sent back to slavery.

After Laura had helped prepare the breakfast, she went out the back door of the house and looked up to the Heights. It was still dark, but the rain was falling less heavily now. She could hear rustling sounds. Was there movement between the trees? She shrank back in fear to the side of the house and strained to see.

A bolt of lightning streaked across the sky, and in its pale light, she saw men in the red uniforms of the British Army swarming up the hill on foot. There was a great clap of thunder and at the very same moment, the firing of guns.

Laura ran into the house and up the stairs and took a deep breath before entering her daughters' room. Then she went in and spoke to them with a quiet firmness that did not reveal her fear. "Harriet, get dressed quickly, and Charlotte, since you're already dressed, you can get the baby ready." Laura had trained her children well before the crisis, and they knew now that they must do exactly as she said.

But before they could go down the stairs, they heard men's

voices and a loud banging at the back door. All four froze in fear as Laura called out, "Who is it?"

The voices were not distinguishable at first. Then they heard James above the noise of the others, "It's me, Laura." While the children huddled together at the top of the stairs, Laura ran down to the door and pulled up the latch lock.

James burst into the room with three other men. Their red jackets and white breeches were soaking wet and spattered with mud, and the sickening smell of wet wool and blood filled the hallway. The four of them carried a very large man in a gold-trimmed scarlet uniform. Bob held a candle up, and in its flickering light Laura saw that the officer's chest was soaked in blood.

"Quick, Fan," Laura whispered as she stared at the wounded man. "Bring water and cloths."

Her husband's face was ashen, for the man they carried was their own General, Isaac Brock. "Up the stairs," gasped James, his arms under one shoulder of his commander.

The frightened children scurried back to their room, and Laura followed to hand Charles over to Charlotte. She closed their door tightly behind her as the men climbed the stairs very slowly with their precious burden.

The door to her bedroom was still open when she left the girls, and she could see the men by the bed, bending over the General. James came out alone to her and closed the door behind him.

"Laura, General Brock cannot be helped now. Tell Fan not to bring the water. In case the body is found here, we are removing his uniform so he can't be identified by the enemy. We do not want them to know our leader is dead; nor do we want them to have the body. They'll not recognize him out of uniform."

"What are we to do? . . . the children, James?"

"Go to the country. There is still some cover of darkness. Go through the village to the north side and then straight west. You'll be safe there. For now, the Americans want Queenston. The countryside is safe."

"But where are they? I thought the fighting must be at the Landing."

"We thought so too. We had it well guarded, but somehow they found a way to the Heights up the sheer cliffs through the fishermen's pass. Only a few from Niagara know that way. Someone has betrayed us."

"Where are the General's men?"

"They aren't here yet. When General Brock heard the cannon, he thought it was a ruse to draw his men away from their stronghold at Fort George so the enemy could attack there. He didn't believe it was possible for them to climb that cliff, let alone find their way. He felt the real fighting would come at the Landing, and he knew we were well prepared to hold out there until he could bring his men. So he left his men and came himself to investigate the situation."

"It must have been three in the morning when I heard that cannon. Did the sound come from across the river?"

"No, it was our own cannon stationed halfway up the Heights above Queenston. Our men shot it for a warning to us, then spiked it, making it useless, and fled down the hill. They never reached the bottom because the warning sound revealed their position, and they were shot."

"Why didn't General Brock wait for more men before he attacked?"

"If he'd waited, he wouldn't have been able to stop the Americans from marching in and taking Queenston. We held them back, and Colonel Macdonell should be here any minute to lead the next attack. The Americans have retreated for the moment."

The solemn-faced soldiers hurried out of the bedroom, and James said, "I must go, Laura. You and the children hurry away. Bob and Fan will help."

James and the other men rushed down the stairs and were gone.

"Come quickly," Laura called to her children, opening their door. They crowded behind her as they went down the stairs.

Bob and Fan, who were waiting in the hall, helped put a cape on Charles, and they all hurried outside. The raw, wet wind cut through them as they walked along the street leading away from the Heights.

It seemed to take forever to reach the north end of town. It had started to rain again when they got there, and they met scores of wet and dirty Canadian and British soldiers marching down the main road toward them. Bob cheered loudly when Captain Runchey's company of black soldiers came into sight.

The family turned up a side street, then headed north and west. Before long they were on the outskirts of Queenston.

"We'll cut across country now," said Laura. She knew that any farm family would take them in, but the farther they went from Queenston, the safer they would be. She decided to head for the Chrysler or Clement farm.

They walked on in broad daylight now and the rain had almost stopped. A silly rhyme that her father used to repeat started ringing in Laura's ears: "If it rains before seven, it'll stop before eleven." Barely four months had passed since his death, and she thought of him often. But if he were alive now, he would surely be grieved by this war. How torn he would have been, for he had friends on both sides.

The sound of gunshots echoed from the Heights behind them. Looking back, she could see flashes of gunsmoke. "God, please keep James safe," she pleaded silently as she pushed along.

"Aren't we ever gonna get there?" Harriet grumbled.

"How about a ride?" Bob asked, lifting the small girl onto his broad shoulders. Harriet smiled from her perch at the others, who were still walking.

"May I carry Charles a piece, Ma'am?" Fan asked.

"I'll be all right. He's asleep and it's not far now." Laura's arms did ache though, for Charles was a big baby. Laura turned to look back and saw other groups of women and children coming from the southeast.

The road was muddy in places, and as they reached the woods near the back of the Clements' farm, she said, "Climb through this rail fence here and we'll cut off at least a mile from going around on the road." They all squeezed through between the rails and pushed along a trail through the bush. The grass along the edges was long and very wet, but at least they were free of the mud on the road.

Finally, they saw the big grey flat-board barn and the log cabin beyond. As they approached the house, Mrs. Clement swung the door wide open and reached out for the baby. Her usually jolly face was sober as she laid Charles on the bed in the adjoining room.

Pale-faced, the girls huddled together on the long bench by the hearth. The fire felt good.

"Will you have some porridge for yourself and the young-uns?" asked Mrs. Clement. "It'll warm your insides."

"I think we'll just rest first, thank you," Laura said, collapsing into a chair before the fire.

Mrs. Clement nodded and turned her kind eyes away to stir the big pot of oatmeal porridge that she had already prepared for any who might come that day.

*****

Much later in the morning, Laura was cutting bread for the noon meal and the children were playing outside near the house when suddenly she heard a loud knock at the front door. She went to open it and was not surprised to see Mrs. Law, another woman fleeing from Queenston, along with her eleven-year-old son, John. The Laws lived across town from the Secords, but they had met many times in the Secords' general store.

"We've just come from Queenston," she said. Her face had lost all of its colour, and glassy-eyed, she passed Laura as she mumbled, "The fighting is bad. My husband and older son have been killed in the battle. I fear the Americans will take Queenston."

Her red-headed son stared straight ahead too and sat down silently on a chair just inside the door. He did not look like his usual self at all, with his face so pale even the freckles were faded. The stubborn expression on his face and his wild-looking hair reminded Laura of someone.

"Mama, Charles is crying," Charlotte called from the bedroom. Laura went in to calm the baby and to coax him to eat a little.

When she came back into the kitchen, Mrs. Clement, Fan, and Charlotte had set the table for all of them. It was a simple meal of bread, turnips, and fried pork, with a glass of milk for each child.

"I'll call the others," Laura said, going to the door. Her children came running to the house, but young John Law was not with them.

Mrs. Law, who had sat in a numbed state on the kitchen couch since her arrival, suddenly came to life,screaming, "Where's my baby boy?" She stared wildly about and then rushed out of the house.

Laura looked at Mrs. Clement, who gave her a knowing glance. The woman had just lost her husband and older boy that morning. No wonder she was panicking. Laura remembered now who young John reminded her of. He looked just like Red, that unforgettable fugitive from a different battle. But now she and her children were the fugitives.

"We must all help her look," Laura said, breaking off her thoughts. The older children raced outside to hunt while Laura and Mrs. Clement started searching through the house.

"More than likely he's crawled into a corner in the barn somewhere. That young'un is havin' hisself a good cry where no one cin see him," Mrs. Clement said.

Laura was looking behind the barrels on the back stoop when she noticed the elderly Mr. Clement heading towards the house.

"Was he in the barn?" Mrs. Clement asked anxiously, coming up behind Laura.

"No, but since you've not found him, I cin go back and check agin."

Mr. Clement turned to go back to the barn, but stopped abruptly at Mrs. Clement's cry, "Joseph, your musket's missin'—and your cartridge pouch too! Don't you always keep 'em in back of the pantry?"

"Yep, haven't moved them for weeks."

Laura and Mrs. Clement looked at each other. They knew they would have to call Mrs. Law to tell her.

Mrs. Law came quickly, her eyes red from crying, but she looked hopeful as she searched their eyes for confirmation that her son was found.

"My husband's musket and box of cartridges are missing," Mrs. Clement said slowly. They were all afraid to see her reaction, but Mrs. Law was silent as her face turned even paler than before.

Just then the other children rushed up the steps. "We couldn't find a trace of him," said Charlotte.

Mrs. Law groaned weakly and crumpled onto the stoop, holding her head in her hands. "I know my son," she cried out. "He's gone to get the men who killed his father and brother. My son, my son. . . ."

Laura stared at Mrs. Law and then at the Clements. Could such a young boy really have gone to the battlefield? Surely his mother was not thinking sensibly in her grief.

Mr. Clement broke the silence. "You may be right. I haven't no other reason for my musket disappearin'. It was there this mornin'."

Mrs. Law got up then and stood shakily on her feet, but she was looking very determined. "I'm bringing him back if I have to drag him with my own two hands. I'll not lose all my family on the same day."

"We'll go together," Laura said. "I want to go home anyway to see if there is any news of James. Fan and Bob and my older daughter will watch the younger ones, Mrs. Clement, if I may leave the children here. My baby takes milk from a cup now."

"Certainly they cin stay here. I wouldn't want the young-uns goin' back to Queenston, and I don't rightly think you should be goin' back there yourself either, Laura."

"I'll be fine."

"What good cin you do? Better to stay away." Then she looked at Mrs. Law. "Still, May here could use the company . . . but like as not, dear, you'll find John halfway there, shootin' at a rabbit."

"No, I won't. I know my son."

TWENTY-THREE

A strange stillness had settled over the town of Queenston. The streets were deserted and the pungent smell of sulphur hung thick in the damp air.

The women kept tramping down the empty street toward Laura's home at the foot of the Heights. As they reached the Secord yard, they heard the gunfire start again, and before Laura could stop her, Mrs. Law rushed toward the Heights.

"John . . . John," she was screaming.

A musketball tore through her petticoat and grazed her leg. She fell instantly to the ground. Then with blood soaking through her stocking from just above her ankle, she struggled to her feet. Unsteadily, she limped in and out among the men as she asked, "Have you seen a young boy?"

Laura stood still at the edge of her own dooryard, unable to do anything to help. Then a bareheaded soldier came limping towards Laura. She recognized him at once. It was Josh's younger brother, Elijah. Laura grabbed him just before he fell against her. With her support, he reached the house.

Inside he slumped onto the couch in the hallway. "It's just my leg," he said. "There's others worse off."

"Have you seen James?"

"Not since early this morning. He was leading his men into the fighting."

"If you're all right, I'm going to look for my friend and her young son," Laura said. He nodded.

She rushed back to the edge of the lawn. Then she saw them. Mrs. Law was dragging her son, who was kicking and screaming at her. She walked with a bad limp, and her stocking was soaked in blood. Laura ran to them and took one of John's hands. With their combined effort, they pulled the hysterical boy into the house.

Inside, Laura poured water into a bowl to bathe the wounds of her friends. John had stopped fighting his mother now and was standing beside her looking down with surprise at the blood on her torn petticoat and leg.

Laura worked rapidly on Mrs. Law's wound. Now that she had put her leg up on the kitchen bench, the bleeding was starting to ease. "It's good it bled like that," Laura said. "It'll clean the wound."

Laura knew that Mrs. Law must be in pain, but she showed no evidence of it. Her thoughts were only for her son. "Don't let John get out again," she begged. "I'm afraid the boy's gone a bit daft."

"I'll talk to him," Laura promised. She had been watching him out of the corner of her eye as she worked on his mother's wound. He was sitting quietly on a footstool by the kitchen window, staring straight ahead.

Laura approached the boy and stood beside him for a moment before she spoke. He looked up at her sullenly. "Your mother is going to need your help to get back to the Clements' farm, John," Laura said in a quiet but firm voice. He looked at her again and said nothing. Laura waited.

"I've used up all my ammunition anyway," John answered finally, "but I got some of 'em."

Laura turned away and walked to the bake table to tear strips of linen to bind Elijah's wound. He was wincing with pain now. She could hear John talking to his mother in the background.

"I hope your leg doesn't hurt too much to walk, Mother. I figure I should be taking back Mr. Clement's musket. I wouldn't want him to think I stole it. I figure I can work to pay him back for the cartridges."

"Don't worry 'bout it, son. I'll pay for them. We'd best be going now, but I'm going to need you to hang onto."

Before Laura could tend to Elijah again, she heard the door opening, and in stumbled half a dozen redcoated Queenston men.

"We've pushed them back up the Heights, but they've still got possession of the top," said Joe Pine, one of the Lincoln militia.

"They're on the defensive. They're not attacking Queenston anymore."

"The Yanks are in control of the Heights and down around the cannon, but it's not working. Our men took care of that."

"Are you going back to attack?" Laura asked.

"Not now. We'll hold Queenston if they attack us, but we're waiting for Major General Sheaffe to come up from Fort George, and the Mohawks from Chippawa."

"Have many men been killed?"

"I don't know. I don't think so. But General Brock . . . General Brock. . . ."

"I know."

"And Macdonell fell too, but he's still breathing."

"The doctor says he'll not make it," said Joe.

"Have you seen James?" she asked.

The men hesitated then, and Joe looked down. She realized that he knew about her husband. "Please tell me," she said.

"He's alive, but he's wounded and behind enemy lines. He fell just left of the cannon."

"How long before Sheaffe's men are expected?"

"Two or three hours at least."

"James will be lying helplessly in the middle of a battle!"

"I'm afraid so, Laura."

Laura looked down then and spoke quietly to the men. She knew what she must do. "Help yourselves to anything in the kitchen—bread, cheese, milk," she said. They did not need urging, for they must keep up their strength. As they went into the kitchen, she slipped unnoticed out the back door.

At the foot of the Heights, she broke her run and walked briskly to the left in the direction of the cannon.

"Where are you going, Laura? The enemy have control of the Heights," called a local volunteer soldier who was standing guard.

"I know. They also have my husband. He's wounded. I'm going for him." The soldier looked to the others for help, but not a man stepped forward to stop her.

Her ankle-length white petticoat stood out starkly among the soldiers' dull red uniforms. Her hair was tucked under her white cap.

Enemy soldiers saw the white figure approaching and alerted others. White was the symbol of parley and sometimes surrender between fighting soldiers. They watched with anticipation until they discerned that the approaching figure was only a slender young woman. What had she come for?

"Oh, dear God, please help me," Laura breathed as she kept on advancing toward the enemy line.

Laura hesitated then, for she had come upon the very battle site. The enemy were stationed just beyond. Dead and wounded soldiers lay before her. She trembled as she heard their groaning. As she ran fearfully from one to the next to find her husband, she forgot that the enemy soldiers were watching her intently.

Suddenly she saw James. He was lying very still on the ground between two standing American soldiers. One soldier had raised the butt of his gun in the air ready to strike.

"No!" Laura shouted.

The soldier looked up.

She ran and threw herself over James' body and screamed, "Kill me, not my husband!"

"Why not kill both of you?" the soldier snarled as he grabbed her arm and pulled her to her feet.

"She's too pretty to kill," the other soldier yelled, and yanked her over beside him.

Laura gasped for breath as she struggled to free herself.

"Stop!" A sharp command rang out.

Laura looked into the face of an American officer who had come up beside her.

"I apologize, Ma'am, for the conduct of my men," he said politely. Then he turned aside and barked, "Page and Johnson, take these two under guard."

Two more soldiers stepped forward from the other side of the battle site. They grabbed the weapons of the soldiers who had threatened Laura, then walked the offenders on up the Heights, where they disappeared among the trees.

"You may take your husband home," the Captain told Laura.

"Thank you," Laura said, with tears falling down her cheeks. Already she was beside James holding his head in her hands.

"Please, James, try to sit up. Then you can lean on me."

He did not move.

"Here! Adams . . . Durham," the Captain commanded. "Help this man to his home."

Another pair of soldiers stepped forward, tied their coats together, and lifted James onto the makeshift stretcher. They started slowly down the hill. James' arms hung down limp.

Laura turned to the American captain who had helped. "Thank you. Thank you, Mr. . . ."

"Captain Wool."

"Thank you, Captain Wool."

Then she ran to the men who were carrying James and directed them toward the Canadian line.

She walked in front and to one side so that the Canadian soldiers would see her first and allow the Americans to pass. When they reached the place where the Queenston men were guarding the ground they had gained, James roused himself a little and groaned. Then he slipped into unconsciousness again.

"We'd better take him directly to bed and not change coats here," the one soldier said.

The Queenston guards understood the situation and did not object. "I'll go with you to make sure that you get back safely after you leave James," one of them volunteered.

They reached the house and carried James to a bed in the girls' room. Laura did not dare lead them to the other bedroom and the body of General Brock.

She thanked them at the door. They nodded and were gone. The soldiers standing in her kitchen were watching in amazement.

"Please go for the doctor," she said, putting a kettle of water to boil. A soldier nodded and left by the back door.

She went back upstairs to James, who was groaning weakly. She could see two wounds, one in his leg and the other in his shoulder. She went to the girls' nightstand to get a jug of water. When she came back to the bed, James was calling her name, delirious now with fever.

"I'm here, James," she said, placing a cool cloth on his forehead.

Finally, she heard noise below and heavy steps. She walked out of the bedroom to see the doctor and another soldier at the foot of the stairs.

"Dr. Greenfield, thank God you've come," she cried out. The

doctor started up the stairs to see James. Laura stared in disbelief at his clothes, splattered with blood and pieces of flesh. Even his face and hands were dirty with mud, blood, and grime. The stench from his clothes was worse than the smell of James' fresh wounds. Up in the room, Laura quickly poured water from her pitcher into the china basin and handed the doctor a bar of her own strong lye soap.

He hesitated at first and then proceeded to wash his hands. He would please the lady, he decided. He had no energy left to quarrel with her.

She watched anxiously while the doctor examined James. He was conscious now and groaned feebly as the doctor probed his wounds. Finally the doctor said, "I've got the ball from his shoulder, but I can't get the one in his knee."

Laura was relieved when James lapsed back into unconsciousness. For a few minutes, he was free from the pain and could not hear the doctor's comments. Dr. Greenfield finished dressing the wounds and walked out into the hall with Laura. "He will get better, won't he?" Laura asked.

"I can't say. Only God knows that, Laura. I'll venture to say, though, that if he lives through the night, he may make it. However, we'll have to amputate the leg if infection sets in, and with the bullet still there, it's bound to."

A feeling of powerlessness overcame Laura, and she grabbed the railing of the staircase to steady herself.

"These powders may help a little to keep the pain down. I'm sorry I can't leave more," the doctor said. "I must go now. There's to be another battle soon. I have to be ready for the injured."

Back in the kitchen, the kettle was boiling madly, and all the soldiers had gone except for the wounded Elijah. Dr. Greenfield took a look at his wound and said he was in no danger, but he'd be useless in the battle. Then the doctor left for the battlefield.

"Where have the soldiers gone?" Laura asked Josh's younger brother.

"To take the Heights," he said weakly. "Sheaffe's arrived and they've gone to form up with his men."

As Laura hastened back up the stairs and into the bedroom, the thunder of cannon and spatter of heavy musket fire filled the house. "Thank you, God, that James is not out there in the middle of it," she mumbled aloud. At least there was that relief. But turning towards James, who was moaning now and moving his head back and forth on the pillow, she wondered if there was any reason to hope.

*****

Laura emptied the dirty water into the pail and poured fresh, cool water into the china washbowl. She squeezed her damp cloth and laid it across her husband's forehead. Already she had cut away his dirty, blood-soaked uniform and removed it from his body. She laid fresh, dry towels under his arms and legs and sides. Then with a clean cloth, she dipped into the water and continued to bathe her husband's burning body as James slipped in and out of consciousness. James was shifting restlessly in the bed and flailing his arms about as he continued to mumble meaningless sounds, and his temperature kept rising.

Only when he finally lay still did she notice how quiet it was outside. She rushed to the open window and listened intently. There was no gunfire.

"Is it over?" She could hardly believe that. Even if the shooting had stopped, it did not necessarily mean that she and James were out of danger. It was quite possible that Queenston had been taken by the enemy, and that American soldiers were already on their way to take possession of all the houses in the town.

It was then that she remembered the body of General Brock in the other bedroom. If American soldiers came to take over the house, there would be no way of hiding the body from them, and she had heard that they did not always treat the bodies of leaders with respect. Then she remembered that they would not recognize him, since his uniform had been changed. Her mind turned back to the danger at hand. She would have no way of defending herself and her husband from a band of celebrating soldiers. Only God could protect them now. Otherwise, they were completely at the mercy of the enemy.

She looked down at James again. For now, he was her greatest concern; his pain was as bad as ever. Glancing at the washstand, she noticed that the water was low in the pitcher. She took it up and ran downstairs for more water. As she went by the clock in the hall, she noticed that it was five o'clock in the afternoon. Somehow it seemed much later.

Out at the well beside the house, she rolled down the bucket, looking up toward the Heights as she worked. Near the bottom of the slope, not far from the edge of her yard, she could see men coming toward her. They were Queenston men. She recognized their dull red coats.

"We've gained the Heights," they shouted as they came nearer. "We've held it for two hours now. It's ours!"

"We've taken more than nine hundred American prisoners. They'll be marching them through the town."

Laura saw the blue-coated captives not far behind. Even the ones with blood-soaked wounds were forced to limp along. She stood riveted to the spot, looking at the haggard faces of the defeated soldiers, suddenly aware of the suffering of the other side. Then she saw one man who looked familiar. It was Captain Wool. Blood trickled from a shallow wound on the side of his face, and his eyes looked glassy. The soldiers had stopped the prisoners to assemble them into lines, with Captain Wool in front.

Laura grabbed her pail of water and the dipper that hung on a nail by the side of the well and ran to the side of the road. She handed the dipper of water to Captain Wool, who gulped the water down, then handed the dipper back to his men. As each one drank, the pain in their faces went away for a moment and then returned.

Captain Wool had not realized who she was. Then as he looked up to say, "Thank you," a glimmer of recognition crossed his face.

A Queenston soldier handed her the empty pail and she turned to refill it, but by the time it was full, the men had started marching down the road again in long lines.

Laura raced back to the house, where Elijah was still lying on the couch in the hallway. "We've won," she said, handing him a cup of water. He sighed and smiled.

At that moment Laura heard someone at the door. Before she could rush to open it, James' brother David came in. "We've taken the Heights, Laura," he said. "Where's James? They told me you got him."

Laura led him up the stairs to the girls' room where James lay. James did not recognize either his wife or his brother.

"The fever is high," she said. "I'm trying to keep it down with the cold water."

"Be careful, Laura. You don't want him going into pneumonia."

Laura remembered General Brock's body in their other bedroom. "David," she asked, "will they be coming for General Brock now?"

"I thought you knew," he said, surprised. "They came for his body early this morning. He was only here for a short time. They took him to a safer place, farther from the American line."

"I didn't know," she said. "We could have taken James to his own room then. . . . Still he was better on this side of the house, farther from the noise of the battle. He needs stronger medicine, David. Will you try to find the doctor and get something more?"

"I'll try, but he's very busy. . . . Goodbye, Laura." He turned then and hurried down the stairs and out the door.

Laura shook a little as she went back into the bedroom. Her hands trembling, she squeezed the excess moisture from her cloth and bathed her husband's brow. His eyelids opened, but he looked beyond her. His deep, blue eyes were clouded now and heavily bloodshot.

"Laura, Laura," he whispered, still not looking at her.

"I'm here, James."

He moved his hand and she took it. He strengthened his grip. She knew he must realize she was there caring for him.

"Who's . . . winning?" He could barely say the words.

"We won, James. We've taken the Heights. It's a definite victory."

He relaxed his hold then and slipped back into semi-consciousness. This time he seemed more peaceful, and Laura felt he was resting.

*****

Long past dark, Laura was still sitting at his bedside in the light of the flickering candles. Hearing footsteps on the stairs, she went out into the hallway and saw David Secord coming up the steps. His face was lined and smudged with dirt. Obviously he had not rested since the battle. Laura looked at him expectantly, hoping that he had brought more medication.

"How is he?" he asked as Laura held the bedroom door open.

"A little better, I think. He's resting more comfortably and he recognized me a short time ago, but he still feels very hot. And he's in a lot of pain."

David looked down at his younger brother. "The doctor's too busy to come now," he sighed. "He's run short of supplies, but we're expecting more from the fort."

"Is it really over?" she asked, looking for reassurance, though she herself had seen the enemy prisoners led through the town.

"Yes, for now."

"Was it a long battle on the Heights?"

"Not at the last. We had them surrounded and pushed them to the edge. Then Sheaffe gave the order that if they surrendered, their lives would be spared."

"What happened then?"

"They couldn't hear him in all the confusion. They were jumping off the cliff to their deaths to avoid death by British bayonets or Indian scalping knives."

"But those prisoners who went by. . . ."

"Yes, we took some prisoners. I ran into their lines and shouted Sheaffe's promise. Then they listened."

"How did they know they could trust you?"

"My wife's father and brother were among them, and they reassured the others. They were just ready to jump too when they saw me and stopped."

"Thank God! But how brutal war is when men must fight their own kin! Were many of our men killed?"

"Fourteen, we think—far fewer than we expected—but two of those were Brock and Macdonell. The price for the Heights was high. There never has been a general like Brock and never will be again."

"I know. James loved him too, as we all did."

"There's great mourning now, and it will spread all across Canada this week as the news gets out. He gave his life to hold the line till reinforcements came. If he had waited, they'd have taken Queenston." Then, breaking off abruptly, he turned toward the stairs again. "I must go now. Come down with me so you can latch the door."

"Why?"

"We think we have them all, but a few American deserters may be roaming about."

"Oh, I didn't realize we were still in danger," she said, following her brother-in-law.

"I wish I could stay to help."

"We'll manage. Your men need you." Laura knew that David Secord was a Major.

"Good night, Laura."

"Good night."

Laura dropped the latch across the door and turned back into the kitchen, where she picked up clean cloths and a kettle of hot water. Hurrying back up the stairs to her husband, she knew it would be a long night.

TWENTY-FOUR

When the autumn sun rose on the morning of October 14, Laura was still sitting beside her husband's bed, tired beyond measure. She had attended him all night as the wounds in his knee and shoulder became more and more inflamed. Not long after sunrise, James came fully awake for the first time since Laura had rescued him. Drops of perspiration fell from his forehead as he wrestled with his pain. Laura almost wished that he would slip back into unconsciousness. Finally, he fell into a fitful sleep.

Laura sat by the bedside. She had not slept since the day before yesterday. As she leaned over onto the bed, exhausted, she prayed for strength and for James. "It's all in your hands now. Oh, God, prepare us for whatever comes." The doctor's grim prediction was still in her mind.

If there were more battles, James would not be going, she thought with some satisfaction. Then she wondered what James would think about that. He had so wanted to defend his land. Unlike so many of the settlers, he had not been indifferent to the American attack. He was convinced that the invaders had to be defeated. How would he feel if he could not continue as Sergeant of his militia regiment?

*****

Laura awakened to the sound of James calling her name. She did not know how long she had been sleeping. As she raised her head, she saw that he was tossing with fever again and moaning in pain.

She ran down to the kitchen, selected some herbs, and ground them together in a wooden cup. Hooking a kettle over the fire, she waited for what seemed like hours before it boiled. The tea would soothe the pain, even if it didn't take it away.

Back in the girls' room, she held some of the tea to James' lips and put cold compresses on his wounds to cool the inflammation. His knee now looked worse than his shoulder.

The fever was rising again. Laura poured more water into the jug. Using clean linen cloths, she continued to bathe his body. She even managed to comb out some of his blood-caked hair. Then his increasing groans told her she would have to stop, and he lapsed back into sleep.

Laura stood up to stretch, still keeping her eyes on her husband. She remembered again the doctor's warning about James' leg. "Oh, dear God, please don't let it happen. Please, don't let James lose his leg." The thought of it made her sick in the stomach. Would they have to come in and hold him down while the doctor sawed off his leg above the knee? She almost fainted at the picture that flashed before her eyes.

She turned and held the back of her chair to get control of herself again. The room was still going black. She sat down and held her head in her lap.

The feeling finally passed and she got up to go downstairs to prepare food for herself and James. As she reached the foot of the stairs, she heard someone at the back door and rushing out of the kitchen into the hall, she lifted the latch.

Her brother, Charles, stood there in his uniform. She reached up and wrapped both arms around him. "Charles, you're safe. Are you all right?"

"Yes, I'm fine," he answered almost lightly.

"I guess you weren't in the battles yesterday."

"I was in the second one on the Heights. My first battle, Laura."

"Charles, how awful for you."

"I thought it would be, but it wasn't. I was with Major Thomas Merritt's Niagara Light Dragoons. His son William Hamilton Merritt and I were together through it all. I can tell you, we were dreading if after the events of the morning. We were too late for the first battle. We had come galloping into Queenston from Fort George only to find out the terrible news that Brock had fallen and the Yanks had taken the Heights. We were told to wait for Major-General Sheaffe."

"The waiting must have been hard."

"I'll admit, Laura, I was fearful. We all were. We'd just lost Brock and found out the Yanks had control of the Heights. It was as though the impossible had just happened. We thought about two-thirds of the Canadian and British forces would be cut down even if we did win the battle. Sheaffe led our troops the long way around from Fort George and out through the country. Then we crossed back again to attack from the west. It was the most tense ride of my life."

"Did you attack from the west?"

"The infantry, the 41st Regiment and the local militia, went up the Heights from the west in lines along with a battery of guns drawn by farm horses. We rode on the right flank."

"Expecting the worst?"

"Yes, but it was all over in ten minutes. We lost only fourteen men and we'd expected to be slaughtered. We could hardly believe it when they surrendered. It was all over so fast, and we were still alive."

"Thank God."

"Well . . . the Mohawks, on the right flank too, were there ahead of us, along with Captain Runchey's Company of black soldiers. They surprised the Americans from the southwest and kept interrupting them with skirmishes while they were trying to build fortifications. So by the time we got there, the enemy was vulnerable to our attack. Thank God for the Mohawks and the black soldiers!"

"I only hope the Americans stay home now."

"I doubt they will, but we've driven them out for now and probably for the winter. Their casualties were high. We took over nine hundred prisoners, and they had over two hundred and fifty dead and several wounded. How is James?"

"Come and see. I can't leave him for long."

Charles followed her up the stairs.

James' eyes were open now, and he brightened a bit at the sight of Charles in uniform and mumbled, "Are we holding the Heights?"

"We sure are. I doubt they'll ever try that again."

"But . . . General Brock. . . ."

"I know," said Charles.

James grimaced with the pain though he tried not to show it, and Laura nodded to Charles as she held the door. "I'll be right back, James," said Laura going out behind Charles.

She followed Charles down the stairs. "Please try to get the doctor to come and see James again or at least get some pain medicine. He had so little to give him when he came before."

"I'll try."

Laura prepared more herbal tea, then returned to James' room. She kept on bathing him, and as night approached she cleaned his wounds again.

When she was finished, James looked up at her and said in a whisper, "Laura, try to rest. I'll call you if I need you."

She looked across at Harriet's bed.

"Go ahead, Laura."

Fully dressed, she crawled into the bed and did not even stretch out before her eyes closed. James' face convulsed with pain but, breathing deeply, he did not cry out as he looked at his wife asleep across the room.

*****

"It's the gun salute . . . for General Brock," James murmured to Laura. The sound of cannon going off nearby shook the air. Then they heard a salute from across the river.

"That sound came from Lewiston," said Laura. "Even his enemy salutes General Brock."

"He would have ordered the same for an enemy general."

Laura did not answer. Instead she said, "I'll go for more fresh water to clean your wounds, James."

"Laura, the pain has eased a little now. Can't we just leave them alone?"

"I suppose, but I'll need water anyway to be ready for later."

Laura left him then. She knew he was thinking about the funeral and other wounded men in his company who would not be there either.

The doctor had finally called and said that James was out of immediate danger. He had given her special instructions for the knee wound.

As Laura went out the back door, heading for the well, a brisk wind blew about and moved the leaves along the ground. Looking up, she noticed how bare the trees had become in the last few days. The wind had blown away the leaves and left them looking bleak and lonely on the cold morning. Perhaps even the Heights mourned General Brock.

Still . . . Upper Canada had remained under British control and James was alive. She bowed her head for a moment and whispered thanks to God.

Laura knew that most people were thinking the war would soon be over. No one really wanted it in the first place, since many, like themselves, had close friends and relatives across the line. It was a political war forced on the Americans by their new government, which had succumbed to the pressure of the war hawks. Surely the American forces had been beaten so decisively at Queenston Heights that they would be called home, and it would all be over before Christmas. She was thankful that neither she nor Mira had sons old enough to go to war and fight against each other. And Josh was so busy on his farm, she doubted he would ever be called into active duty, though she knew he had been called upon to train in a reserve force in case the States were invaded.

As she pulled her bucket up over the low stone wall around the opening of the well, she heard children's voices. Setting down the pail, she turned to see Charlotte running around the corner of the house and Harriet following close behind. Bob and Fan were walking behind with Charles.

Laura put down her bucket and held out her arms, a wide smile spreading across her face. She hardly remembered what it felt like to smile. Charles threw his arms around her neck as she took him from Fan.

"Mama, mama," he cried as he hugged her.

"We heard Papa was wounded," Charlotte said. "How serious is it?"

"He's improving. He's still very weak, but not as feverish."

"They made us bring them back, Ma'am," said Fan. "They just wouldn't believe your brother, Charles. He told us you and Mister James was all right."

"I'm so glad to be home," Harriet twirled around with joy. "I'm glad this war is over. We thought it would never end!"

"Yes, dear, it's over, but you'll all need to be very quiet, for your father was badly wounded. He's in your room and too weak to go back to his own yet. You girls may sleep in our room. Charlotte, you can watch Charles in the cradle. . . . I must stay near your father; he still needs me. Now come quietly, and you may see him, but only for a minute."

Without further words, Laura, the children, and Fan and Bob crept up the stairs to where James lay. Laura held the door as they went in one at a time to see him.

Harriet, who was last, looked up at her mother with the same deep blue eyes as her father's. They looked larger than usual just now in her pale face as she said, "Oh, Mama, we will all have to pray hard tonight for Papa."

*****

Laura sat knitting a stocking in a chair beside James, who was sleeping more peacefully now. She had sent the children to bed a couple of hours ago, and Bob and Fan had also retired early to their quarters in the cabin by the bakehouse. A flickering candle on the night stand gave only a dim light, but Laura did not really need it, for she was not even looking at her swiftly moving fingers.

Though a steady rain was pelting against the window, she felt no chill; Bob had built a good fire in the fireplace, and it was warming the room. She could see lights flickering in the windows of the house next door and thought of her friends who had come home that day. Queenston was getting back to normal. The worst appeared to be over. Surely the Americans would not come back again.

TWENTY-FIVE

"It's a bloody disgrace," said James. "Sheaffe should have stood his ground and fought, instead of destroying his own ship and running with his troops."

Spring had finally come and with it the unexpected news that York had been invaded and captured. A Canadian frigate, the *Isaac Brock*, had been burned in the harbour by order of Major-General Sheaffe before he withdrew his men. Within a day, the Americans had taken over. Now James was sitting in the armchair beside the kitchen window fuming over what he felt was an act of great cowardice.

"Thank God for Strachan up there at York. If he hadn't taken over and negotiated with the enemy, it would have been even worse. Imagine an Anglican preacher having to take charge instead of the military."

"The poor people," Laura said as she thought of the looting.

"The Reverend Doctor blames the plundering on our own leader, Sheaffe. When the fleeing British army blew up the York Magazine, a huge boulder killed several Americans and their leader, General Pike, just as he was moving in to take York. The American soldiers were furious at the loss and spent their anger against the people and property of York."

"Please don't concern yourself with it, James. Nothing can be done now."

"Strachan's right, Laura. He's right. This country will be ruined by Sheaffe's defensive warfare. We need another Brock with the courage to lead his men. His offensive tactics worked. Sheaffe will not only bring us defeat. He'll make us a laughingstock while he's at it."

Laura was not sure who was right, but she was certain that James' irritation wasn't doing him any good. His shoulder wound had healed, but he was still unable to put his full weight on the leg with the wounded knee. Even after the long winter, it had not healed. In fact, just lately the wound seemed to have become more infected, and James spent most of his time in their room, with his leg stretched out on a fat feather pillow. The throbbing pain was unbearable when he stood.

Laura helped James back up to his room and had just returned to the kitchen when she heard a heavy pounding on the front door. She set down the bread pans she was bringing out and reached for a cloth to wipe her hands. Who would be passing by so early in the morning?

She pulled open the door and stood in surprise as three grey-coated American soldiers stared at her. Word had come to Queenston that the American forces were moving around the western tip of Lake Ontario to Burlington Bay and towards Newark, but she had not expected to see enemy soldiers at Queenston. Perhaps these were advance scouts.

"May we have water and food, Missus?" one of the soldiers asked politely.

She noticed how boyish their faces looked. They reminded Laura of her brother Charles. "Yes," she replied.

They were armed and she knew she had to do as they said. She prayed that James would not call out for her. They might become alarmed if they heard a man's voice and shoot her husband before they realized how weak he was. And if she volunteered to tell them about him, would they believe her or would they think it was a trick?

They followed her directly into the kitchen. Laura was surprised to see them take their shakos from their heads and put them on the hall table as they passed through. Then the three young soldiers sat down quietly on the bench beside the kitchen table as she laid out dishes for their meal. She noticed that they were looking around the room with admiration. One nudged the other and pointed to her glassed-in cabinet in the corner. Most of the good dishes displayed there had come from Great Barrington and had belonged to her mother before her. She took in a deep breath as she watched them and her anger grew. Yet she said nothing.

"I must go out to the cellar to get meat," she said quietly. She hoped they would not follow to see where she kept their food supply, so she added, "You might like to sit in the parlour while you wait."

They nodded and followed her as she led them into her best room. They smiled with satisfaction and two of them slumped down on the sofa while the third sat in the large chair nearer the warmth of the fireplace. As he leaned back in comfort, he stretched out his long legs until they nearly reached the hearth.

"Reminds me of home," he said to the other two.

Seeing them quietly settled, Laura ran out the back door to Bob and Fan, who were working at the large oven in the bakehouse. She told them about the soldiers and gave instructions for the meal.

Laura saw Charlotte and her other children returning from the store. "Go back to our store," she said, after explaining what had happened.

"Shall I take Charles with us?" Charlotte asked.

"No, Charlotte, he'll be fine with me. You run along now. Go to the other side of the shed and don't pass where they can see you from the parlour window." Charlotte was now a beautiful girl of fifteen with curly dark hair. She looked very much like her cousin Phoebe.

Laura took the fresh coffee pot from the hearth, put it on a tray with three cups, and took the tray in to the men in the front room.

"Your meal will be ready soon," she told them."Thank you, Missus," they said.

"You'd think I'd invited them to dinner," Laura grumbled to herself.

She shut the door behind her as she came out of the parlour, then silently went up the stairs and across to James' room. She held her finger to her lips, and James, alerted by her pale countenance, knew that all was not well. She quickly whispered into his ear and left.

She brought a fresh apron down from the linen cupboard in case the men had seen her and wondered why she had gone upstairs. To her relief the door to the parlour was still closed. They had probably not noticed anything.

She had not been in her kitchen long when Bob and Fan came in with the steaming food. They had prepared fresh creamed potatoes and carrots, and pork fried in maple syrup. Some apple pies were baking now, to be ready by the time the Americans finished their first course. Bob and Fan set the serving dishes on the table and went back out to the bakehouse.

Laura took out some of her best dishes. Perhaps if she treated the soldiers well, they would leave her house without taking anything. She could not forget the stories she had heard of the plundering of York even after a peace treaty was signed. The American officers had not been able to control their men, or had pretended they were not able.

The three young soldiers ate as though they hadn't had a good meal in weeks. When Fan came in with steaming apple pies, Laura added a large chunk of cheese to each plate.

"It's just like Ma's pie," the youngest one said when he ate his first bite. He smiled openly at Laura. "I'll be glad, Missus, when this is all over and we can go back home."

"Not me," his older friend said. "When we come for good to this country, we'll divide the land, and I'll take this here for my share." He looked around the room and rested his eyes on Laura's built-in china cabinet.

Suddenly unable to contain her outrage, Laura burst out, "You scoundrel, all you'll ever get here will be six feet of earth."

They were silent after that. She was no longer the hostess and they her guests. They were the enemy. The soldiers looked at Laura suspiciously as they finished their last few mouthfuls of pie and left without losing any time.

As Laura watched them go, she regretted her outburst. "I was wrong to be so vindictive. They were mostly polite and took nothing from me except food, which I would gladly give to any hungry strangers. I had no right to speak to them the way I did, even if they were enemy scouts." Laura was not sure that they really were scouts, and she could not leave James to find out.

She heard soon enough. A few days later, on May 27, 1813, the Americans attacked and took Newark, so those soldiers must have been advance scouts. Her brother Charles had been at Newark with the Provincial Dragoons, trying to defend the town. It had been a bloody battle, with heavy losses on both sides. The British were outnumbered four to one.

Two days after news of the battle reached her, Laura had gone to St. David's to see if Charles' fiancee, Elizabeth, or her mother, Hannah, had received any word from Charles. She was surprised to find Charles there himself. He had been injured and was resting in one of the bedrooms upstairs. He described the slaughter to Laura. "In one plot of land no wider than fifteen feet and no longer than two hundred yards, there were at least four hundred wounded and dead men. If my friend William had not seen me lying there and dragged me to safety and taken me on the back of his horse, I'd have died."

"Rest now, Charles," Laura had said.

Glassy-eyed with fever, Charles insisted on continuing. "Brigadier-General Vincent. . . ."

"Who's he?"

"The commander of the Centre Division. He ordered us out. He said the fort was lost. He ordered the magazine blown up and started us on the road to Queenston. Then he directed us across by St. David's. William brought me right here to the Secords. I'd never have made it on my own."

Elizabeth walked into the room with a bowl of water and clean towels.

"I know you'll take good care of him," Laura said to Charles' frail fiancee, who looked almost as pale as Charles.

"He'll be fine," Elizabeth said for Charles' sake as she tried to smile.

*****

Although the doctor had not been able to take the bullet out of her husband's knee, his salves had been helping the wound lately, and James had been able to sit for a short time each day. Laura hurried home because he would be ready to get up now, and she wanted to tell him the news about Newark before someone else did. She hoped it would not set him back again.

When she came to her backyard, Laura noticed two horses tied by the fence. She hurried towards her house wondering who had come for a meal this time.

From the hallway, Laura could hear the voice of the young enemy soldier who had liked her apple pie.

"So they've come back to claim 'this here' property," she thought.

Passing through the hall, Laura saw two shakos on the hall table. In the kitchen, Fan was rushing around preparing food.

As Laura approached the soldiers, she controlled her feelings and greeted them as if they had just come by on a visit. "So . . . you've come back for more of that pie like your ma's," she said to the younger one.

He smiled and said a bit bashfully, "Thank you, Missus. We'd like that."

They were sitting on the bench beside the table.

"And where's your other friend? There were three of you last time?"

The young soldier looked down. "You were right about the six feet of earth, Missus."

The third man had been killed at Newark.

TWENTY-SIX

"I've come for some of your baking, Missus," the old woman said in a squeaky voice that did not seem quite real. Laura stared at the large, bent figure standing at her kitchen door. A close-knit woolen shawl covered her head and crossed over her short-gown. The front of a beribboned mob cap poked out over her forehead. Her heavy petticoats hung well over her shoes as she waited on the back stoop, holding her empty round basket.

Laura did not hesitate to welcome her, for she had never forgotten her outburst against the three young American soldiers. When she learned that the youngest soldier had been killed as well as the oldest one, she had felt even deeper regret for the harsh words she had spoken. She had had no real wish to see them killed. She only wanted them called home, and peace again at Queenston.

Never again did she give food grudgingly to a soldier. "Love your enemies, do good to them that hate you . . ." she remembered. Now she kept food prepared and ready to serve to anyone who passed her way. Most often it was the enemy. Praise for Laura Secord's apple pie and candied maple sugar spread through the lines as more and more American soldiers received her hospitality. So Laura was not surprised to see this woman at her door.

"What would you like?" Laura said in a pleasant voice. The coarse-featured old lady shifted from one foot to the other. It was late at night and Laura could see that she was tired. James and the children were already in bed and the servants, Bob and Fan, had retired to their quarters.

"I'd pay for a bite to eat, Missus," the woman continued in a squeaky voice. The woman looked down and shifted uncomfortably again.

Laura looked sadly at the bent figure and said, "Come in, please. If you wish, you may rest in the kitchen while I prepare you a bite." The woman stepped forward and hurried inside.

She sat down heavily in the rocking chair by the window, and Laura began to warm potatoes and cook eggs in an iron frying pan over a low fire in the hearth. This war had made her unduly suspicious, she decided, for she couldn't help wondering about the old woman. Why was she far from home? In these times, local women did not travel far.

When Laura turned from stirring her potatoes, the woman said, "Do you have extra butter? I supply butter regularly to the troops stationed out of town, and I have none left."

"And where is your home?" Laura asked.

"Eh?" the woman asked. She cupped one hand around her ear as she looked up at Laura.

"Your home? Where are you from?"

"Near Stoney Creek. Have you any butter for sale?"

"I'll get a few bowlsful from the fruit cellar later. . . . You are a long way from home."

Laura hurried about the room. Well, at least the woman had offered to pay. She sighed as she took a tin plate from the cupboard and placed it on the table. With a long wooden ladle, she pushed the hot potatoes and eggs onto the large plate. She was just about to tell the woman to sit at the table when she noticed her at the other side of the room, peering into the china cabinet.

"Your food is ready," Laura said a little crisply.

The woman turned around quickly then, but spoke in the same shaky voice. "You must have brought these dishes from the old country." She slid along the bench seat beside the table. Her long unfashionable petticoats dragged along the floor.

"No, they came from Great Barrington, Massachusetts," said Laura. "They were my mother's."

The woman suddenly choked on the huge mouthful she had just scooped up, and Laura rushed over to a pail on the bake table. She dipped out a cup of water and handed it to her.

"Here," she said. "This may help. You needn't hurry. Take your time eating." She was beginning to feel sorry for the woman.

Laura bent over the fireplace to cover the coals with ashes, for it was a warm day in late May and she hoped the fire would not heat the rest of the house. In this position squatting over the hearth, she glimpsed across at the woman, who was still clearing her throat.

Beneath the table, her feet were spread wide apart and her boots were not a woman's. She knew that sometimes women wore their husband's boots, but these boots were different; they were military boots. A British soldier would not try to hide his identity, and neither would an American soldier. A cold chill gripped her as she realized he must be a scavenger. He could well be more dangerous than the enemy, but she knew she must feed him anyway. She stayed crouched there, poking the ashes and trying to compose herself. She must go along with his disguise for now, and then figure out a way to lure him outside, give him the butter, and then hurry back inside and lock the door. Maybe she would come to no harm. She slowly straightened up and turned towards the table.

His plate was empty. "Let's go out for the butter now," she said quietly, but her hand shook a little as she picked up the plate from the table, and it slid suddenly from her hand and hit the floor with a clatter. She bent over quickly to pick it up, but her hand still shook as she felt the eyes of this person close upon her.

"Don't be afraid, Laura Ingersoll," said a low, smooth voice.

Laura turned and stared at the figure before her. She had not been called Laura Ingersoll for years now. Who was this person? "I was Laura Ingersoll before I married. My husband is James Secord, a sergeant with the first Lincoln Militia."

"Laura . . . I'm Red," the man said in a strong masculine voice, pulling the heavy grey wig from his head and letting a shock of thick red hair fall over his forehead.

Laura stared in disbelief. The man's unruly hair was standing on end, just as it had when she had first met him, and his face, though fuller now, had broken into that lopsided smile she could never forget. It truly was Red.

"Red!" she shouted and rushed over to him, but hesitated and dropped her arms without throwing them around him.

Still smiling, he said in a low voice, "Be quiet, Laura. I'm on the run again." He grabbed the wig from the table and pulled it back over his head. "But tell me about yourself."

"First, I'll get you some of my apple pie," she said, cutting him a huge wedge.

"Thank you," he said. "Now tell me."

"Well, we came to Upper Canada in 1795," said Laura, taking a chair by the window. "Father ran the tavern at Queenston at first. Then he set up farming out at the La Tranche River."

Red was eating the pie slowly as she talked. "He must be torn by this war."

"Yes, he would have been, for Mira and her husband and family are in the States, but he died just as it began. He never knew."

"And Sally?"

"She's at Port Credit, running the inn there. They lost the farm." She swallowed as she thought about her father. Then she looked up at Red and asked, "And you, Red. Why didn't you ever write? I waited and waited for you to write."

"I did. I wrote to the Judge and I wrote to you too."

"There was no return address on your letter to the Judge, and I never received any letters."

"I didn't write you at the same time as I wrote to the Judge. But I wrote you not long afterwards. My letter must have been lost. Then I wrote again a few years after that. I guess you'd moved to Canada by then. I never forgot you, Laura, but I gave up hope of ever seeing you again." His voice was deep with emotion as he stared at her now, and his fork lay still beside his plate.

He was a handsome man, she thought, probably a few years younger than James—more her age. He adjusted his wig with one hand, and his pale green eyes swept softly across her face. She had forgotten that she had removed her mob cap in the evening heat before he had come, and her shining, brown hair hung down long now across her back and shoulders. He silently admired her as she sat there by the window with the evening shadows falling across her face.

They sat in silence for a few minutes as though the years had not passed between them. Finally he stood and walked over to her. He took her hand in both of his and said simply, "Thank you again, Laura."

She looked up into his handsome face and remembered the boy she had cared so much about and had waited and waited to hear from.

"Mama!" It was Charles, crying out in his sleep.

Laura came back to the present with a start and pulled her hand free. The child did not call out again. Then she looked back at Red still standing there and started to wonder. Here was Red—running again. And why? There could be only one reason. He must be deserting. Why else would he be in such a disguise and wearing soldier's boots? "And you, Red," she asked. "Where are you going?" Then, in a lower voice, "I mean, who or what are you running from this time?" But there was no sting in her tone.

"I'm sorry. I can't explain." He sounded embarrassed.

She knew he was hiding from someone, or he would not be dressed as he was. Suddenly her feelings changed and she said, "There was some excuse then, but now you're a man. What justifies your running now?"

His voice became guarded. "You're right," he said. "And I must go. May I buy the butter?" He grabbed up his large basket and handed it to her. She knew he wanted it for a cover, as it was not unusual for peddlers to go through a camp of soldiers, selling their goods. This way he would pass undetected.

"I'll fill it from the cold cellar." She walked briskly to the door.

In about five minutes, she was back, and he was sitting on the back stoop. She handed him the basket filled with wooden bowls of butter, packed in ice chips and sawdust.

He put a handful of money in her hand, but she did not even look at it as she saw him go out the door. For some reason, he had irritated her. Perhaps it was his irresponsibility. It seemed he would never grow up.

Then her heart softened as she thought of the poor shivering boy back on the road to Great Barrington. "God go with you," she called out gently.

He turned then and smiled, "We'll meet again, Laura. I will come back to see you."

She smiled sadly at Red, limping like an old woman as he went along the road to St. David's. She was quite sure she would never see him again.

TWENTY-SEVEN

The sultry summer days grew longer and hotter as the war that was to have ended so quickly dragged on into its twelfth month. The Americans controlled a large part of the Niagara Peninsula. Sheaffe had been recalled to England, and Brigadier-General John Vincent, commander of Britain's Centre Division, had withdrawn to Burlington Heights and disbanded the local volunteers. With three thousand American soldiers to seven hundred Canadian, the outcome of the war appeared to be inevitable. In the northern part of the Niagara Peninsula, the only local men still fighting were the cavalry of Captain William Hamilton Merritt.

Only one leader, an Irishman named James FitzGibbon, still dared to inhabit the lower region of the Peninsula. He had been an officer under Brock and had learned from him and admired his war strategy. His small, trained band, known to the Americans as the Bloody Boys, made lightning-speed skirmishes against the enemy. They travelled from place to place, signalling each other with cow bells.

*****

The evening of June 21, 1813, Laura was helping James up the stairs to bed. That afternoon the temperature had reached 98 degrees, and it was so hot on the second floor that James had spent the afternoon lying on the sofa in the parlour. His wound was still inflamed and gave him a lot of pain when he tried to stand on it. She noticed his weight on her shoulder more than usual this night. The heat was taking its toll.

They had barely reached the top of the stairs when Laura heard loud knocking at the front door. Wearily, she realized that it would probably be enemy soldiers looking for food. They must be newcomers too. Soldiers who had been here before came to the back door that led to the kitchen.

The knocking had become louder, and she could hear sounds of shouting and jeering. This was a rougher bunch than usual. But she could not lock them out. "Dear God, protect us," she prayed as she led James into their room, then raced back down the stairs.

With a trembling hand, she opened the door and looked up at a tall man with a long face and a large nose. His piercing blue eyes stared at her coldly as he gave orders to his men. "Search the place."

Laura spoke out firmly and pleasantly, "I'll be glad to show you about. My wounded husband has been given permission by the American officers to stay at home, and my young children have gone to bed for the night."

Their leader nodded to two of his men, indicating that they should go with him, and they followed Laura up the stairs. Laura could hear the other men searching the yard and the rooms below.

When Laura and the men returned to the main floor, she opened the door to the parlour and said, "I'll prepare you a meal quickly while you wait in here if you wish."

Their leader agreed and his men entered. He stayed in the hallway, looking out the window.

"I'm going to the bakehouse to call my servants to help," she explained as she went outside. He followed not far behind, and when he saw only the two black servants, he returned to the back stoop.

Bob and Fan had already prepared most of the meal. Laura now kept partially cooked food in her deep cellar so that the preparation would not take long. She was thankful that they had the fireplace and pit in the bakehouse. A fire inside tonight would have made the upstairs unbearable for sleeping.

In about twenty minutes, the meal was ready and Laura brought the serving dishes into the kitchen. She set the table and called the rough men in from the parlour. They slid eagerly along the benches on either side of the table. Laura had opened both the front and back windows, and just as they were ready to eat, a pleasant breeze blew through the room and across the table.

They didn't notice. They helped themselves to huge portions and started eating right away, not like most of the other soldiers, who had waited until they were served. Their total concentration on their eating had one advantage, though. It gave Laura a chance to tiptoe up the stairs to check on her family.

The girls were not yet asleep, and she tried to reassure them with a smile. Then she looked in on James. He motioned her over to him, and as she bent her head toward him, he whispered, "It's that bastard Chapin and his turncoat partisans." She nodded and stepped back out into the hall. She dared not stay longer, lest she arouse suspicion. Trembling, she held the stair railing for a few seconds before she returned to the kitchen.

Laura set her last three pies on the table in front of the leader. Without thanks, he grabbed one, helped himself to a large piece, and passed the rest on to his men, who had already eaten plenty. They hardly noticed her as they continued to eat and talk.

Laura went out the back door and sat on the stoop, where it was a little cooler. She could hear the conversation of the men inside coming out through the kitchen window.

"That green sliver is getting too bold, Doctor. The men sure didn't expect to run into him at Deffield's Inn today," a voice said. Before the war, Chapin had been a surgeon in Fort Erie and later Buffalo.

"I'd think the two of them could have beat him up at least, even if they didn't capture him," Chapin replied.

"He took them by surprise, Doctor."

"Taking a man by surprise is his style, and I plan to do something about it."

"Do you think Boerstler will take your advice, sir?" another voice asked.

"Of course, he will. He'd be a fool not to," Chapin bragged. "Now's our chance to get rid of that green sliver and his Bloody Boys. Boerstler will listen to me."

"So, Captain, we attack the day after tomorrow?"

"Yes, we'll combine forces with all Boerstler's troops at Fort George and march down on the last foothold in the Niagara Peninsula. When he's wiped out, Upper Canada is ours!"

"He's a tough one though. It may not be easy."

"He doesn't have nearly as many men as we do. Besides, we'll take him by surprise."

Laura sat frozen to the stoop. What if they came out and saw her sitting there? Surely they must know she was about. Perhaps it did not matter. What good could hearing them do her? She was behind enemy lines and it would be impossible for her to take the news to FitzGibbon.

Laura walked quietly to the well and sat on the far side of the low stone wall around the well opening. From there she could hear voices and guffaws but could not distinguish words. The front door slammed. She had taken the bucket from the well and set it on the low foundation wall when she heard footsteps coming toward her. Turning around, she saw Chapin and his men standing beside her. She gulped down her fear and handed Chapin the dipper. To her relief, all he did was take a drink and offer his men the same. Then the churlish crew went on their way. Laura breathed a prayer of thanks as she went back into the house and walked upstairs to see James. They had not ransacked her home, as had happened twice before, and they had not harmed her family.

Laura could see the relief in James' face when she told him the guerrillas were gone. Before she could say a word about what she had overheard, Charles cried out in his sleep. The heat was making him restless. She went to the cradle and wiped Charles' face with a cool cloth, her mind racing. Lieutenant FitzGibbon should be warned. He must not be taken by surprise. As it was, he would be far outnumbered by Boerstler's troops. She needed to talk to James.

When Laura finally turned back to her husband, she knew his pain was bad tonight. His dark head lay still against the pillow, his face was pale and his eyes intense. As usual, he did not complain, but he was obviously in no condition to talk. She had to tell him though, and she did, recounting all the details she had heard.

"We can't be sure there even will be an attack," James whispered. "Chapin is known to be a braggart. He has no real power. Boerstler may well not listen to his suggestion. You've probably," he grunted in pain, "only heard the ravings of a man impressed . . . with his own importance."

"Still, I wish your brother David or someone else would happen along so I could tell them."

"That won't happen now. All our men have been evacuated. There's no point in their risking coming into enemy territory."

"I also heard Chapin and his men talking about a run-in two of their men had with FitzGibbon just today. It seems he beat them up at Deffield's Inn singlehandedly. As far as I could tell, Chapin has a personal grudge against FitzGibbon."

"Ah . . . " James frowned. "And if he does persuade Boerstler, all of Upper Canada is in danger. FitzGibbon and his men are the only soldiers left inland in the southern part of the Peninsula. They've set up now at De Cew's house at Beaver Dams. The rumour is that De Haren's men to the north and Bisshopp's, stationed even farther north on the southern shore of Lake Ontario, are outnumbered by the enemy. If they take FitzGibbon, they've got the Peninsula and they may soon have Upper Canada!"

"James, somebody ought to tell Lieutenant FitzGibbon they are coming."

"Well, if I crawled on my hands and knees, I could not get there in time."

"Well, suppose I go?"

"You go? With the country in so disturbed a state? I doubt a man could get through, let alone a woman."

"You forget, James, that God will take care of me."

James was silent then for some time before he finally said to her, "We can pray to know what to do."

*****

Half an hour later Laura slipped out of the room and down to the kitchen to set the table for the next day's breakfast so that all might go smoothly if she was not there.

She thought of her children and her husband who needed her. Did she really have a choice? How could she risk going to carry her message to FitzGibbon?

TWENTY-EIGHT

In the darkness, Laura lay still against James' shoulder, battling with her decision. When dawn came, she had made her choice. She knew that she must go. She sat up quietly on the edge of the bed, but James woke up and reached out to her. Wondering how to tell him her decision, she turned and grasped his hand and squeezed it.

But he knew. "God go with you, Laura," he whispered.

In a moment, she had pushed her feet into her shoes and slipped into an ankle-length petticoat and yellow-flowered short overgown.

Laura felt refreshed from her short but sound sleep. A cool, light breeze blew in through the window. Before she left the room, she pulled the cradle nearer to the bed so her husband could rock the baby if he awakened. Just then, Charles did wake up and cried in the darkness. She stopped to push back the damp curls from the child's forehead and stroked his temples until she felt him relax into a quiet sleep. She hoped it would be a cooler day for the baby. It might be—a light, cool breeze blew in from the window.

Down in the kitchen, she hastily ate the bread and cheese she had set out the evening before, not knowing when she would be eating again. Taking a lunch would certainly arouse suspicion if she were stopped by a sentry.

As she slipped out into the darkness, she prepared herself to answer any guard or scout who might question her. There was a possibility she might meet one; neighbours had reported seeing enemy scouts from Fort George in the area lately. She hurried along toward the cowpath that led to St. David's, a route that was used less frequently than the main road. From St. David's, she would go through the Black Swamp, where she knew she would not need to fear the patrols, for they would not risk encountering dangerous rattlesnakes and the quicksand in the swamp. She trembled at the thought. It would take long hours to get through the swamp and walk along the trail to Twelve Mile Creek. From there she would still have to find her way to the lieutenant.

"Halt!" a man shouted as she jumped down from the rail fence onto the cow trail. "Where do you think you're going?"

She turned slowly to face him. In the half-light, she could not tell if he was one of Chapin's guerrillas or an enemy scout from Fort George. She did not hesitate to answer. "I'm going to visit my brother, Charles Ingersoll, wounded and sick at the home of Mrs. Stephen Secord, a widow in St. David's."

"Why are you leaving so early? The sun is just rising."

"It's cooler now. I've found the heat so tiring lately, I could faint along the way if I waited until the heat of the day. I've come this way across the fields through the shade trees, This path is cooler than the main road to St. David's."

The guard walked closer and scrutinized her carefully. No doubt the pale, thin woman really did need to travel in the fresh morning air. He believed her story because he knew of her brother in St. David's and the other wounded men who had been allowed to stay in the area. He nodded her on.

The light was increasing now as she hurried ahead, and she could see a farm woman with her dog rounding up some cows for the morning milking.

By about 6:00 a.m. when Laura reached her sister-in-law's home in St. David's, the sun had risen. She rapped lightly on the back door. A startled Hannah Secord opened it to see Laura standing on her back stoop. Her surprise soon turned to alarm as she said, "Whatever is it, Laura? What is the matter? Is it James?"

"No . . . the family is well."

"Come in, come in. . . . Now, what is it?" she asked as Laura sat down in the nearest chair. No one else was in the room, but still Laura put her finger to her lips to show the need for secrecy.

Instantly Hannah knew her message concerned the war. In these times, walls were sometimes too thin. In the Peninsula, where there was such a mixture of people, Loyalists and American settlers, one just couldn't be certain who was loyal to whom.

"May I see my brother?" Laura asked. "I have come before the heat gets too unbearable."

"By all means, Laura, but first come with me for a bite of

breakfast." Inside the kitchen, Hannah closed the door and fastened the windows tightly.

Charles' fiancee, Elizabeth, stood by the table, setting the dishes for the morning meal. She turned in surprise when Laura came into the room. "Oh, Laura . . . have you come to see Charles? He is improving." She recovered herself. "It's slow, but he is a little better."

"I'm grateful for your care and devotion, Elizabeth."

Elizabeth blushed and turned away. She went to the cupboard for bread and butter to set before Laura.

"Now, Laura, you may speak," Hannah whispered.

Laura quickly explained about Chapin's plan of attack on FitzGibbon.

"My dear, you are attempting the impossible. The road from St. David's to Beaver Dams is regularly patrolled by enemy scouts. You would not be allowed to pass through. It's simply an impossible task."

"But I don't need to go by that road. I'll travel west and a little north across country from here to Shipman's Corners. That'll take me through the Great Black Swamp. No soldier will be looking for anyone there."

"What are you saying, Laura? You can't go through that swamp. If you do avoid the quicksand, you may very well be bitten by a rattlesnake."

"I have to get this message to them. James can't go, and I can't think of anyone else who can. I feel certain that God has let me hear this message. I must go. He will direct me through the swamp and beyond."

"Oh, Laura. I'm afraid for you."

"I'm going with you," Elizabeth volunteered. "If we come to quicksand, I can help. We'll walk a piece apart and if one of us is sucked in, the other will be able to help. That swamp is just too dangerous for anyone alone."

"It's too dangerous for anyone at all," Hannah mumbled. "You're too frail to attempt it, Elizabeth."

"May I go with you, Laura?"

"You and Hannah decide. But while you're thinking about it, can you take me up to see Charles, Elizabeth? I'd like to see him for a minute. Is he awake?"

As they went up the stairs, they knew he was awake, for they could hear low groaning. The sound stopped when they entered the room.

Charles was sitting on the edge of the bed, but he slumped back onto the pillows as they came over to him. Perspiration stood out on his face.

"Oh, Charles!" said Laura.

"It only hurts when I move, but I can't go on lying here when my dragoons need me. I must be ready soon to return to the troop."

"The fever comes back when he moves around much," Elizabeth explained.

"I won't stay long, Charles. I just came to check on you before the day was too hot."

Laura squeezed her brother's hand. They did not talk long, for Charles was obviously in great pain, and Laura was able to excuse herself soon without arousing his suspicion. She did not want him to carry the burden of her day. She left the room quickly, with Elizabeth close behind.

When they reached the lower hall, Elizabeth said, "I'm going with you as far as Shipman's Corners. I must tell Mother."

Laura slowly started away from the house and down the lane, but Elizabeth caught up to her before she reached the road. There they turned and waved to Hannah, who stood in the doorway.

They scanned the horizon for any sign of an approaching horse or man. All was still as they reached the edge of the swamp. Laura tried to appear confident so the fear would leave Elizabeth's eyes. But she found that difficult as they entered into the dense undergrowth of the woods.

Elizabeth tried to smile. "It's best we walk apart."

"Yes, in case of quicksand. I think we should each get a sturdy stick to feel ahead of us," Laura advised. She thought of another use for the sticks but she didn't mention that. The sticks would help fight wild animals or snakes.

Armed with an old branch, Laura led the way through the thick brush and undergrowth. Neither of them spoke. They were using all their energy to push ahead. The branches caught and tore at their petticoats as they fought their way through them. They kept swatting at mosquitoes and horse flies that were coming for them in swarms.

Suddenly Laura felt one foot sinking. Slowly and steadily, she pulled back while she leaned on her other leg and her stick. She gradually drew her foot from the mud, but her shoe was gone. When Elizabeth came up close behind her and saw Laura's shoe was lost, she offered one of hers. "No, I can't take it," Laura said.

"I'm only going to Shipman's Corners. You have to last much longer. Take it. You have to get through," Elizabeth replied more forcefully.

Reluctantly, Laura accepted the shoe. It was too tight but it protected her foot well. They went on ahead. As they came to a thicket of thorny bushes, Elizabeth bravely kept from crying out as she stepped on a sharp stone.

Eventually the ground below them seemed less swampy. "I think it's not far now," Laura said. They could see some huge rocks ahead, the ideal spot for a rattlesnake. They moved slowly, looking and listening for rattlers.

They had just passed the rocky outcropping when Elizabeth declared, "I'm sorry. I have to rest." She lowered herself to a small rock at the side of the path.

As Laura turned back to her, she saw that her foot was bleeding where she had cut it on the stone. "I'll not wear this any longer," Laura said, and put the shoe in Elizabeth's hand. The younger woman hesitated at first and then accepted it.

"We must continue on," encouraged Laura, "if I'm to reach De Cew's by tonight."

It was then that they heard the distinct sound of a rattler about to strike. They froze like statues.

Laura had no time to put words to her prayer. She instinctively held her breath as she waited. Then they heard a slithering in the bushes, and other sounds became stronger. Laura knew they had been saved from the disaster. Shaken, but strengthened in her resolve to complete the mission, she turned to the terrified Elizabeth.

"I can't . . . go . . . farther. I can't . . ." Elizabeth said with a scarcely audible sob.

"We're almost there, Elizabeth. Look through the branches and trees. I can see clear sky . . . a blue patch . . . the end of the swamp."

"Well, there's no sound now," Elizabeth responded. "I guess it's better to go on."

In no time they were in the light again and out of the dangers in the swamp. Then the full heat of the windless late June day hit them, and their eyes stung with pain. Elizabeth staggered at first as she adjusted to the light and the intensity of the heat. Laura put out her hand and steadied her. Sweating heavily, they reached the main road that led to Shipman's Corners.

As the houses of the little settlement came into view, Laura said, "I'm going south now."

"No, Laura. Come with me," Elizabeth pleaded. "It's too far and too dangerous. You'll never make it."

"No, Elizabeth, I'm going on," Laura replied.

Elizabeth turned north to Shipman's Corners, and Laura took the road to the south.

TWENTY-NINE

Twelve Mile Creek didn't usually flow this fast in the month of June, but that night it raced to the lake with the speed of a small river. The spring rains had turned it into a torrent of rough waves that swirled out toward the banks and jackknifed back into the main current. Even the tree-trunk bridge that lay across the creek was completely under water in three places. Laura was struggling over it, half-stumbling, half-crawling in the darkening dusk. Her cap had been torn off by an overhanging branch, and her thick brown hair now hung down in wet strings and lay flat against her back. She knew if she made it about two-thirds of the way, she could wade the remaining distance to the shore through the reeds that clustered up against the opposite bank.

About halfway across, a rush of water washed her shoe away and wrapped the hem of her petticoat around the stub of a branch. She tore the petticoat loose and pushed forward. Slowly, she scraped along the trunk, testing each hold. She knew that she must not falter now; the water was getting deeper. Inch by inch she drew nearer to the opposite bank.

Finally she reached the thick marsh reeds that swayed in a gentler current along the edge of the creek. She tightened her hold on the tree trunk and cast one leg down into the water until she could feel the mud oozing over the sides of her remaining shoe. Then she slipped off the trunk and started wading towards the bank, waist-deep in the swirling water. By now she was barefoot; her second shoe had refused to come out of the murky creek-bed.

As she parted the last bunch of reeds, the total fatigue she'd been labouring under for the last two hours enveloped her like a dark cloud. She dropped heavily onto the grassy bank and fell into a half-sleep.

Crickets chirped gently in the quiet darkness, but they could not blot out the memory of that rough vengeful voice. "Now's our chance to get rid of that green sliver and his Bloody Boys."

She was jolted awake by a rustling sound. Before she knew what she was doing, she jumped to her feet and stared ahead. A familiar choking smell assailed her. It was a skunk. Squinting through the darkness, she could see it sauntering up the hill in front of her. A false alarm, but it reminded her that she was putting herself in danger lying there in the open. And besides, she had to get the message through.

She struggled forward up the rough ground. It was painful without shoes, and she felt almost too weak to climb the steep hill ahead. She was thankful, though, that she knew the area well. Many times she and her husband and small children had picnicked here. Was it really only last summer that the children had chased each other along this hillside?

If she could just reach the top of the hill, she would only have to cross a couple of low, flat fields and one more hill. From there, on that second rise of land, she knew she would be able to see the house of the Lieutenant.

As she pushed her tired body up the hill, waves of doubt began to wash over her. There really was no reason for the Lieutenant to believe her message. Perhaps, as James had suggested, Chapin had only been bragging to his guerrillas. After all, her only evidence of the planned attack was a snippet of a conversation overheard through a window. FitzGibbon might just laugh at her or pity her, thinking she had become confused from the pressures of the war or the heat of the day. She could just imagine him saying, "Madam, I'm truly sorry; I'll be needin' hard facts." Laura put these thoughts out of her mind and kept going up the hill.

The night was darker now. A thin wash of moonlight was all that lit the way. Without slowing her pace, she reached ahead to part the tall grass and weeds. She flinched as she stepped on a sharp stone, but the throbbing of her foot was soon lost in the pain she felt all over her body. She had been running, stumbling, walking for sixteen hours, and it seemed that every muscle was screaming in pain. She did not even stop to check the new wound.

When she reached the top of the hill, she stopped abruptly,

trembling at an unexpected sight. There were clusters of tents and groups of men around campfires silhouetted against the sky.

At least a dozen men started to move towards her. As they came closer, she recognized the Mohawk leggings that some of them were wearing, but she could not guess the identity of the others. She wondered if they were on the side of the Lieutenant. Whoever they were, they were now moving swiftly in her direction. As they come closer, she saw that they were staring at her with cold eyes and moving in to surround her. The two on the right pointed at her and began shouting to each other in a language she did not understand. She gasped in fear, but even as that terrible feeling of weakness came over her, she knew she must show courage.

Marching directly to the one who appeared to be a chief, and pointing to the next hill, she said in a firm, sharp voice, "Lead me to Lieutenant FitzGibbon." She knew the Lieutenant and his men were camped in the direction she was pointing. Surely he would understand.

But the chief just stood and looked at her. She motioned and pointed to the chief, then to herself and then to the camp over the hill. Repeating all these motions and saying the Lieutenant's name over and over, she kept the chief's attention. Then she pointed to the distant northeast and shouted, "The enemy is coming!"

The chief studied her closely, and finally his brow relaxed a little and his eyes became softer. He nodded, then turned and spoke to his men, but they looked suspiciously at her and spoke to each other in low voices.

Her heart pounded. She found it harder than ever to control her fear, but she was too tired to run away. All she could do was stand and wait.

The chief finally indicated that she should go with him toward the Lieutenant's camp. He and two of his men strode along beside her. She walked briskly with pain in every step, fearing that the chief would change his mind before they got there. Her breath was coming in short gasps almost as if she were running again.

Laura had no idea how long it would take to reach the top of the last knoll. All she knew was that she could finally see the stone house where the Lieutenant was stationed. As soon as it was in sight, one of the Mohawks ran ahead. She could go no faster though. If she did, she would fall, and she knew that she must not fall now, so near the end of her journey.

The darkness seemed to close in on her when she finally reached the yard in front of the house. The Lieutenant, carrying a lantern, was coming out the front door and down the stone steps to meet them. She could not make out his features; her eyes were so blurred from fatigue.

She staggered as she reached him and gasped out her message. "I am the wife of Sergeant James Secord, who was wounded in active duty at the Battle of Queenston Heights."

Lieutenant FitzGibbon breathed in sharply and stared at her in disbelief. Then he recovered himself and stared at her with his cool green eyes .

Laura tried to focus on the face before her. It looked familiar somehow. "Since my husband is not able to travel, I have brought this message. The enemy under Colonel Boerstler and directed by Chapin's guerrillas plan a surprise attack tomorrow. They have a much larger force than you."

"Who told you this?"

She hesitated. Would the Lieutenant take seriously the gossip of Chapin and his men? Could she tell him that the wine she served may well have loosened their tongues? "My husband does not wish to reveal his source, but he says to tell you it is a reliable one."

"How could you possibly have come by the road from St. David's? Enemy scouts are patrolling all the way to Queenston along that route."

"I know. I came 'round by the Great Black Swamp and passed nearly to Shipman's Corners. Then I went south and across Twelve Mile Creek to the Mohawks' camp."

The Lieutenant's eyes narrowed with suspicion as he examined her wet, torn, blood-stained clothes, her scratched arms and legs, and her bleeding feet. "My God, Laura Ingersoll! If it's not Laura Ingersoll, I'll be . . . and you walked. My God, that's nineteen miles in this burning heat!"

How does he know my name? thought Laura, who was trembling with fatigue. She looked up at him but could not make out the face exactly. It was a blur, and so were the other faces around him. Then, for a short moment, everything came into focus.

It was Red. That was why he knew her name—Lieutenant James FitzGibbon was Red!

"Laura, I don't know how your husband got this information, but I believe you. You risked your life to get it here." Then, turning to one of his officers who had come up behind him, he commanded, "Here, Sam, help this lady up to the Turneys' house. She's about to faint. Move sharp now."

Red turned and walked briskly back to his headquarters. It was going to be a long night.

THIRTY

The first clank of cow bells sounded loudly in the morning air. Then four more rang out over the fields, one after the other, at even intervals.

"They've come," FitzGibbon announced to his men. It was 7:00 a.m. on the twenty-fourth of June. FitzGibbon and his force of forty-five men had been waiting since late in the evening of the twenty-second when Laura had brought them her message.

Lieutenant FitzGibbon did one more quick calculation of the resources available to him. He had sent word to Major De Haren, who was camped a couple of miles to the north. At most, though, he reckoned De Haren had no more than two hundred men. The opposing enemy force was made up of five hundred or more trained soldiers. Still, the warriors who were supporting him were even now hidden in the beech woods ready to harass the approaching force.

The warriors included the Caughnawagas from Quebec under Dominique Ducharme and the Grand River Mohawks led by the young John Brant. Brant was ably assisted by his second cousin, Captain William Johnson Kerr, and the tribe's adopted Scottish leader, John Norton. The Indians numbered well over two hundred, and he knew he could depend on them to complete their task, for they had proved their value and their loyalty many times in this war. And especially now, his situation would be hopeless without them.

The Lieutenant had instructed the Indians to employ their usual tactic, attacking the fringe of the enemy from their secure position in the woods nearby. But if face-to-face fighting followed, how long would they last? They were not accustomed to that kind of warfare.

At best, his circumstances were not good, even though he had received sufficient warning. If only De Haren's troops would arrive now, he might have a chance. Without them, he would be far outnumbered by the attacking Americans. Yet he would not back down without a fight. FitzGibbon shook off his dreary thoughts and hurried to a high point just to the right of the Mountain Road that came from St. David's to De Cew's.

The enemy, unaware their every move was being watched, moved steadily ahead. They had just completed a long march the day before in the oppressive heat. That night, as they slept in a nearby farmer's field, no light or fire was allowed since that would reveal their position to the residents of Queenston. Extra scouts and guards had gone ahead of them as they marched out of the field, to make sure no one could possibly surprise the advancing troops.

Lieutenant FitzGibbon walked to a high spot on the top of a hill and looked over the cornfield. Soldiers in grey uniforms led the way. Next came the Colonel on his horse, followed by what must be three hundred walking soldiers. Their dark blue shakos, blue coats and white breeches would make them easily recognized targets. Behind the infantry came their train of artillery, with horse teams pulling wagons of ammunition while other teams pulled large and small field guns. More companies followed, each one led by its officer. In the rear were two dozen cavalrymen. The harnesses on their horses and brass plates on their caps flashed in the light of the morning sun.

Through his field glass, FitzGibbon saw the advance guard return after they had reconnoitred the woods. The main body of troops then proceeded to enter the beech woods. They were only a few miles now from his camp. When would the Mohawks and Caughnawagas attack the enemy? Watching the troops disappear into the woods, he drew in his breath and waited for the sounds of battle.

Suddenly rifle shots and the piercing war cries of the warriors broke the silence of the morning. For a moment, relief swept over him.

Then he faced again the truth of his precarious position. What good were his forty-five soldiers and two hundred warriors against a trained enemy force of over five hundred regulars who had more ammunition and supplies? Reinforcements could well come to them from Fort George before his own help might arrive. De

Haren should have been here some time ago if he was really only two miles away, as he had thought.

If the Americans emerged on the west side of the beech woods, only two short miles would lie between them and his men. Even with severe losses to the enemy, the Bloody Boys would be far outnumbered. He swallowed as he thought of his loyal crew, men of the brave 49th Regiment with their scant numbers and meagre resources, fighting a well-supplied American army of five hundred. He could not let this happen.

When the enemy began to emerge from the far end of the woods, the Indians would lose ground. Only FitzGibbon's trained men could fight in the clearing, and those men would be swamped.

FitzGibbon's plan was too fantastic to dwell on for long. He moved speedily to the far end of the field, and reaching his men, he had his bugler sound the "cease fire." Almost to his own surprise, the Indian attackers immediately fell silent in the woods and their firing stopped.

Holding high a white handkerchief firmly tied to his sword, he rode forward at a measured pace from the west toward the beech woods. FitzGibbon kept riding ahead in silence, the white handkerchief fluttering weakly in the wind. There was not a single movement from the enemy side and he was getting dangerously close to their lines, where he would be completely vulnerable.

Finally he saw an enemy soldier coming towards him on a large white horse, holding another white flag. The horse cantered ahead at a controlled speed, then lightly pawed the ground when its master drew the reins in tightly to bring the steed to a stop.

"Good morning, sir," the officer said. "I am Roderick McDowell, First Regiment of Artillery, United States Army."

FitzGibbon put his bold plan into words. "My pleasure, sir. I am Lieutenant James FitzGibbon of His Majesty's Forty-ninth. I am instructed by Major De Harem to offer you the opportunity to surrender and avoid unnecessary bloodshed." The officer did not reply. "You are surrounded by a large force of British and cannot escape," FitzGibbon continued. "My Indian allies, incensed by their losses in this morning's battle, are ready to close in for a massacre. Only a fast surrender will ensure your safety."

"Thank you, Lieutenant. I shall relay Major De Haren's message to Colonel Boerstler," Captain McDowell replied. Nodding, he turned then and galloped back to his lines.

FitzGibbon waited patiently, but his thoughts were racing ahead. He was planning the reply he would make if the Colonel refused to surrender.

Just then, a British officer rode toward him from his own lines. "I'm Captain Hall from Chippawa. We heard firing and I've come with my twenty dragoons. We're at your service, Lieutenant."

"Thank you, Captain Hall. Please return to your lines, but I may call you back shortly. In the absence of Major De Haren, you will serve as the Major." Captain Hall looked puzzled. "Only in the eyes of the enemy," FitzGibbon told him and laughed loudly. Quite puzzled, Captain Hall nodded and returned to his men.

In a short time, Captain McDowell returned with his commander's message. "Colonel Boerstler says he is not in the habit of surrendering to an army he has never seen."

With an expression of confidence, FitzGibbon replied, "If that is his wish, I shall ask my superior officer if I may escort him to see our troops."

FitzGibbon abruptly pulled his horse's right rein, and the animal turned so suddenly its raised tail cut the air in a semi-circle. He galloped back to his men, went directly to Hall, and saluted him.

The amazed officer still did not realize what was happening. In a low voice, he stammered, "Lieutenant, I don't understand."

"Captain, you don't need to. But for the present just pretend you are my superior officer. I want the enemy to believe that. If all goes well, you will be no closer to them than you are now. Later, it won't matter anyway if they do know you aren't Major De Haren." As he spoke, FitzGibbon gestured with his hands and pointed to the enemy. He shook his head several times and pointed again.

Hall was becoming more confused. "It's all for effect," FitzGibbon said. "They may be watching."

Finally, he nodded his head and saluted Hall. Still holding his horse's reins, he mounted lightly and cantered back to the enemy.

Colonel Boerstler, the commander of the American forces, advanced slowly. Even though his horse was moving at an even speed, the officer grimaced with each shift in position. FitzGibbon looked at the grave-faced Colonel and sized him up. He was not a big man and he had a sallow, pale complexion. Then he looked down and saw that blood had hardened on the Colonel's uniform just above his saddle and down his leg. The Colonel sat with great discomfort on his horse.

FitzGibbon saluted the Colonel. "I am sorry, Sir," FitzGibbon said, "but Major De Haren refuses to put his troops on display for the enemy."

Weakened from his loss of blood, Boerstler hesitated, "We need time to decide. Ask Major De Haren to give us until sundown."

"Sundown!" shouted the agitated FitzGibbon. "No, Colonel Boerstler, we cannot give you the time you request. I can't promise you any more than five minutes, with my Indian allies chafing to avenge the death of their friends." FitzGibbon forced himself to speak more slowly. "I am aware that the Americans accuse us of stimulating the Indians to destroy you, whereas we have ever used our best endeavour, and almost always successfully, to protect you."

In extreme pain, Colonel Boerstler replied, "Can you in fact ensure the safety of my men?"

Heartened by his reply but reluctant to show it, FitzGibbon avowed, "I can only give you this assurance; the Indians must take my life before they shall attack you."

"Your assurance is sufficient!" Boerstler exclaimed and held out his hand to FitzGibbon.

With great reserve and considerable gravity, FitzGibbon took the officer's hand. He dared not look too jubilant.

Then, as he started to discuss the details for surrender, he noticed a horse galloping speedily toward him. To his amazement, the real Major De Haren was rapidly approaching, accompanied by his aide.

FitzGibbon turned then and rode back to meet him. After he had saluted, he quickly asked, "Do you have your troops?"

"No, Lieutenant," the Major replied, "they're miles away, but I'm here. I'll take over now."

"Sir, I already have control. They have surr. . . ."

As Major De Haren brushed by FitzGibbon to face the enemy with no knowledge of the negotiations underway, FitzGibbon groaned. Would all be lost now?

Inflamed, he turned and raced his horse to De Haren's side and said in a low, bold tone so only the Major could hear, "Not another word, sir; not another word; these men are my prisoners."

Before the Major had time to reply, FitzGibbon addressed him loudly so that the enemy could hear. "Shall I proceed to disarm the American troops?"

De Haren answered, "You have my permission."

As the American troops lined up before them, FitzGibbon watched De Haren, who was now beside Boerstler. Would De Haren say something that might give away the ruse? Then in a flash, he thought of a solution. He barked a command to the soldiers. "American troops, right face. Quick march." Boerstler nodded to his officers, and they repeated the command to the men. As the troops marched straight ahead, the two leaders had to move apart and were prevented from talking any more.

Now the Americans were approaching the wooded area where FitzGibbon's men were waiting, so the Lieutenant addressed De Haren, "Sir, shall the American troops ground their arms here?"

"No," he answered harshly. "Let them march through between our men and ground their arms on the other side."

FitzGibbon seethed inwardly. In his desire to humiliate the enemy by forcing them to lay down their arms before their conquerors, the British officer had forgotten one important fact. Would five hundred men lay down their arms when they saw they were facing a force of only forty-five? He thought not.

Lieutenant FitzGibbon drew a deep breath. "Sir, do you think it prudent to march them through with arms in their hands in the presence of the Indians?" he shouted to De Haren.

"For God's sake, sir, do what this officer bids you!" Colonel Boerstler shouted to De Haren.

"Do so," De Haren told him.

"Americans, halt! . . . Front! . . . Ground your arms!" FitzGibbon shouted. The command was passed on by the American officers.

They obeyed promptly. The Indians rushed out of the woods and headed straight for the soldiers. They had been promised the enemy's weapons in return for doing them no harm. A few American soldiers, terrorized as they watched the Indians approach, reached down for their muskets.

Instantly FitzGibbon's voice rang out, "Americans, don't touch your arms! Not a hair of your head shall be hurt. Remember, I am here."

Lieutenant FitzGibbon was starting to relax now. He knew he could rely on the word of the chiefs.

He turned to Colonel Boerstler, "Come with me," he commanded in a kindly, courteous tone. "I will take you to my headquarters at the De Cew house where you will receive care for your wounds."

THIRTY-ONE

Laura awakened from her sleep to the sound of guns. At first, startled by the realization that she was in strange surroundings, she swung her feet abruptly to the floor. Pain shot to her head. Gingerly, she started towards the door. Then she remembered where she was and sat down on the side of the bed.

She did recall reaching Lieutenant FitzGibbon with her message about the surprise attack, and she also remembered the officer bringing her here. A woman had opened the door for her and directed the officer to take Laura upstairs.

"I must have slept right off," she thought as she looked around the small, clean room. She remembered nothing about the room from the night before. Just past the two oak posts at the foot of her bed, the pale blue chintz curtains blew gently in the breeze. Nearer the door there was a small washstand with a jug and bowl, clean towels, and a dish of soft soap.

The gunfire started again as Laura headed for the door. She winced. Her feet were wrapped in strips of a white linen shift. The very windows rattled with the noise of battle.

"Hello," Laura called out at the top of the stairs.

She heard light steps below. A woman hurried up the straight, steep stairs toward her.

"Mrs. Secord, how are you?" she asked before she reached the top of the stairs.

"I'm quite well," Laura replied, "... although a little light-headed, I'm afraid."

"Just you go right back to bed," the woman said as she took her hand. "I'm Mary Turney. A soldier and my husband brought you here the night before last. You were worn right out."

Laura did not know the Turneys, but she recognized the name and knew the farm house where she had slept. "The night before last.... You mean, I've slept since then?"

"Yes, you have."

"And the fighting? Has it been going on all this time?"

"Oh, no. The fighting just got started. Lieutenant FitzGibbon sent men out to watch. They watched through all that night and yesterday and last night."

"So now they've come."

"I don't rightly know, but they must have, for there's shooting and all. It's no turkey shoot that's going on. I'm certain I heard cannons."

"Did British soldiers arrive in time to help?"

"Don't you worry yourself. Lieutenant FitzGibbon is taking care of it. His men have been planning for it ever since you came. You just sit right on your bed until I get back up here with some soup. That light head will be gone in no time."

Laura lay on the bed and thought of her meeting with FitzGibbon. At the time, she was sure he was really Red, but now she was beginning to doubt it. After all, she had been in a state of extreme exhaustion at the time and could easily have been confused. But whether FitzGibbon was really Red or not, the important thing was that she had delivered her message, and FitzGibbon, whoever he was, had acted on it.

Before long Mrs. Turney came back with a bowl of soup and a cup of steaming coffee and hurried back downstairs to her baby. As Laura sipped the hot coffee, her thoughts went back to Queenston.

She wondered how her family had fared as the American army marched through. Had her daughters and Fan and Bob been able to carry on in her absence? If she were missed by the scouts, would the authorities accept the explanation that she was visiting her brother in St. David's? Then as she took sips of the soup, she realized that the American soldiers would be too busy planning an attack to look for a missing wife and mother. Her family were fine, no doubt. The danger was possibly nearer at hand.

"You finished that soup yet?" Mrs. Turney called up to Laura.

"Yes, thank you."

"Can I bring you some more?"

"No, thank you."

Mrs. Turney climbed the steep stairs and puffed a little as she put down a pair of leather slippers for Laura. "You may need these when you feel like getting up. Here, let me help you with the bandages." She moved toward Laura.

"No. Thank you. I can do this myself."

"Well, if you're sure you can manage. . . . I should get back down to my kitchen work. But just you call if there's anything else you need." Mrs. Turney turned and left the room and walked heavily down the stairs.

Laura slowly unwrapped her bandaged feet. They were still swollen but not too painful now, and she was able to fit them into the slippers. For a minute, she lay back on the bed and tried to sleep. But she was too restless now. She needed to be doing something to take her mind off her family—and the battle being waged a few fields away. She felt her way down the narrow back stairs and then went on out to the kitchen.

"I'd like to help," she told Mrs. Turney, who was peeling potatoes at the sink.

"Now, that's not necessary. You just go back to bed."

"No, I'd really rather work. It'll pass the time."

* * * * *

At about four o'clock that afternoon, the firing stopped. Laura and Mrs. Turney sat silently in the kitchen, listening for the whoops of victorious Indians. If they heard these, they would know that the victory had gone to Upper Canada.

Finally, Mrs. Turney said, "We'd best be preparing some supper." She bustled over to the pantry and came out with the leftover potatoes and the iron spider frying pan, which she set on the bake table. "Here, you slice these, dear." She handed Laura a knife and went back to her pantry for more victuals.

Laura's hands trembled a little as she sliced the potatoes. She was straining to hear the sounds that did not come. She started chopping the sliced potatoes.

"We don't need those potatoes for mincemeat," Mrs. Turney said, then added more gently, "Thank you, dear. They'll do just fine."

Laura nodded as she looked down at the potatoes, all chopped into little bits.

It was nearly five when they heard the sound of someone running toward the house. Mrs. Turney whipped the door open, and her husband burst in.

"They've surrendered. The battle's over. And the Lieutenant wants to see Mrs. Secord before I take her home." It was then they heard the jubilant whoops of the victorious Mohawks and Caughnawagas.

* * * * *

The following afternoon, Red was sitting alone at his desk in the De Cew house when Laura entered. She had not been dreaming; it really was Red.

When the door closed behind the soldier who had shown her in, FitzGibbon reached out for Laura's hand and clasped it in both of his. "They surrendered without a battle," he declared. "And it's all because of you that we were ready for them. We would have lost without your warning. How can I thank you?"

She gave him a mischievous smile and said, "I always seem to be getting you out of tight spots, don't I?"

He laughed that merry boyish laugh that she remembered from so many years ago and motioned her to a chair by his desk. Pulling his own out from behind his desk, he sat close beside her.

She drew her swollen feet in under her chair and looked up to find him still staring at her. He seemed to be speechless.

"So FitzGibbon is your real name?" she asked, still nagged by lingering doubts.

"Yes, it's James FitzGibbon, but I couldn't tell you that when I visited your home, for I was going on a fishing expedition into the enemy camp to discover their strengths and resources."

"I understand that," she said, "but I do not understand the rest. What are you doing in Canada and how did you find your way into the British army?"

"Well, after I sailed back to Ireland, I ended up back home on Bantry Bay. I worked hard on my father's small farm and occasionally caught a salmon to help feed the family. Then when I was fifteen a French fleet invaded our area, and troops were sent in from England to protect us. The first regiment to appear in our village were the Devon and Cornwall Fencibles, who were billeted in our homes. Their quiet behaviour and gratitude for our hospitality astounded me, for the whole village had little use for the English."

"So you ran away and joined the army when you were old enough."

"Not exactly. I had neither the money nor the education to become a commissioned officer and so was reluctant at first to join up."

"So how did it happen?"

"Friends and a lot of luck." A sad expression crept across his face, and Laura did not question him further, for she had heard that FitzGibbon was a protégé of the great Sir Isaac Brock.

"Well, it is our good fortune that you were here to save us from the enemy. Otherwise, all Upper Canada would have been lost some time ago." She spoke more formally now, but as she stood up, she added, "And Red, you know I've never forgotten you over the years. There were many times when I missed you and wondered what had become of you."

Red smiled a proud lieutenant's smile, but there was something impish in it. "Now don't say you were pining. You've had plenty to keep you occupied, with a husband and children."

"Of course, but you still had a special place in my heart. Don't slip out of sight again, Red. Come and see me and my family as soon as you can."

"I will, Laura." He rose from his chair.

Laura smiled at her old friend and stood to leave. Then a look of fear crept into her eyes. "I have just one request, Red."

"What is it?"

"Please don't tell anyone that I brought you this message. We are not safe from the enemy. Today you have won the battle, but tomorrow who knows who will rule the Peninsula?"

"Don't concern yourself with that Laura," said FitzGibbon, his eyes twinkling. "Nothing will be said, but I feel confident we will drive the Americans back home."

"I hope you are right, Red. God be with you in our defence."

* * * * *

Mr. Turney's vegetable wagon was creeping along at a snail's pace towards Queenston. Laura was sitting up on the buckboard beside the farmer, trying not to shout to him to hurry along. She had been gone for only four days, but she was getting more anxious about her family the closer they got to the village.

"I'll just keep moving slow and easy up to your house, Mrs. Secord," Mr. Turney said, peering through the gathering dusk. "No point in arousing suspicion. We have the Americans on the run now, but who knows what next month will bring?"

Laura nodded, but she was still impatient. This trip back to Queenston seemed to be taking longer than the trek to De Cew's. Finally, as they reached the edge of the village, they turned out from the woods that lined the roadway and started down her street. She could hear the creak of the well-crank turning in the backyard, but apart from that, all was silent. The red roses overhanging the front walk stood quiet; it was as if nothing had happened.

Mr. Turney pulled the reins tightly, and his horses stopped in front of the house, "Everything seems to be fine," he said, turning to Laura, "but I'll wait here in case you need help. If all is well, you can wave me on. If you don't need me, I must leave. I have business to attend to at the Landing."

Laura jumped down lightly from the side of the wagon as he finished speaking. She winced a little as her feet touched the ground. "Thank you," she said. "Thank you for everything."

Ignoring the pain in her bruised feet, Laura ran up the path towards the front door. The smell of roses gathered in around her like a bride's veil. She walked up the stone steps and threw open the door. Inside, the hall was quiet and dark. All she could hear was the clock ticking in the parlour. The kitchen was empty, but the table had been set for the next morning's breakfast. Laura ran back to the front door and waved Mr. Turney on.

"I'm home, James, I'm home," she shouted, running back down the hall towards the stairs. She raised the muddied hem of her borrowed petticoat and ran up the steps. James had still not answered her; the upper hallway was as silent as the downstairs. But when she looked up towards the bedroom, she saw him. He was standing, but he was so weak that he had to lean against the doorway.

She ran to him and threw her arms gently around him.

"Thank God, thank God," James whispered, clasping her to him.

For a minute they stood there, silently holding each other.

Then he asked, "Laura, did you reach FitzGibbon?"

"Yes, and the American soldiers have surrendered. The British have control of the Peninsula again."

"Do the Americans know how their surprise was found out?"

"I asked FitzGibbon not to reveal my part in case there were more American attacks. He will keep my secret. We are safe, James. We are safe."

James limped back to his chair and sank into it, grimacing with pain. In the dying light of the sun, Laura could see deep lines around his mouth that she had not noticed before. She sat on the footstool beside his chair and reached across to take his hand. It was warm and strong, which gave her hope that his health would soon be completely restored.

Together, they sat looking out the window toward the Heights and watched the day end.

EPILOGUE

The war with the Americans ended eighteen months after Laura's walk, and peace came to Queenston. No Canadian territory was lost in the conflict, and, as a nation, the United States never invaded Canada again. James was restored to health, but the bullet never was removed from his knee, and he always walked with a limp. At Kingston in January 1814, Lieutenant FitzGibbon was promoted to Captain of his own company of the Glengarry Light Infantry, in recognition for capturing the American forces at Beaver Dams. He later rose to Colonel and Acting Adjutant General in Upper Canada. Laura continued to care for her family and two more daughters, Laura and Hannah, born after the war.

The major events described in this story actually happened, but Laura had five children at the beginning of the war: Mary (13), Charlotte (10), Harriet (6), Charles (3), and a baby Appy. The character of Elizabeth is drawn from Laura's sister Elizabeth and step-sister Nancy. The relationship between Laura and FitzGibbon is fictitious.

James' business in Queenston did not recover from the plundering and damage of the war, but his business troubles came to an end when he was appointed Registrar for the District Surrogate Court of Niagara. Five years later, he became Judge of the District Court. After resigning from that position in 1835, he became Collector of Customs in Chippawa. The income from that job and his small military pension were enough to keep his family living comfortably in a cottage with a rose-covered porch on the bank of the Chippawa Creek.

In 1841, less than a decade after he took the customs' job, James died. He was sixty-seven and Laura was sixty-five at the time. He was buried in Drummond Hill Cemetery in Niagara Falls, the site of the battle of Lundy's Lane, the last and the bloodiest fight of the war of 1812-14, where many of his fellow soldiers had fallen.

Laura never received official recognition during her lifetime from the British colonial government or the Canadian government for her part in the victory at Beaver Dams, and in later years, historians questioned whether Laura had actually brought FitzGibbon any information he did not already have. Laura's descendants were quite sure that FitzGibbon's victory was the result of Laura's message, and they would not give up searching for proof. Through the efforts of one of these descendants, Henry Cartwright Secord, a certificate written by FitzGibbon in 1820 testifying to the fact that Laura Secord had brought him a message of an impending attack at Beaver Dams, was located in 1934. Its contents were similar to those of an existing certificate that FitzGibbon had written in 1837, but its date, closer to the time of the event made it more valid.

Then, in 1959, the third and most important certificate was found in the National Archives at Ottawa. In it, FitzGibbon gave the exact date of Laura Secord's walk and drew attention to the fact that her message reached him first. He pointed out that "Mrs. Secord and her Family were entire Strangers to [him] before the 22nd of June 1813, and her exertions therefore could have been made from public motives only." But it was the following statement that provided the best proof that FitzGibbon was unaware of the planned attack by Chapin and his guerrillas: "*In consequence of this information*," he wrote, "I placed Indians under Norton together with my Detachment in a Situation to intercept the American Detachment." After this discovery, Laura Secord's heroic act and its direct benefit to FitzGibbon were recognized and described in textbooks.

Laura did receive recognition for her heroism from the British government when she was in her eighties. In 1860, Albert Edward, Prince of Wales, then a young man of nineteen, was visiting Niagara. He had been asked to officiate at a Queenston Heights ceremony in which Laura's name appeared on the list of war veterans presented to the Prince. He became interested in Laura's story, as she was the only woman among the veterans. In 1861, after he returned home, he sent her £100 in gold in appreciation for her service to her country. Prince Albert Edward later became King Edward VII.

Laura Secord died on October 17, 1868, twenty-seven years after her husband's death. She was ninety-three years old. In 1901 a monument was erected above her grave in Drummond Hill Cemetery, where she is buried beside James. Beneath a sculptured bust of this courageous woman is the following inscription:

TO PERPETUATE
THE NAME AND FAME OF
LAURA SECORD
WHO WALKED ALONE NEARLY 20
MILES BY CIRCUITOUS, DIFFICULT
AND PERILOUS ROUTE THROUGH WOODS
AND SWAMPS AND OVER MIRY ROADS
TO WARN A BRITISH OUTPOST AT
DE CEW'S FALLS OF AN INTENDED ATTACK
AND THEREBY ENABLED LIEUT. FITZGIBBON
ON THE 24TH JUNE, 1813, WITH LESS
THAN 50 MEN OF H.M. 49TH REGT.
ABOUT 15 MILITIA MEN AND A SMALL
FORCE OF SIX NATION AND OTHER INDIANS
UNDER CAPTAIN WILLIAM JOHNSON KERR
AND DOMINIQUE DUCHARME, TO SURPRISE
AND ATTACK THE ENEMY AT BEECHWOODS
(OR BEAVER DAMS), AND AFTER A SHORT
ENGAGEMENT TO CAPTURE COL. BOERSTLER
OF THE U.S. ARMY AND HIS ENTIRE FORCE
OF 542 MEN WITH TWO FIELD PIECES.

The Government of Canada erected a second monument to Laura Secord in 1910. This monument stands twelve feet high, not far from Brock's gigantic monument on Queenston Heights. This is its inscription:

TO LAURA INGERSOLL SECORD
WHO SAVED HER HUSBAND'S LIFE
IN THE BATTLE OF THESE HEIGHTS
OCTOBER 13TH, 1812
AND WHO RISKED HER OWN
IN CONVEYING TO CAPT. FITZGIBBON
INFORMATION BY WHICH HE WON
THE VICTORY OF BEAVER DAMS.

This second monument is not far from the place where Laura found and rescued her husband during the Battle of Queenston Heights. Many have come to read the inscription and to look out over the Niagara River as James and Laura did more than a century ago.

NOTES

The following are explanatory notes and sources for quotations and ref*erences.* The numbers along the left refer to the page numbers in *Laura's Choice.*

15 "Better . . . than the halter." (These words were the slogan of the men in Shay's rebellion.) Judge Whiting in the records of the Massachusetts Supreme Judicial Court in the Suffock County Courthouse in Boston under #160304 in Marion L. Starkey, *A Little Rebellion* (New York: Alfred A. Knopf Inc., 1955), p. 174.

160 "As sure as you do, I will have you indicted for murder." Laura Secord as related by her granddaughter, Mrs. Cockburn, in Emma A. Currie, *The Story of Laura Secord and Canadian Reminiscences* (Toronto: William Briggs, 1900), p. 69.

192 "When we come for good to this country, we'll divide the land, and I'll take this here for my share." American soldier as told to Mrs. Curzon in *The Story of Laura Secord*, p. 66.

192 "You scoundrel, all you'll ever get here will be six feet of earth." Laura Secord in *The Story of Laura Secord*, p. 66.

194 "You were right about the six feet of earth, missus." American soldier in *The Story of Laura Secord*, p. 66.

204 "James, somebody ought to tell Lieutenant FitzGibbon they are coming." Laura Secord as related by Laura Secord Clark, Granddaughter of Laura Secord, to Mrs. George S. Henry. *Ontario Dept. of Public Records and Archives*, Misc., 1933 and Ruth McKenzie, *Laura Secord, The Legend and the Lady* (Toronto: McClelland & Stewart, 1971), p. 51.

204 "Well, if I crawled on my hands and knees, I could not get there in time." James Secord in *Laura Secord*, p. 51.

204 "Well, suppose I go?" Laura Secord in *Laura Secord*, p. 51.

204 "You go, with the country in so disturbed a state? I do not think any man could get through, let alone a woman." James Secord in *Laura Secord*, p. 51.

204 "You forget, James, that God will take care of me." Laura Secord in *Laura Secord*, p. 51.

220 "I am aware . . . to protect you." FitzGibbon in Mary Agnes FitzGibbon, *A Veteran of 1812: The Life of James FitzGibbon* (Toronto: William Briggs, 1894), p. 88.

220 "I can only give . . . shall attack you." FitzGibbon in *A Veteran of 1812*, p. 89.

221 "Not another word . . . are my prisoners." FitzGibbon in *A Veteran of 1812*, p. 90.

221 "American troops, right face. Quick march." FitzGibbon in *A Veteran of 1812*, p. 90.

221 ". . . shall the American troops ground their arms here?" FitzGibbon in *A Veteran of 1812*, p. 90.

221 "Let . . . on the other side." Major De Haren in *A Veteran of 1812*, p. 91.

221 ". . . do you think it prudent . . . of the Indians?" FitzGibbon in *A Veteran of 1812*, p. 91.

221 "For God's sake, sir, do what this officer bids you!" Boerstler in *A Veteran of 1812*, p. 91.

221 "Do so." De Haren in *A Veteran of 1812*, p. 91.

221 "Americans, halt! . . . Ground your arms!" FitzGibbon in *A Veteran of 1812*, p. 91.

222 "Americans, don't touch your arms! . . . Rember, I am here." FitzGibbon in *A Veteran of 1812*, p. 91.

223 ". . . slept right off." Laura Secord in *A Veteran of 1812*, p. 85.

ABOUT THE AUTHOR

Connie Brummel Crook, a former teacher and avid history buff, is taking seriously the creative English lessons she taught for many years. She is now spending much of her time writing, seeking to bring to life the exciting experiences of Canada's pioneer families. Crook's aim is to give readers some Canadian heroes by making their stories come alive through gripping, suspense-filled novels.

Crook lives in Peterborough, Ontario. She and her husband, Albert, have two daughters and four grandchildren. She is a former teacher and vitally interested in providing excellent period novels for schools. This is her second book; *Flight,* the story of a Loyalist family's escape to Canada, is her first.